Ignatius I. Murphy

Life of Colonel Daniel E. Hungerford

Ignatius I. Murphy

Life of Colonel Daniel E. Hungerford

ISBN/EAN: 9783337381042

Printed in Europe, USA, Canada, Australia, Japan

Cover: Foto ©Raphael Reischuk / pixelio.de

More available books at **www.hansebooks.com**

LIFE

OF

COLONEL DANIEL E. HUNGERFORD

BY

I. I. MURPHY

HARTFORD, CONN.
PRESS OF THE CASE, LOCKWOOD & BRAINARD COMPANY
1891

PREFACE.

At the Re-union of the Veterans of the Mexican War, held at the Hotel Continental, Paris, September 14, 1889, to celebrate the capture of the Capital of Mexico by the army of the United States, in the year 1847, an eloquent tribute was paid by one of the speakers to Colonel Daniel E. Hungerford, who bore a conspicuous part in that great historic event.

As Colonel Hungerford's modesty of character would never permit him to chronicle his own brave deeds, he has been persuaded by many friends that it was due to his family, and those who have the privilege of his close friendship, to allow his heroic achievements to be recorded in this form.

I crave the indulgence of the reader for my execution of this work, which is due to the truth of history, that brave deeds should be kept in lasting remembrance, and that the generations of Hungerfords to come should be inspired to emulate his noble example as a gentleman and a soldier.

I. I. MURPHY.

December 5, 1889.

DANIEL E. HUNGERFORD.

CHAPTER I.

Ancestry of Daniel E. Hungerford — Description of Farleigh Castle, Ancestral Home of the Hungerford Family — The Chapel — The Monuments in the Chapel —
The Vault — The Church — The present Farleigh
House.

NO one has ever heard Colonel Hungerford
boast of his ancestry. Thorough and
consistent American as he is, he believes that
a man makes his own destiny, and should be
judged by the results of his own life work.
Yet I find by examining the records that he
has much cause for honest pride and satisfaction in the history of the Hungerfords that
have gone before him, many distinguished in
the civil and military annals of their time, as
shown by special favors and exaltations of
rank from the sovereigns under whom they
lived.

Military genius seems to have been the
prominent trait of the Hungerford race, and
as the following pages unfold themselves, the

1

reader will conclude that the military ardor
and warlike spirit of his forefathers have not
been discredited through Colonel Hungerford's
endeavors.   Under the "Stars and Stripes," on
many a hard-fought field, in the Mexican War,
the Indian campaigns, and the Civil War,
he has taken no mean part, having on more
than one occasion won the most honorable
mention from his superior officers.

To look at Colonel Hungerford, the casual
observer would never suppose, from his erect
form, soldierly bearing, and elastic step, that
three score and ten years were his to record,
years filled with so many stirring incidents,
midnight, marches, bloody battles, thrilling
escapes. With what satisfaction cannot the
old soldier look back, and tell the story of
those years to his kindred and friends, among
the peaceful refinements of his delightful
home. Let many, many years still be yours,
and may the relentless reaper long spare your
life to those who love you best!

Quoting freely from the work of Rev.
J. E. Jackson, compiled from authentic
sources, and treating of the history of the
Hungerford family, and Farleigh Castle, their

ancestral home, it seems that the Hungerfords originally came from a town of that name, Farleigh, in England. They had great wealth, were contributors to monastic foundations, and to the building of churches and almshouses. They were prominent supporters of the House of Lancaster, and in that cause suffered severely both in life and fortune.

Sir Robert de Hungerford, Knight of the Shire of Wilts, flourished about 1325. A monument to him is still standing in Hungerford Church. His nephew, Sir Thomas, was Speaker of the House of Commons during the last Parliament of King Edward the Third, having been recommended for that office by the Duke of Lancaster. This Sir Thomas came into possession of Farleigh Castle, situated in Somerset County, England, in 1369. It had been previously occupied by the Bishop of Lincoln, afterwards Lord Treasurer and Chancellor. From that time till 1686 it continued to be the principal seat of his descendants in the county of Somerset. In that county their possessions were considerable, but in Wilts there were hardly any districts in which they were not at some time or another land-owners.

The Hungerford crest is a wheat sheaf or

garb, rising out of a ducal coronet. Through their own and the adjoining counties, their crest could be seen on many church windows and buildings, it being the custom of the nobility to affix their crests to their posses-sions.

Sir Thomas died in 1398, and was buried at Farleigh. He was succeeded by his son, Walter, Lord Hungerford, Heytesbury, and Homet, K.G., High Treasurer of England in the reign of Henry the Sixth. He was a most distinguished person, and exercised great in-fluence during his time. The castle was com-pleted by him. He built for the convenience of his parishioners a church (the present one) standing outside the walls, instead of the older one within them. He died in 1449, and was buried in Salisbury Cathedral, in the "Iron Chapel," which exists to this day.

Robert, second Lord Hungerford, married Margaret, heiress of the Botreaux family of Cornwall. This Lord performed signal mili-tary service in foreign lands. His death occurred in 1459, and he was buried in a family chapel (now destroyed) on the north side of Salisbury Cathedral. His lady, Mar-garet, founded the almshouse at Heytesbury, which still remains. A monument to him is in the row between the arches on the south side of the nave of Salisbury Cathedral.

Robert, the third Lord Hungerford and Molyns (in right of his wife, the heiress of that family), was killed in the Wars of the Roses, 1461. His son and successor was Sir Thomas Hungerford, who lived at Rowdon, near Chippenham. His death occurred in 1469. At this time the estates were wrongfully taken from the family by Edward the Fourth, and given to his brother, Richard, Duke of Gloucester. In 1470 a composition was made between the Duke and Margaret, Lady Hungerford and Botreaux, by which he took Farleigh and Hungerford Court, and she Heytesbury. The Duke of Gloucester is not known to have resided there, but his brother, George, Duke of Clarence, seems to have done so, for in this castle was born, on the fourteenth of August, 1573, his daughter Margaret Plantagenet, Countess of Salisbury. In 1483 the Duke of Gloucester transferred Farleigh Castle to John Howard, Duke of Norfolk, who, two years after, was killed at Bosworth. Sir Thomas Hungerford, who died, as before stated, in 1469 at Salisbury, left one daughter and heiress, who married Edward, Lord Hastings, and carried into that family a vast number of manors. Farleigh was not of that number. By special arrangement it was kept in the male line, and in 1485, after the Duke of Norfolk's death, it was restored by Henry the Seventh to the eldest of the second line of Hungerford, Sir Walter. He lived at Heytesbury, and died there in 1516. The next owner, his son, Sir Edward, married a Zouche, and their coat-of-arms, on stained glass, is now in Farleigh Church. He also lived at Heytesbury, his death occurring in 1521. His son Walter was created Lord Hungerford of Heytesbury, 1536, he dying 1540. At his death the estates again passed into the hands of the Crown. They were administered by Lord Seymour of Sudely (brother of Protector Somerset), as "High Steward of the lands of the Late Lord Hungerford, and Keeper of the Castle and King's Park of Farleigh, Hungerford." The office was afterwards filled by John Bonham and Sir Ralph Hopton of Witham, near Frome. Sir Walter, son of the Lord Hungerford who died in 1540, finally recovered the lands. He was a famous military man, and was known as a great warrior. He had an only son, Edward, who died in his father's lifetime, and at Sir Walter's death, 1596, the estate passed to his brother, Sir

Edward. He died without issue in 1607. This Sir Edward purchased Corsham Manor.

Sir Walter, who died in 1596, left three daughters, one of whom, Lucy, married a kinsman of a junior branch of the family, Sir Anthony Hungerford, of Black Bourton, County Oxon. She had a son, Edward, afterwards Sir Edward Corsham, to whom, being his great nephew, the Sir Edward of 1607 bequeathed his estates; thus the Black Bourton branch succeeded to Farleigh.

Cicely (Tufton), Lady Hungerford, widow of the Sir Edward who died in 1607, re-married Francis Manners, sixth Earl of Rutland, who, in right of his wife, held the estates. He died in 1632, the Countess in 1653. It does not appear whether they lived at Farleigh or not. Sir Edward, the great nephew above mentioned, took a gallant part in the Civil War of Charles the First. Farleigh Castle seems to have been still held by the Countess of Rutland, when it was seized as a garrison for the Crown, Sir Edward, at the time, living at Corsham, which, as just mentioned, had been purchased by his great uncle. He married Margaret, daughter and co-heiress of William Halliday, Alderman of London. He died without issue in 1648. His lady founded the Alms-

house at Corsham. She died in 1672. Anthony Hungerford, Esq., of Black Bourton, his
half brother, succeeded him. The date of his
death was 1657. His widow, Rachel, had the
Castle and Park, until her death in 1679. He
was the father of Sir Edward Hungerford, K.
B, the "spendthrift," who squandered his
fortunes and sold the estates in 1686. His
brother, Thomas Hungerford, described as "of
generous and adventuresome disposition," is
the one from whom Daniel Elihu Hungerford is
directly descended. He came to America
about 1628.

The history of Farleigh Castle is very clear,
and easily traced. We find that Sir Thomas
Hungerford, who came into possession, as previously stated, in 1369, made many additions
to the original edifice. He added the moat,
towers, etc., and it was further strengthened
and beautified by his son, the High Treasurer of England. In that condition, Farleigh
Castle continued to the end of its history, without much alteration; for John Aubrey, of
Easton Piers, the celebrated antiquary, who
visited the place about 1650-70, says it was then
one of the two houses (Old Stourton House
being the other) that were almost entirely
the same as they had been in the time of the

old English barons. The oldest known description of Farleigh Castle is the following, by Leland, the Antiquary, who made a passing visit in the locality, about 1540-2. I extract as below, preserving the old English:

"From Through-bridge to Castelle Farley about a 3 miles by good corne, pasture, and nere Farley self plenty of wood. Or I came to the Castelle I passed over Frome water passing by there yn a roky valey and botom where the water brekith into armelettes and makith Islettes but soon metyng agayn with the principale streame, whereby there be in the causey divers smaul bridges. This water rennith hard under the botom of this Castelle, and there driveth a mylle. The Castelle is set on a rokky hill. There be diverse party towres in the utter (outer) warde of the Castelle. And in this utter warde ys an auncient chapelle, and a new chapelle annexid unto it. Under the arch of this chapelle lyith, but sumwhat more to the old chapelle warde, one of the Hungerfordes with his wife.

"Ther longgid 2 chauntre prestes to this chapelle; and they had a praty mansion at the very est end of it. The gate-house of the inner court of the castelle is fair, and ther be the armes of the Hungerfordes richley made yn stone.

"The haule and 3 chambres withyn the second court be stately. There is a commune saying that one of the Hungerfordes builded this part of the castelle by the prey of the Duke of Orleaunce whom he had taken prisoner. Ther is a parke by Farley Castelle. Ther is also a litle above the Castelle, a village."

When the Crown took possession of the estates in 1540, the following description is

2

given in the survey taken by the officer of the Crown:

The Castell of Farlegh Hungerforde.

"The sayde Castell standeth in a parke lenyng unto a hill syde, portly, and very strongly buylded, havyng inward and outward wardes, and in the inward wardes, many fayre chambres, a fayre large hall, on the hedde of which hall iij or iiij goodly greate chambres, with fayre and strong roffes, and dyvers other fayre lodginges, with all manner howses of offices."

It appears that each of the round towers of the castle was surmounted by a conical roof of the extinguisher shape, common in the old French and Scottish Castles, as was also the case at Nunney Castle (Symond's Diary). In the British Museum (Add. Mss. 18,674) a drawing has lately been found which represents Farleigh Castle as it was about 1746. This also shows the conical tops to the tower, and the west front.

The castle seems to have figured extensively in the military history of the time. Archaeologia, Vol. XIV., page 121, says, "In Dec. 1644, a writ issued from the King at Oxford addressed to "Our trusty Sir Robert Walsh, Kt. Whereas there are now remayning good numbers of suits of Apparell for the clothing of our army, at our city of Bristol, Nunney Castle

and Farley Castle. Our will and pleasure is
that you immediately repair unto the said
places, and demand to receive the said cloath-
ing into your custody, and convey them to our
army."

On the fourth of the same month, Edmund
Turnor, Esq., was appointed by Letters Patent
to look after the various expenses of the King's
Castles in the West:

"Charles, by the grace of God, etc, to Edmund Turnor,
Esq, Treasurer of our Garrisons of Bristol, Bath, Berke-
ley Castle, Nunney, Farley Castle and Portishead
Point :

"Whereas, for the good and safetie of our people, we
have thought fit to place and settle several garrisons in the
said Castles and places, and for the well ordering of the
same : We appoint you the said Edmund Turnor to be
Treasurer of the said garrisons, from 1st Nov. last."

A newspaper of the day, "Perfect occur-
rences," the sixth of September, 1644, says:
"Two Parliamentary officers, Wanzey and
Dowett, drew out each a troop of horse and
dragoons from their stations at Brickworth and
West Deane (near Salisbury) and went across
the country towards Farleigh. Dowett arrived
at the Castle; but he declined making any attempt upon it, and then marched into Somersetshire, with a view of beating up the neighborhood of Philip's Norton."

In March, 1645, Sir William Waller attacked Sir Francis Doddington at Trowbridge, who fell back and occupied Farley
Castle. The newspaper "Vicars' Burning
Bush III. 286, says: "We understand that Farleigh Castle in Somersetshire (whereof Colonel
Hungerford, brother of Sir Edward, is Governor) after a brave resistance has been finally
compelled to surrender."

Sir Edward Hungerford, K.B., who sold
Farleigh, died in London, and was buried in
the old church of St. Martin's-in-the-Fields. It
has often been said that he reached the extraor-
dinary age of 115 years, but this is an entire
mistake, which has arisen from confounding
him with his uncle, Sir Edward, whose monument is in the center of the side chapel. The
uncle having died in 1648 aged 52 (as is proved
by the date on his tomb), must have been born
1596. The nephew, who sold Farleigh, died
1711. The difference between 1596 and 1711 is
exactly 115 years, but the error lies in apply-
ing to one individual dates that apply to two.
The last Sir Edward was born 1632, and consequently was 79 years old at his death, instead
of 115. He had by his first wife, Jane Hele of
Devonshire, a son, Edward, and a daughter,
Rachel, afterwards Viscountess Massareene.

The son, following several precedents in the
family, married the Lady Alethea Compton,
who, had she lived, would have inherited a
moiety of the Dorset and Clifford estates, but
both she and her husband died young. Sir
Edward had by his third wife another son,
who died in 1748.

In the great sale by Sir Edward were included the manors of Farleigh, Tellisford,
Wick Farm, Hinton Abbey, Norton St.
Philips, Rowley, Wellow, Road, and Lang-
ham, with lands elsewhere in the neighborhood. The whole was bought by Mr. Henry
Baynton of Spy Park. He and Lady Anne
(Wilmot, sister of the Earl of Rochester), his
wife, resided here. In 1702, soon after his
death, the estates were sold again. The ma-
norial lands at Farleigh were bought by Mr.
Joseph Houlton, ancestor of the present pro-
prietor, but the castle itself did not come into
possession of the Houltons until purchased by
them from Mr. Cooper's family in 1730, by
which time it had begun to fall to decay, and
the materials to be used for other purposes.

The principal entrance of Farleigh Castle
was on the southeast side, where the shell
of the gatehouse still remains. Over the arch
is a single sickle cut in stone, the oldest device

used by the Hungerford family. Above this
is a window, and higher up, though sometimes
hidden by ivy, is a carved shield of their arms,
surmounted by a helmet and crest, and the
letters E. H., for Edward Hungerford. The
single apartment above the archway was a
guard room, with a door leading on to the
walls. There is no trace of a portcullis, but
there are holes for the beams of a drawbridge.
From this entrance a narrow moat, walled and
paved with Keynsham stone, went half way
round along the upper, or south and west
sides. The remains of it were lately found
under the ground, in front of the archway,
and some portion of it may still be seen in the
orchard on the left hand. The water was supplied by pipes from a spring called the King's
Pond, nearly three-quarters of a mile off. As
the ground on the lower sides toward the north
and east falls away very abruptly, the water
was held up by a strong dam at both ends.
The dam on the west side was removed a few
years ago. On the sides where there was no
moat, the Castle was protected by the steepness
of the knoll on which it stands.

UPPER OR OUTER COURT.

It will be seen by the plate of the ground
plan, that the general area was divided into

two courts, the upper and lower. The first is entered directly on passing through the gate-house. It contained the stables, guard rooms, etc., and was formerly pitched all over with stone. To the left, on entering, is a high wall running around this upper court. This upper wall formed the back of the stables, etc., as the holes for the beams of the flooring are still to be seen in it. There were one or two small towers or bastions on this side, one of which is entered by a crumbling arch, a smaller one is farther on. The high wall went on to another entrance, exactly opposite to that already described. Two fragments of thick masonry still remain to mark where this second entrance was. In a corner close by it were lately the lower steps of a winding staircase, by which the rampart on this side was mounted. Through this gate was the exit to the Castle Park, which lay on the west and north sides. A carriage road led from it, winding under the walls and across the river by a bridge (of which some traces are still left in the bank), round to the Trowbridge Road. The Park extended nearly to Iford, and included the hills on both sides of the river.

Farleigh Lodge Farm was a gamekeeper's house, and at the Dogkennel Farm (as it is

still called) near Iford, the hounds were kept.
The kitchen garden of the Castle was on the
south side, now an orchard.

THE LOWER COURT.

The upper court ended where a line of
wooden rails now crosses the Castle yard. Immediately on passing through these rails,
where formerly was a pair of high iron gates,
the visitor stands on the site of another gate-
house, which formed the entrance to the dwelling-house. On each side of this site are two
small square sunk gardens, that on the right
being considerably lower than the Castle yard.
The gate-house that stood between them is described by Leland as " Fair, and there the
Arms of the Hungerfords richly made in
stone." It seems to have been flanked by
small turrets, the foundation of one being still
to be seen. On this spot, the visitor may suppose himself to be standing immediately under
the south front of the dwelling-house. This
was in the shape of a hollow square or quadrangle, with a round tower at each corner; of
two of these towers, portions still remain, and
they are those which formed the ends of the
south front. The other two, now wholly destroyed, were, of course, at the opposite corners

of the quadrangle; and the intervals from tower to tower were filled up with the rooms. An old woman, called Betty Sheppard, granddaughter to Townsend, the last Sir Edward Hungerford's gamekeeper, had handed down to elderly people, who were still living at Farleigh, (1832--45.) sundry stories about the place. She used to show the Chapel to strangers, and she remembered the Castle when it was perfect. There was, immediately on passing through the inner gate-house (now destroyed) a large flight of about twenty steps, leading up to the hall. This hall, according to her account, was so large that a broad-wheel wagon might have turned round in it. The walls were painted with figures of men in armor, and on horseback. The rooms just mentioned were, according to the antiquary previously quoted, "stately," and were built by one of the Hungerfords who had taken prisoner the Duke of Orleans. The same authority also states that the Duke (father of Louis, the Twelfth King of France) was taken prisoner at the battle of Agincourt by Sir Walter Hungerford, then owner of Farleigh and a great man in Henry the Fifth's reign.

Of the coats of arms in the windows or on the walls, many notes were taken on the spot by Le Vive, an antiquary (1701) who made a visit here at that time. The notes are still preserved.

A fine hall table, said to have been part of the furniture, is preserved at Hinton Abbey, and various fragments, such as carved heads, mullions of windows, mantel-pieces, etc., have been recognized in cottages. In the neighboring church of Laverton, the front of the gallery was (a few years ago) made up of balustrades from the Castle.

On leveling the ground in the northwest corner of the lower courtyard in 1845, the foundations of some rooms were brought to light. The remains of an ash pit, furnace, oven, and flue, show that the back of the house lay on that side. The principal front, as drawn in Buck's "Antiquities," faced east, rising immediately on the edge of the bank on which the Castle stands. On the north side, where the bank falls most suddenly, there was a thick outer wall or facing of masonry. The front of the house on that side did not stand forward quite upon this outer edge, but stood back several feet within it, leaving space for a narrow strip of ground, the pitching of which still remains under the turf.

THE TOWERS.

Of the two that are left, that which first meets the eye on passing under the entrance gateway formed the west end of the south front of the quadrangular dwelling-house. It was higher than the one at the other end nearer the chapel, and contained a ground floor room and three stories. The walls are in some parts eight feet thick, so as to allow stairs or small apartments within them. The rooms were of course circular, about fourteen feet across, and eight feet high. It was for many years held together by a network of ivy, growing from a single stem, nearly two yards wide.

On November 5, 1842, the ivy accidentally caught fire, and was entirely destroyed. The tower being thus deprived of its girders, a large part soon afterwards fell down, showing the interior, as it is now seen.

On September 18, 1846, Prince Louis Napoleon, afterwards Napoleon the Third, Emperor of the French, visited the ruins of Farleigh Castle. He sat down on a piece of timber, lying in the Castle yard, and made a sketch of this picturesque tower. He afterwards lunched at Farleigh House, and greatly admired a fine bust of his uncle, Napoleon the First, which was in the parlor, naming the probable age at which it was taken.

In the other tower nearer the chapel, there was a ground floor room and only two stories, in one of which are three large windows commanding a pretty view down two valleys, east and north.

Of the third and fourth towers now destroyed that which was in the northeast corner was standing as late as 1797, when, having been partially undermined by plunderers for stone, it fell down after a hard frost.

The towers had not subterranean chambers, but the foundations are laid in circular courses of masonry, each lower course being broader than the one above, until the lowest of all becomes a solid floor, underlying the whole.

They seem to have had different names: one was called the " Red Cap," another in the northwest corner " Hazlewell," perhaps from a spring below the Castle, near the watercress beds. " Red Cap" was the favorite appellation of a class of spirits which was supposed to haunt old castles.

The Castle Chapel, dedicated to St. Leonard, stands in the upper court yard, but within the area of a small cemetery, the level of which is

several feet below the Castle yard. The
parapeted wall round it is modern. This
chapel, or more probably an older building on
the same site, was in ancient times the Church
of the Parish, but when the Hungerfords converted their house into a castle, and enclosed
it with high walls and a drawbridge, it was
necessary to provide for the parishioners a
church outside, to which they might have free
access at all times. Accordingly, when the
parish church then standing here was appropri-
ated by them as a domestic chapel, another
(the present Church of Farleigh) was built on
the ridge to the south of the Castle. This was
done by Walter Lord Hungerford, High Treasurer of England, 1443. The chapel is about
fifty-six feet long by twenty wide. It is entered at the west end by an open porch, the
roof of which is of oak, embossed with sickles
and the arms of the Hungerfords. The descent
into the building is by a few steps, the floor
being below the level of the cemetery. There
is neither aisle nor distinct chancel; but the
latter is represented by a slight elevation of
the pavement, for about nine feet from the
east wall. The windows are of precisely the
same style as those of the parish church, the
only difference being that the east window of

the one is the west in the other. The stained
glass now there is of modern insertion. The
west window has decorated tracery. There
were formerly side windows: on the south side,
five, and on the north side, three. They were
also of the same pattern as the side windows
now in Farleigh Church. Being much dilapi-
dated, they were blocked up some years ago.
The roof seems to have had a covered ceiling.
The font, now in the chapel, was brought from
the present parish church in 1833.

The chapel was at one time much neglected;
and in Grose's "Antiquities," (1774) it is drawn
as half-roofless. It was repaired in 1779, and
again in 1806. Having been long disused as a
place for religious service, it has become a
sort of repository for curiosities, found in and
about Farleigh. Besides a large quantity of
common soldiers' armor of various patterns,
hanging about the walls, some of which are
relics of the old armor of the castle, there
is a miscellaneous collection of things either
found or brought here from time to time.
Among these are a heavy saddle tree, and
military boots of the Commonwealth fashion,
antique wooden stirrups, bits for bridles, old
Castle keys, fragments of carved stone, etc., etc.
There are also some good specimens of carved

oak furniture. On some of the arms is an H between two sickles. An old settle with the arms of Hungerford cut on the panels came from Farleigh Church, where it had been one of the open seats, the rest having been at one time all of the same kind.

Some trunks and papers were left in the chapel by the Hungerfords, but they were afterwards taken away by them, except some papers which were allowed to remain undisturbed. Among these papers were two letters written by Oliver Cromwell. Both were addressed to Anthony Hungerford, Esq., of the Black Bourton branch of the family, father of the Spendthrift, Sir Edward. One of the letters is quite legible, and reads as follows:

"Sir, I am very sorrye my occacion will not permit mee to returne (i. e., to reply) to you as I would. I have not yett fully spoken with the gentleman I sent to waite upon you. When I shall doe it, I shall bee enabled to bee more particular, beinge unwilling to detaine your servante any longer. With my service to your lady and family, I take leave, and rest

Your affectionate servante,
O. CROMWELL.

July 30, 1652.

"For my honoured friend Mr Hungerford, the elder at his house, these."

The walls towards the eastern end were stenciled in foliated pattern. On one side of the altar is a gigantic representation of St. George and the Dragon, and near this are traces of a figure of a knight, kneeling, bearing on his coat the arms of Hungerford. On the east wall is a painted consecration cross.

Over the east window, in black and white upon the wall, is a shield of Hungerford quarterings, having for supporters a griffin and a large bird, intended for a raven, collared and chained.

The side chapel, commonly called St. Anne's, is on the north side of the principal chapel, and measures twenty by fifteen feet. Under the arch between them lies the tomb of Sir Thomas Hungerford, who died in 1398, and his wife, who died in 1411-12, so that this side chapel was probably built by their son Walter, Lord Hungerford, K. G.

In the will of Joan, Lady Hungerford (1412), she says that she desires to be buried next to her husband "in the chapel of St. Anne, in the north part of the said church of Farleigh." In later times, it seems to have been principally used as a mausoleum. About 1650, it was embellished, and the vault underneath was enlarged by Margaret (Halliday), Lady of Sir

Edward Hungerford, K. B. The walls and beams were covered with coats of arms, and figures of angels in various fantastic dresses and attitudes, blowing trumpets, etc., the Apostles, with their respective emblems; also the representation of the interior of some church with altar, tombs, and effigies, all in fresco. The floor was inlaid with black and white marble in lozenge shape, and gilded iron gates with arms and crests were placed between the two chapels.

The coats of arms on the walls of the side chapel are somewhat indistinct, but they can still be easily recognized by the aid of an original manuscript, dating from 1760, which is still preserved.

On the north wall, there are three shields; on the same wall between the window and the east end, there are sixteen coats of arms. On the east wall, eight coats of arms. The four on the south wall, and the four on the west wall, are now obliterated, but they were existing in 1760.

The first monument is to Sir Thomas Hungerford, and Joanna, his second wife. She was the daughter and co-heir of Sir Edmond Hussey, Knight of Holbrook, County Somerset. They were buried within this side chapel.

4

The effigies bore the arms of their respective families. Sir Walter, the Knight's son, afterwards Lord Hungerford, appears to have been the first who adopted a garb or wheat-sheaf between two sickles, which appears on his later seals, as well as on his K. G. escutcheon in St. George's Chapel, Windsor.

The last will of Joane, Lady Hungerford, contains a curious order about her funeral: "Joane, Lady Hungerford, February 1, 1411. My body to be buried in the Chapel of St. Anne, in the Parish Church of Farleigh Hungerford, next to the grave of my husband. I will, that with all possible speed after my decease, my executors cause three thousand masses to be said for my soul, and for the souls of all the faithful, deceased: Also I desire on my burial day that twelve torches and two tapers burn about my body, and that twelve poor women holding the said torches be cloathed in russet, with linen hoods, and having stockings and shoes suitable. I will that the two hundred marks now in the hands of my son, Sir Walter Hungerford, be given to found a perpetual chantry of one chaplain, to celebrate divine service in the chapel of St. Anne, in the north part of the said Church of Farleigh for the health of my soul, and the soul of my husband, and the souls of all our ancestors, for ever."

Sir Walter's "of Farleigh" tomb is in the southeast corner of the large chapel. He was the seventh in descent from Sir Thomas, and he died in 1596. The inscription is curiously cut. It reads as follows: "Tyme tryeth truth." The tomb is of freestone, painted in red, green, and gold, the colors of the Hungerford livery, taken from one of their oldest coats of arms.

Sir Edward Hungerford and his wife lie in the northeast corner of the smaller chapel.

Sir Edward Hungerford of Corsham, K. B., and Margaret (Halliday), his wife. This Sir Edward was great nephew to the earlier Sir Edward, mentioned above. He was commander of the Wiltshire forces for the Commonwealth, in the Civil Wars of Charles the First. He besieged Wardor Castle when it was defended by Blanche, Lady Arundel. He lived chiefly at Corsham (which his great uncle purchased in 1602). His death occurred in 1648. His lady was daughter and co-heir of William Halliday, a wealthy alderman of London. Her will charged her estate with "five pounds per annum for the repair of the vault at Farleigh Castle, when it shall be defective; the

same to be kept in stock in the meantyme."
She was the foundress of the large almshouse
at Corsham, which, under the same will, is
also maintained by money from the estate.
She died in 1672. The monument is very fine,
and is said to have cost eleven hundred
pounds. It is of black and white marble, the
upper slab being a single piece, eight feet long
by five feet wide. At the head of the tomb is
a shield of fifteen quarterings of the husband's
family. In the center, on an escutcheon, is the
coat of arms of her own family, and underneath, the motto," Dieu mon Appuy" (God is
my support). At the other end of the monument are the arms of the Hungerfords, single ;
at her husband's feet, the crest of Hungerford ;
at her own, that of Halliday. From an inscription upon it, it appears that her mother,
Susan, Mrs. Halliday, married, as her second
husband, an Earl of Warwick (Robert Rich,
the third Earl of that family), and that the
monument was erected during the life of the
Lady Hungerford whose figure lies upon it.

The translation of the inscription is as follows :

" Laid on this tomb you see the effigies of a worthy pair."

Sir Edward Hungerford, Knight of the Honorable order of the Bath, Son of the illustrious Anthony Hungerford of Black Borton, in Co. Oxford, Knight by Lucy his wife, who was descended from the noble line of Hungerford of Farley Castle, Co. Somerset.

Margaret Lady Hungerford his beloved wife, Daughter and co-heiress of William Halliday, an eminent citizen and Alderman of London by Susan, his wife, after-wards Countess of Warwick.

In her praise, much might truly be said, but surviving, she forbids it, let this be hereafter.

For { God, His country, His kindred } He lived 52 years.

And fell most peacefully asleep, 23 October, in the year of Salvation, 1648.

The record of the death of Susan his wife, above spoken of, is found in the register of St. Andrew's, Holborn. It reads as follows: "1645–6, Jany 21, Dame Susan, Lady to the Rt. Honorable Robert Rich, Earl of Warwick, died in Warwick House, Holborn, 16th and was buried in St. Lawrence Church, near Guildhall, London the 21st."

Against the east end wall is a circular copper plate which for many years lay loose on one of the coffins in the vault below, and was originally on the lid of a cylindrical leaden urn, which contained the heart of this Sir Edward. The arms on it are the same as those at the head of his monument.

Translation.

"Within are deposited the mortal remains of the most illustrious Sir Edward Hungerford of Corsham in the Co.

Wilts, Knight of the Honourable Order of the Bath, eldest Son of Sir Anthony Hungerford, of Black Bourton, in the Co. of Oxford, Knight by his wife Dame Lucy Hungerford, daughter of Sir Walter Hungerford, of Farley, Hungerford, in Co. Somerset, Knight, of which most eminent and ancient line of Farley Hungerford, he was the last. He was united in happy marriage for 27 years with Dame Margaret, daughter and co-heir of William Halliday, Citizen and Alderman of London. He died on the 10th before the Calends of November [*i. e.*, 23 October] 1648, in the 52nd year of his age."

The following lines formerly painted on the window are mentioned as being there in 1703:

"In the vault, under this monument, lyeth Sir Edward Hungerford, Knight of the Honorable Order of the Bath, only son of Sir Anthony Hungerford, by Lucy, daughter and co-heir of Sir Walter Hungerford of Farleigh Castle."

"Margaret, Lady Hungerford, wife and relict of Sir Edward Hungerford, daughter and co-heir of William Hallyday, Alderman of the City of London, and Susan, his wife, (who was afterwards Countess of Warwick) out of her pious affection to the memory of her deceased husband, beautified this Chapel, and erected this monument at her own cost; and designs, when it shall please God to take her out of this world, to rest by her husband in this vault."

The vault is under the side chapel, and is entered from the outside by a descent of eleven steps. Over the outer entrance is a cross, cut in stone. It is the arms of Sandys, a family into which one of the Hungerfords married. At the foot of the steps are two arched doorways, filled up with stone. The vault is well built of ashler, and is arched. On the farther side, lying across two stone trenches, are the leaden coffins of four males, two females, and two children. They are, most probably, those members of the Hungerford family whose monuments are in the chapel above.

In the year 1760, on one of these plates lying on a coffin was this inscription: "The Body of the Lady Jane Hungerford, Wife of Sir Edward Hungerford of Farley, Hungerford, Co. Somerset, and Daughter and Heir unto Sir John Hele, of Wembury in the Co. of Devon, K^t, who deceased 18 day of May, 1664."

The whole number of interments of this family known to have taken place here is as follows:

(1) Sir Thomas Hungerford, 1398,   } No. 1.
(2) Joanna, Lady H., his second wife, 1412, }

(3) Edward Hungerford, 1585, } No. 3,
(4) Sir Walter of Farleigh, 1596, }

(5) Sir Edward (half brother of Sir Walter), 1607, } No. 4.
(6) Dame Jane (wife of Sir Edward), }

(7) Mrs. Mary Shaa (sister of Sir Edward), 1613, No. 5.

(8) Sir Edward of Corsham, 1648, } No. 6.
(9) Margaret (Halliday), his wife, 1672, }

(10) Jane (Hele), first wife of the Sir Edward who sold Farleigh, 1664.

(11) Jane (Culne), second wife of the above, 1674.

The name of the last mentioned is entered as the first interment in the present register of Farleigh.

Gough, in his work, "Sepulchral Monuments," assigns to the other five coffins the following names:

(12) Giles Hungerford.
(13) An infant of Jane (Hele) Lady H.
(14) Culne Hungerford.
(15) Edward Hungerford (son of the last owner).
(16) Lady Alethea (Compton), his wife.

Farleigh Hungerford Church is dedicated, like the Chapel, to St. Leonard. It was built by Walter, Lord Hungerford, K. G., High Treasurer of England in the reign of King Henry the Sixth, and, together with the churchyard, was consecrated on St. Leonard's Day, November sixth, 1443. Before that time, the parish church, as has been already stated, was on the site of the Castle chapel, close to what was then the principal house of the owners of Farleigh. It is of perpendicular architecture, and consists of a tower, nave, chancel, and south porch, about ninety-six feet long by thirty feet wide, walls included.

The tower is at the west end, fifty-four feet high to the parapet, and is finished with a short pyramidal steeple, covered with stone tile; the stair leading up to the top within the

wall to which an extra thickness is given, so as
to have outside the appearance of a flat but-
tress. The west window has three lights and
a semi-circular head, with perpendicular mullions and tracery. The vestry window is
modern; and the glass in it, bearing the device
of a sickle, was collected from the neighboring cottages. There is a doorway at the west
end.

There were five bells in 1791 (Collinson's
"Somerset" III. 362). Now there are four,
and two of these bear the inscription, "Philip
Palmar, 1681." The crest of the Hungerfords,
a wheat-sheaf between two sickles rising out
of a ducal coronet, is upon the bells.

The nave is twenty-four feet wide, and has
no aisles. There are six square-headed windows, three on each side, of which five have
double lights trefoiled. In the heads of the
lights are roses of different colors; in the center of three vine leaves. In the window nearest the chancel on the north side is a portrait
in old yellow glass with helmet and chain
gorget, surrounded by sickles, and the letters
T. H. It is commonly supposed to represent
Sir Thomas Hungerford, the purchaser of Farleigh. The side windows of the chancel are of
the same pattern as those in the nave. As

late as 1789, there was much ancient stained
glass in them; each window containing two
figures on ornamented grounds such as our
Lady, St. George, St. Mary Magdalene, etc.;
also the arms of the Hungerfords. In the top
of the chancel windows remains of this old
glass may still be seen; a knot of three sickles
interlaced, with the coat of arms of the Hungerfords in the center of them.

On one of the windows of the south side is
an ancient piece of stained glass. On it is the
shield of a Sir Edward Hungerford, who died
in 1521, and Jane Zouche, his first wife.

In old times, the castle was, of course,
known as the "Great House" of the village;
and the Park in those days lay north and west
of the Castle, in the direction of Iford and
Hinton. It included within a circuit of about
three miles what are now the Park Farm, Farleigh Lodge Farm, Dog Kennel Farm, and the
Wiltshire Park Farm.

The present Farleigh House is an old building with modern front. In the time of the
Hungerfords, it was occupied by their principal
tenants. It had gabled fronts, east and south,
and the parish road to Tellisford passed close
to the hall door. When Sir Edward Hungerford sold his property in 1686, Mr. Edward

Wayte was in occupation of this house and the farm adjoining, under (as is believed) a lease for three lives. The lease was transferred to Mr. Daniel Drake, who, in 1694, assigned his term to Dr. William Harris, Master of Winchester College. The rest of the Farleigh estate had in a similar manner been leased in various parcels on lives by the Hungerfords, except the Castle farm, which was the only one, in fact, of which Joseph Houlton, Esq., obtained immediate possession, when the purchase was made in 1700. Having afterwards, in 1705, by marriage with the co-heiress of the Whites of Grittleton in Wilts, obtained that property, Mr. Houlton resided there, and never at Farleigh. The Farleigh estate, in 1715, was placed in settlement on the marriage of his eldest son, Mr. Joseph Houlton, Junior, with Miss Hooke of Bristol. In the following year, 1716, upon the death of a Mrs. Wilson, the lease of the house and farm expired, and the younger Mr. Houlton, then living in St. James' Square, Bristol, removed to Farleigh, and was the first of his family who resided there. He converted part of the farm into the present park. At his death he left one surviving daughter, and sole heiress, Mary Houlton, who had married, in 1746, James

Frampton, Esq., of Moreton, Dorset County.
She died without issue in 1762.   Mr. Frampton
continued to enjoy the estate during his life,
and at his death, in 1784, it reverted to his late
wife's cousin, Robert Houlton, Esq., of Bristol.
He died the following year, 1785, and was succeeded by his only son, Joseph Houlton, Esq.,
who died in 1806, and was the father of the
Lieut.-Col. John Houlton.   By the latter gentleman, who died in 1839, the house was changed
and enlarged to its present style of architecture.
John Houlton, Esq., his eldest son, inherited
the property at his father's death, and he having died in 1868, his son, the present owner,
Francis Houlton, Esq., came into possession.

CHAPTER II.

THE family of Hungerford can be said to
be rooted in the soil of America. Six
generations have lived and died in this country
since the first Hungerford. Thomas, brother
of Sir Edward Hungerford, K. B., landed
on the shores of New England in 1628. As
noted in the previous chapter, Daniel Elihu
Hungerford traces his descent by direct line
from him. The town register of Norwich,
Connecticut, states that Thomas Hungerford
acquired property there in 1630, and the
register of Hartford, Connecticut, also bears
his name as the owner of land in the township,
the date of the entry being 1639. The first
town in Connecticut that Thomas Hungerford
lived in was New London, but he did not remain there more than a few years, and the
records just quoted show that he became possessed of property in other parts of the State.

The father of Daniel Elihu Hungerford,

Amos Hungerford, was born March 12, 1777, at Lyme, Connecticut. His mother, China Harrison, cousin of General William H. Harrison, President of the United States in 1840, was born June 13, 1784. They were married at Lyme, Connecticut, January 15, 1802. His father fought in the War of 1812 against the British. His grandfather, Nathaniel Hungerford, fought in the Revolution. He was the son of Green Hungerford, and Green the son of Thomas, Jr., whose father, Thomas, was the original Hungerford, who had come to America, as before stated, in 1628.

Below is the descent in the regular order:

Thomas, Sen.
Thomas, Jun.
Green.
Nathaniel.
Amos.
Daniel Elihu.

The uncles of Daniel Elihu were Josiah, Jehiel, Nathaniel, Elihu, and Stephen Hungerford.

Daniel Elihu Hungerford, the subject of this sketch, first saw the light in Frankfort, Herkimer County, New York State. He was one of a large family, being the youngest of seven sons. His adventures began early in life. When but two years old, the family left his native place, and moved to Utica, Oneida County, in the same State. Baby Dan was a vigorous and healthy youngster, and often proved more than a match for his nurse. One day, venturing too near the banks of the Erie Canal, close to which his parents lived, he fell in. But Providence was kind to him, and he was rescued, none the worse for the accident.

Recognizing the benefits of a good education, his father placed him at school at an early age; he showed aptitude in his studies, and he soon became the leader not only among the boys of his own age, but even of his elders. On the playground he was always first; none ran faster, played longer, or fought more battles than young Dan. The first day he distinguished himself by fighting the biggest boy in the school; it seemed that wishing to put upon the new comer, and desiring to test his mettle, one of his classmates endeavored to pick a quarrel with him. Now this was not very difficult, for, even at that tender age, Dan was beginning to develop his courageous and combative disposition. Soon the two boys were engaged in a rough-and-tumble encounter, but at last Dan got the upper hand. Then and there he established his reputation. No one

ever interfered with him after that ; he was
thenceforward "facile princeps." The schoolmaster, evidently more amused than annoyed,
and amazed at the daring courage of the new
pupil in fighting a boy so much his superior in
size and strength, did not punish either combat-
ant. He facetiously announced to the class that
that day a Napoleon Bonaparte had come among
them. Dan, having truthfully admitted his
part in the quarrel, did not suffer in the estimation of the worthy pedagogue, though he had
flagrantly violated all order and discipline.
This little incident, trifling in itself, foreshad-
owed the career of the future man, and never
was one prouder than the old schoolmaster
when in later years he heard of the distinguished and daring service that young Hungerford rendered to his country in after life.
But to return to the incidents of his boyhood
days. A friend of his father presented him
with a drum almost as big as himself, which
was his most coveted possession, and his heart's
delight. He soon became quite expert as a
drummer, and many a lively tattoo he played
on it to the great amusement of the boys and
grown people of the neighborhood, who showed
their appreciation of the talents by many a
coin.

It is an old saying, none the less true, that "like father, like son." Young Hungerford not only inherited from his father (who had been a gallant officer in the War of 1812) his military spirit, but also his sterling quality of rigid honesty. His father never failed to illustrate by word and example that honor and honesty were above all price. The following incident would indicate this: The boy had one day in his ninth year found a large sum of money which he brought to his father. The latter commanded him to search for the owner, and restore the property, with the strict injunction not to accept a penny for so doing. "My son," he said, "take no reward; you must be honest without being paid for it; adhere to this through life, and you will not only command the respect of others, but you will also respect yourself." And those who know Colonel Hungerford can bear testimony to how well he has abided by that parental advice.

In 1830, his father being in the transportation business, and owner of a large number of canal boats, took his family for a pleasure trip to Albany and return, railroads, at that time, not having come into general use. When the boat reached Albany, cargo was discharged,

and loaded up for Whitehall, upon Lake
Champlain *via* Champlain Canal.

As it was late in the fall, the family concluded to remain at Waterford until the return
of Mr. Hungerford, who had gone to Utica.
Mr. Hungerford, however, decided to sell his
property there, dispose of his interests, and
settle down with his family at Waterford.

There, we may say, the serious work of
young Hungerford began. He attended the
Saratoga Academy, and soon gave evidence of
where his tastes lay. Before he had been well
acquainted with his classmates, he had begun
to organize them into a military company
after his own crude fashion, equipping them
with paper caps and swords made of laths.
Every Saturday afternoon the worthy citizens
of Waterford were treated to the free spectacle
of Captain Dan, as he was called, and his
youthful recruits, marching through the
principal streets, breasts swelling with con-
scious pride, and hearts burning with patriotic
ardor, as in their mind's eye, they saw the red
coats fleeing before them, routed by the
Yankees to the tune of Yankee Doodle.

No bolts or bars ever could keep young
Dan in the house when the martial music was
playing, and the soldiers passing, though many

a reprimand he received for his hasty exits. One day he followed a detachment of United States troops going through the village *en route* to the West, a distance of ten miles, until, exhausted by fatigue, he could go on no further. His brother, following him in hot pursuit, then effected an easy capture of the young captain, who stoutly said, when pressed for an explanation, that he was only going to fight for his country, and help whip the Britishers. It is thus easily seen that our young hero rightly recognized who had the best claim on his services.

In school Dan was always the leader of the militant section of the boys. He well remembers to this day how the main street of the village served in the fierce snowball fights, as the line of battle which divided the "uptown" and the "downtown" crowds, as the two factions were called. Many a bloody nose and blackened eye came from these encounters, and not to show either of these marks was considered more of disgrace than an honor. Dan, being the commander-in-chief and engineer of his side, naturally took the most prominent part in these engagements, for he seemed to have the inborn nature to command, and was always heedless of danger.

In 1832, politics ran high. Andrew Jackson, the hero of New Orleans, was the candidate of the Democratic party. The Hungerfords were ardent Whigs, but the military career of Jackson appealed most strongly to the sympathies of young Dan. To his youthful mind, any one who could whip the British, as he did at New Orleans, was a great man; none could be greater: he, therefore, resolved to do what he could to elect his favorite. What I will now here narrate shows how he accomplished his desire. There was an odd character in town, Chance by name, whose vote was always for sale to the highest bidder. Then, as now, other means than press and platform were used to persuade the electors to rally to a particular candidate. Whigs and Democrats resorted to every stratagem to secure votes. The elder Hungerford lured, as it were, this Chance to his home, and by luxurious living and many doses of whisky he finally succeeded in convincing him that the Whig candidate was the most deserving of his honest suffrage. Mr. Hungerford, however, did not have much confidence in the fellow's promises, so he thought it prudent to keep him an enforced guest until the time came for depositing his ballot. Young Dan, though, had other plans for his father's guest, namely, that he should vote for Jackson ; so, providing himself with a straight Jackson ticket from the ward worker, the youthful electioneering agent succeeded in gaining admittance to the room where Chance was confined. " Who are you going to vote for?" he asked him. " For whomever your father wants," responded the honest voter. Young Hungerford then handed him the slip of paper, and together they went to the polling station, where young Hungerford had the satisfaction of seeing it duly deposited. Meeting Chance afterwards, Mr. Hungerford asked him how he got out, and for whom did he vote. " Why," he replied, "your son let me out, and I voted the ticket he gave me." " By Jove," exclaimed the father, "beaten by my boy!" The joke was too good to be kept, and it was circulated far and wide throughout the town. It told heavily against the elder Hungerford, but spoke much for the shrewdness of the boy, and by its perpetration the latter acquired no little prominence in Waterford.

At the age of fifteen young Hungerford was appointed deputy-inspector of beef and pork in Waterford, the town being the center of a large trade in those meats. It can readily be supposed that a boy of those years would not

have been entrusted with such a position had
he not special qualifications and been well
thought of by the people of the town. One
day, in the absence of his superior, an attempt
was made to corrupt him ; but the young inspector's integrity was not to be sullied, and he
indignantly refused the bribe, threatening to
bring the offender to justice for endeavoring
to bribe a public official. This refusal to betray a trust showed his high sense of duty and
firm uprightness which in his long and eventful life he has never deviated from.

Dan, notwithstanding his military inclina-
tions, was a hard student at school, and early
manifested a fondness for reading and books.
His father, after much deliberation, decided to
direct his talents to journalism, and to that end,
Dan entered the office of the "Saratoga Observer." But he did not stay there more than a
week for the following reason : the foreman in
the printing establishment, mistaking the material in the boy, ventured to send him for a
pitcher of beer to the neighboring saloon.
But the pitcher was destined not to go beyond
the staircase, for Dan, depositing it on the last
step, left in a high state of indignation for his
home, telling his father, when he reached it,
that he went to the office to learn the printing

trade, and not to run errands to the saloon. His father commended his principle, and sent him back to school.

While on a visit to Troy, the boy was unfortunate enough to contract the loathsome disease, smallpox. For days and nights he lay in a darkened room, with no attendant but a faithful nurse, and no diversion for his convalescing days but his old flintlock musket, which he insisted should accompany him in his isolation. He used to while away the weary hours by taking it apart and putting it together again. Truly, this was a trial to a restive boy. During the height of the direful disease, his physician asked him about dying, as he was then in a dangerous condition. "I would not guess head or tail to live or die," responded the boy, tossing on his bed of agony; but it was ordained otherwise for the courageous lad, for he has since been blessed with long life and good health, except one serious intermission, coming shortly afterwards, which almost nipped in the bud the life of the promising youth, then approaching manhood.

Those whose memories recall the years 1836 and 1837 will remember how nearly the United States and Great Britain became involved in war, owing to the disputed boundary

line between Canada and the State of Maine.
Discussion raged fiercely in the press, the military spirit of the country was aroused, the
victorious banners of 1812 were again unfurled,
and patriotic men throughout the land stood
ready to resist, to the death, the tyranny and
usurpation of the mother country.   Things
had come to such a pass that General Zachary
Taylor, old " Rough and Ready," was ordered
to occupy the principal points on the frontier
to prepare to beat back the threatened invasion.   But the determined attitude and warlike preparations of the United States were in
themselves sufficient.   Great Britain did not
wish, for the third time, to try arms against us,
so over the green table of diplomacy, instead
of on the bloody field of battle, what threatened
to embroil the two nations in wanton strife
was finally satisfactorily adjusted.   During all
this time the burning desire of young Hungerford to enter the military service of his country ·
was only intensified in the presence of the
actual danger.   But he was again stricken
down by a fearful malady.   Pneumonia had
him in its grasp, and at what promised to be
the threshold of his military career.   Once
more, though, his indomitable will and vigorous
constitution which carried no inherited taint,

again snatched him, as it were, from the grave. The disease, however, had left its marks; instead of his hitherto robust form, nothing but bone and muscle remained, and very little of the latter, need it be said. It had its compensating effects, nevertheless; for it had removed all superfluous flesh, and his form had become lithe and athletic. During the whole course of his illness, he felt the bitter disappointment of frustrated hopes, and his one question to the physician was always: "When will I be able to leave my bed? Will I be able to join Taylor's forces?" Happily, his services were not needed; his opportunity came at a future period.

In 1836, another presidential election came round, and Democracy had again an ardent champion in young Hungerford. Though not yet of age, and therefore unable to exercise the elective franchise, this did not prevent the young enthusiast from mixing freely in the political discussions of the hour, and many a speech the beardless boy made for the party that he recognized as the instrument of the country's progress and position among nations, and which had brought it to the eminence which challenged the admiration of the world. Patriotism and love of country characterized

7

the Hungerford family, but in politics Dan took issue with his father and brothers. Democracy, for him, was the party best calculated to bring out the nation's strength, and from that opinion he has never deviated. Firm and consistent in principle, his faith has remained unaltered. Trimming or changing with the fortune of parties his nature abhored.

In 1839, he visited New York. The bustle and life of the great city vividly impressed him. He felt that in such a community he would have full scope for his active mind; the quiet country village was not suited to one of his characteristics. He, therefore, inwardly determined that there he would cast his fortunes with the busy surging crowd, as there his ambitions could be gratified, and he would find ample scope for his energies. But he kept his own counsel till the following summer. Then, seeing his father, he frankly told him that he was old enough, and had the capability to earn his own livelihood, and something more. His father was loath to let the favorite son and the youngest of nine children leave him. But Dan urged strongly : "Think it over, father, and let me know in three days; I am going anyway, but I want your consent," said the boy. Filial affection was strong in young Hungerford, and it wrung his heart to give pain to his good father. At the end of three days his father yielded to his persuasions, having great confidence in the self-reliance of his son, and knowing his fixed principles of honor and honesty; he felt sure that he could carve out his own destiny. With a light heart and an earnest purpose he arrived in the great city; friends he quickly made, and true ones, who admired his pluck and his principles. It was not long before he found a place, and soon the young adventurer was playing his opening part in the drama of life in the great metropolis.

In 1840, he was visited by a brother, who persuaded him to visit another brother, who was doing business in Oneida County, near the old home. Glad of his return, and appreciating his abilities and energies, the brother prevailed upon him to accept an equal partnership in the business.

During this year, Harrison was running for president. The canvass was, up to that period, the most exciting in the history of the country. Young Hungerford entered into the campaign with his accustomed ardor; and though his mother was first cousin to W. H. Harrison himself, this fact did not abate one whit his enthusiasm in favor of the opposing candidate. He stood for principle *quand même*, and both family influence and affinities went for naught with him. All this activity in the duties of citizenship and his high-mindedness of character gained for him popularity and friendships, and won the favor of all those who admire a promising youth.

Country life did not suit young Hungerford. The taste he had already gotten of the busy city only whetted his appetite to be again in the arena, where his energies could have full play. The bartering and petty style of doing business, prevalent in the country town, was ill-suited to him, so once more he turned his face towards New York.

From 1840 to 1842 he attended the military school of Colonel W. W. Tompkins. This was, indeed, congenial to his tastes, and happy days they were for him. Taking a lead in the school, he attracted the attention of many people outside, and his heart was gladdened by his election to the lieutenancy of a militia company. Now his desires were beginning to take practical shape. His ascent was easy and rapid. Soon afterwards followed his commission as captain in the one hundred and ninety-

The People of the State of New-York.

To all to whom these Presents shall come:

KNOW YE, That pursuant to the Constitution and Laws of our said State, WE have appointed and constituted, and by these Presents do appoint and constitute _Daniel E. Huntsfield_ Captain ———————— of our said State, (with rank from 31 August 185 2 ————) to hold the 197 Regiment of Infantry, of our said State, (with rank from 31 August 185 2 ————) to hold the said Office in the manner specified on and by our said Constitution and Laws.

In Testimony Whereof, We have caused our Seal for Military Commissions to be hereunto affixed. Witness, **WILLIAM H. SEWARD,** Esquire, Governor of our said State, General and Commander-in-Chief of all the Militia, and Admiral of the Navy of the same, at our City of Albany, the 1———— day of September in the year of our Lord one thousand eight hundred and fifty-two ————

William H. Seward.

Passed the Adjutant-General's Office.

Rufus King, **Adjutant-General.**

seventh regiment of New York State militia, he having previously served as adjutant.

He wrote at this time various articles on military matters, which excited considerable comment; among others, one advocating military instruction in the public schools. This caused much discussion, and the subject was taken up by instructors throughout the country. The result we see at the present day; hardly one of our States is without a detail of officers of the U. S. Army, teaching military tactics in their universities, and few schools there are, either public or private, in which some military instruction does not form part of the course. How many are there now living who know and appreciate that the first agitation of this matter, so beneficial to the youth of our country and incalculable in its results, came from an article by young Hungerford's pen.

Early in the forties he entered upon the most serious step in his life. A young lady, Mademoiselle Eveline de la Visera, loving and beloved by many, was the choice of the young man's affections. She came of an old French family, her parents being born in France, though herself born in New York city. She had received every advantage, and had gradu-

ated with high honors at the Female Seminary
of Perth Amboy, New Jersey, of which the
Rev. Mr. Halsey was the principal. The
courtship was short; the marriage followed
soon after, and never did wedding bells ring
more cheerily nor peal more merrily than on
that bright morning when those two young
hearts were united. And that union, sealed in
the springtime of their lives, now that the
autumn has come, and the winter approaching,
is but the more firm. Through their long and
eventful lives no cloud has ever rested on the
horizon of their happy married life. When
the country was in danger, Mrs. Hungerford
was not the one to urge her husband to remain
at home. She bade him go where his patriotic
nature called him. And while he was away,
her time was not spent in unavailing regrets;
far from it, her tender heart and nobility of
character found ample scope in ministering to
the wants of the poor soldiers who, returning
to their native town sick and wounded, needed
woman's solace in their sad lot. Without
ostentation or display, Mrs. Hungerford did
her duty and more. It has been hers to test
the truth that "the bravest and noblest on
war's bloody fields are the bravest and truest
in love."

Three children blessed this happy union,
Marie Louise Antoinette, Daniel Dominique,
and Ada Elmire. Under the guidance of that
good mother, herself a lady in every sense of
the word, those children were well fitted to
adorn the high stations they were destined to
fill. The eldest daughter, beautiful and accomplished, was first married to Edmund Gar-
diner Bryant, of Brooklyn, who died, leaving
her a widow at the early age of nineteen. She
then married J. W. Mackay, the "Bonanza
King" of California, one of America's financial
geniuses, whose Aladdin-like career and immense interests have made his name known in
all parts of the world. The second, a son,
whose early loss they had to deplore at the
tender age of four years. The third married
Count Guiseppe Telfener, an Italian nobleman,
residing in Rome. Well may he be proud of
his cultivated American wife, a type of charm-
ing and graceful womanhood, who could com-
pare most favorably with any of the countesses
presented at the Italian Court.

In 1845, he is again in politics. The native
American party was then at its height. The
intense patriotism of young Hungerford caused
him to ally himself with that political organization. Solicited by his friends, he finally con-

sented to allow his name to be used, and he was
elected to public office by his fellow-citizens.
At the same time Harper, of the publishing
firm, was elected mayor.   Hungerford discharged the duties of his office with such satisfaction to all parties that he was unanimously
renominated; and although his party was
beaten by several thousand majority, he came
within nine votes of a re-election.   This spoke
volumes for his popularity among the people.
Nothing could swerve him from his duty, and
though a strong partisan, the sanctity of the
oath of office had for him too great a significance to be lightly considered.   Whether on
the field of battle or in civil life he always
felt that there was no obligation so sacred as
that which a public office imposed.   To be the
custodian of the honor of the people was for
him the highest trust that could be confided.

CHAPTER III.

ABOUT the middle of May, 1846, news of the battles of Gen. Taylor on the Rio Grande reached New York. This kindled the flame of enthusiasm and patriotic ardor. The martial spirit of the country was aroused and thousands gathered in the streets to listen and be fired by the speeches delivered at almost every street corner. The cry was now, "On to the City of Mexico!", as, in a few years later, it was to be "On to Richmond!" though the latter was at our doors, and the former three thousand miles away. Yet volunteers were ready and willing. Young Hungerford, returning from one of the meetings, realized that there was no time to be lost, and he determined to be the first in the breach. He knew that the Halls of the Montezumas would never be taken by speeches in New York city; regi-

8

ments would have to be raised and bloody
battles fought before our flag would fly over
the Mexican capital. A meeting of the Native
American party was called for that night at
American Hall, corner of Broadway and Prince
St. Hungerford attended, but, desirous of more
earnest work than mere lip service, he had prepared a list for the signatures of those who
were willing to enlist in the country's defence.
The meeting was about to adjourn without
anything being done, when Hungerford, bound-
ing on the platform, electrified the meeting by
a fervid, patriotic address. He drew a picture
of the gallant little army of Taylor, hundreds
of miles away from them that night, and looking to them for reinforcements. "Are we," he
asked, "to content ourselves by sympathetic
words? Has not the time for action come?" he
cried. "Will we haul down our flag, and shame-
fully retreat while there are thousands of men
here able to prevent it? Our fathers did not
do this in 1812. Let us show that we are as good
patriots as they." Then, holding the paper in
his hand, he appealed to the young men present who thought as he did, to step forward and
sign, he inscribing his name first. In response
to the young patriots call, one hundred and
fifteen stalwart young Americans signed the

roll. Two days after, he published in the
New York Sun a notice, asking the signers
to meet at California Hall, on West Broadway,
and organize a company of volunteers. It
was signed D. E. Hungerford, Captain, and it
pledged the signers to serve under him ; but
when they came together, Hungerford said he
did not wish to restrict them in choice of their
officers, and he was perfectly willing to shoulder a musket in the ranks, like any one of them.
He therefore resigned his rank, and said he
would come to whatever decision they came to.
The men, however, thought that he, himself,
was the one best capable of leading them, so
they unanimously elected him to the position.
Two lieutenants were chosen at the same time.
That same evening was despatched a letter to
the then Secretary of War, W. L. Marcy, offering their services to the Government. While it
was on the way to Washington, a requisition
was sent to the Governor of New York State at
Albany, to raise seven regiments of volunteers,
subject to a future call, to be mustered into the
U. S. service.

A few days later, he received a letter from
Mr. Marcy, commending him for his alacrity
and patriotism, as being the first to offer troops
from the State of New York. He referred him

to the Governor of the State. The Captain
having made his application to the Governor,
the latter recommended him to ally himself and
company with one of the regiments then forming. The consequence was that he joined the
First New York, thinking that that would be
the first one to see active service. His commission was signed by Silas Wright, with rank
dating from the 4th of June, 1846.

Soon after, Col. Jonathan D. Stevenson
received special permission from the War Department to raise a regiment of infantry to go
to California. The young Captain and his
company received the first offer to form part
of the regiment, but it was refused, as the con-
ditions of the service were too ungenerous.
The Government would not pay the expenses
of transportation of the company to their
homes, after they were mustered out of the
service. This was manifestly unjust, as how
could the men be expected to shoulder the cost
of traveling from one end of the continent to
the other. The Captain was willing, but he
could not induce his men, so he was reluctantly
obliged to decline the offer.

No further call was made till November;
in the meantime, the Captain and his company
met every week for drill, and strict discipline

The People of the State of New-York:

TO ALL TO WHOM THESE PRESENTS SHALL COME,

Know Ye, That in obedience to the requirements of the law of Congress, entitled "An act providing for the prosecution of the existing War between the United States and the Republic of Mexico," approved May 13th, 1846, and in conformity with the requisition of the President of the United States upon the Governor of the State of New-York, made under the authority of the law aforesaid, and pursuant to the Constitution and Laws of our said State, **WE** have appointed and constituted, and by these Presents do appoint and constitute *D. E. Hungerford, Captain, Company E, in the First Regiment of Volunteers* of our said State, under the act of Congress and requisition of the President aforesaid, with rank from *June 1, 1846,* to hold the said office in the manner specified in and by our said Constitution and Laws, and the said act of Congress and the requisition of the President of the United States.

In Testimony Whereof, We have caused our Seal for Military Commissions to be hereunto affixed. Witness, **SILAS WRIGHT,** Governor of our said State, General and Commander-in-Chief of all the Militia and Admiral of the Navy of the same at our City of Albany, the 19th day of June in the year of our Lord one thousand eight hundred and forty-six.

Adjutant-General.

was maintained by him. They drilled at the
State Arsenal, then on Centre Street, opposite
the Tombs. The muskets cost, each, twelve
cents a night ; this and other expenses, not in-
considerable, were all borne by the Captain,
who found the self-imposed task a heavy one.

Gen. Ward B. Burnett, a West Pointer, the
Colonel of the regiment, examined young Hungerford, and was agreeably surprised at the
proficiency he displayed, not only in the duties
of his position, but also in general military
knowledge.

Captain Hungerford kept his company in-
tact until the time for mustering in the United
States service, the other companies being
obliged to fill up their ranks to the required
number. Three companies having to be mustered in before a certain day, it became necessary to distribute Hungerford's company
among the others ; this he unwillingly con-
sented to do, although much against the wish
of his men, who had become greatly attached
to the zealous Captain. Hungerford again
began recruiting, and with a success that only
such energy and devotion could have. Soon
he had another company raised, some members of which came from the western part of
the State as far as Buffalo. It was mustered

into the service of Uncle Sam on the ninth day of December, 1846.

Now he was given the important command of the redoubt, in the rear of the fort, manned by his two companies. Such was the confidence his superior officers had in him. He, realizing the importance of the trust, at once commenced a system of rigid discipline. Though far from being a martinet, he was not oppressive, and he never required more from his men than what he was willing to exemplify by his own adherence to duty.

Here the Captain had an opportunity of showing an example of honesty to his men, and of giving a rebuke to his brother officers. To Captain Hungerford was deputed the payment of the men's clothing. In receiving a sum of money from the paymaster for the necessary expenditures, he was given a hundred dollars too much. Perceiving the error, the Captain returned the excess amount immediately, saying, "I have no use for this." "What is this for?" inquired the paymaster. "A slight mistake," replied the honest officer. "Impossible, I've been in the Pay Department thirty years, and never yet made a mistake." "Is that so? well, it only shows that we are all liable to make a mistake at times," he answered, thrust-

ing back the money. This regard for punc-
tilious honesty was all the more rare, since it
was generally accepted to be perfectly legitimate to profit by a paymaster's error. But
Captain Hungerford's fixed principles of integrity did not permit of such acceptations. How
few in life have this high sense of honor;
therefore all honor to the few who do possess
it. One of the officers present remarked that
he would never have returned the money.
"You would not!" responded the Captain,
"then I am sorry for you; that is not my idea
of an officer's honor." Nothing more was
said, and the Captain walked away in disgust,
and it is to be presumed that the group of officers who had heard the conversation were
duly impressed by the lesson given them by
this stripling young volunteer officer. Let us
hope the impression was lasting.

While awaiting the order for embarkation,
there were many spare hours to be occupied.
These were not spent by Captain Hungerford
after the usual manner of young officers. The
billiard table and card room had no patron in
him; he knew full well that, as there was no
royal road to learning, so success in the military profession was to be won only by assiduous attention to duty, and hard work. What

might have been his hours of leisure were to him hours of labor and severe discipline. And were a desire for self-glorification his ruling spirit, much more would be known of his career than I am permitted to state in this book.

Feeling that he could not properly discharge the duties of his position without a thorough knowledge of what those duties were, and knowing that to instruct others he must first be well instructed himself, he made a complete study of the volume on the " Rules and Regulations of the Army," and the " Articles of War." This gave him not only a comprehensive idea of his strictly military duties, but also of the internal economy of his command. Afterwards, while in active service, he had many times to congratulate himself on this preparation, and he had never cause to regret the time so employed. His accounts were as ready for inspection as his command were proficient in their drill. He became quite an authority in deciding technical points, and many a vexed question was left to his decision.

Life in the fort was uneventful, marked only by discipline, drills, and hours of study. But days of expectation must end, farewell to drilling-grounds, friends, and country must be said. Officers and men were at last thrilled to

the heart by the receipt of the long-coveted
order to embark for Mexico. The last bugle
sounded on shore, and the word for embarkation was given. With alacrity, with joy
mixed with sadness, the order was obeyed.
Words grow faint, and realization indistinct,
and we leave the imagination to supply the
thoughts of that little band marching forth,
with their lives in their hands, saying farewell,
perhaps forever, to those they loved best. But
war is a stern master, and very little heed can
be given to those left behind. Far away, with
Mexico in the distance, fame to be won, — with
all this in view, Captain Hungerford, leading
the way at the head of his company, was the
first to embark. Now for the battles in the
unknown land, teaching was to be put into
practice, the first baptism of blood and fire was
near at hand. Cheerily, even gaily, they set
out, alas! so many never to return. But there
was no quaking in the breasts of those brave
men, to whom the country's honor and safety
were so well entrusted, and never did hearts
beat faster nor with more glorious expectations, as the too slow ship ploughed the waves,
on the long voyage to Mexico. How well they
performed their duty, the success that attended
their arms, the victorious treaty of peace, by

9

which an empire of territory became ours and civilization was advanced — all form part of the nation's history, and make its pages glow with untarnished brilliancy. I will not follow Captain Hungerford through the war. The official records amply testify to his bravery and gallantry. Instead, I will give verbatim a letter he wrote to his brother from the city of Mexico, dated March 7, 1848, and in which he describes the movements he took part in, personal observations, and a general *résumé* of the operations of the army. Seeing clearly and writing clearly, his letter will prove interesting reading, and, being unreserved and free, it may throw a new light on some discussed points. He says:

"I commence to-night a detailed account of the operations and incidents of the campaign in Mexico, in which I have been a participant. Many of the incidents about to be related have come under my own observation.

"On Sunday, January 3, 1847, Captain Charles H. Shaw's and my own company embarked on board the bark *Isabella* at Fort Hamilton, situated at the entrance of New York Harbor. Captain Shaw, being the senior captain, was in command of the detachment. We remained lying off the fort until

the night, when we weighed anchor, and put
to sea with a fair and favorable wind. Our
destination was Point Isabelle, and we made
Brazos Landing on the twenty-fourth. We
remained off the Brazos nearly a week, taking
in water, food, and provisions. We were then
ordered by General Scott to proceed at once to
the Island of Lobos, a small island lying just
off the Mexican Coast. Lobos was designated
as the place of rendezvous for the troops composing the Army of Invasion, under General
Scott. We arrived here and disembarked,
clearing ground sufficient for our encampment;
we pitched our tents for three weeks before
the remainder of our regiment joined us. Our
time was occupied during our sojourn on the
island by drilling and preparing for more
active duties in the field. General Scott arriving with the last of the troops from the Brazos,
we were again embarked on board ship to rendezvous at San Antonis Lizardo, a few miles
above Vera Cruz, where it was intended to
effect a landing upon the coast of Mexico, but
the general-in-chief, altering his plan of landing, ordered the numerous transports of troops
to run down to the Island of Sacrificios, much
nearer the city of Vera Cruz, and just out of
range of the heavy guns of the Castle of San

Juan de Uloa. The island lies off about a
mile from the main land, and affords a good
shelter for shipping, from the heavy 'north-
erns,' which blow so fiercely in this latitude,
and are very dangerous to shipping upon the
coast, probably the worst in the world. From
this point the commander-in-chief proposed to
land his force.

"The disembarking commenced on the 9th
of March, under protection of our men-of-war;
the landing was effected as follows: The First
Division, General Worth, commanding on the
ninth; the Volunteer Division, General Patterson, commanding on the tenth; and the
Second Division, General Twiggs, on the tenth
and eleventh. General Worth met with but
little opposition, owing, probably, to the nature
of the ground, and the deceived Mexicans, not
anticipating a landing on this coast, had made
no preparations for our reception; they, sup-
posing we would attempt the disembarkation
at San Antonis Lizardo, had made rather extensive preparations to oppose us at that point.
On the tenth, we left the water or floating
prison, and sallied forth on terra firma, glad to
have space enough to use our elbows once
more. We formed our line upon the beach,
where we first planted the colors of the

Empire State. It was a grand imposing sight —
our dark blue jackets and white belts contrasting with our bright, shining bayonets, as the
rays of a scorching tropical sun poured down,
casting back a blinding reflection of glittering
fire. The bright, glowing colors upon our
state standard seemed as if rivaling the efful-
gent rays of the rainbow, as it took the gentle
breeze, and loosened its folds to the free breath
of the heavens. We proceed to possess ourselves of the many hills overlooking the city.
Before going farther, it may be well to give
you an idea of the situation of the city, and a
partial description of the immediate surrounding country. Vera Cruz is situated upon the
point of the mainland, apparently running out
into the sea. It is upon a sandy plain.
Directly in front, facing the sea, stands, upon
a small island of coral, the celebrated San
Juan de Uloa. The city is right upon the
shore, indeed, the ocean washes against the
foundations of some of the buildings; to the
rear, a level, sandy plain, extending some two
miles; then rise enormous high hills of loose
sand, apparently lodged there from some unknown causes. Between these hills run the
roads leading to and communicating with the
interior. You will perceive that the city,

being upon a point, by extending our line
straight across, we reach the beach on the
opposite side, and consequently prevent communication between the city and the interior.
General Worth kept more along the beach,
probably with a view of gaining an advantageous position, while, as I stated before, we
proceeded to take possession of the hills. In
effecting this, we had several smart skirmishes
with the enemy's light troops and lancers. We
finally gained a position, and bivouacked for
the night upon the loose sand. I lost, in the
day's operations, one man. It was my turn to
be on guard that night, and a hard tour of duty
I found it. I tore my clothes to pieces, going
among the 'chaparral,' to place and post my
pickets. Nothing of importance happening
during the night to disturb the tranquillity of
the camp, the next morning at an early hour
we marched still further across the hills, and
slept that night upon the brow of a large hill.
A strong 'norther' had sprung up during the
night, and when daylight broke, it was difficult to tell whether there were any human
beings in the vicinity or not, but the doubt was
soon dispelled; officers and soldiers disinter
themselves by throwing off the heaps of sand
which had served them for a blanket, blown

there during the night. Such was the sameness of each day and night until the sixteenth, when we had gained our position proper for the investment of the city. Our position in the line of investment brought us on the Orizaba Road, one of the principal avenues leading from the city. We had cleared a sufficient space for the occupation of the companies in the line of battle, in which order we encamped with a space of twenty or thirty feet intervening between the companies' camps. We cleared also a ground for parade. After a lapse of several days, we got our tents up from the beach, some three or four miles distance, no easy task, there being no other means of transportation than little burros or "jacks," that were caught in the 'chaparral.' There was no practicable road for wagons over the hills of sand, and through the 'chaparral.' While occupying this position, we were frequently called upon to furnish details for the working parties, building and establishing batteries for subjugation of the city. On two occasions, my company was called to the works. The last time I shall never forget. A fierce 'norther' was blowing the sand like a snowdrift, filling our eyes, ears, and mouths, coming with such force as to bring the blood as it

struck the check. That was a terrible night.
On returning to camp, my men became scattered, and some of them did not find their way
back until noon the next day. Provisions
were very scarce; in fact, I do not know what
we would have done, had there not been
plenty of beef found among the 'chaparral.'
We were obliged to send parties from camp
to hunt beef, and supply us in that way.
On one occasion, the nineteenth of March, a
party of beef-hunters from the First Pennsylvania Volunteers was surrounded by a
large force of rancheros who were in our
rear watching an opportunity to break our
lines and gain the city. This little party,
consisting of twenty under command of a
subaltern, were in danger of being cut off
from us. We, lying nearest, intelligence
reached us first of their situation. Col. Burnett ordered four companies under arms, to
march to the assistance and rescue of the
party. The companies were Hungerford's,
Dyckman's, Taylor's, and De Bougard's, which
were promptly got ready. Leaving camp,
we pursued the Orizaba Road, where we
were joined by Col. Wynkoop, of the Pennsylvania Volunteers. With a portion of this
regiment, we followed the road to where it

branches off, when Col. Burnett gave Col. Wynkoop one of his companies to make their respective forces equal. Col. Wynkoop was to follow the road leading to the right and gain the enemy's rear, while Col. Burnett was to take the left, leading through a thick 'chaparral' and breaking into an open plain (where the enemy was supposed to be), and attack in front. After this arrangement, the two colonels took the agreed directions. I was with Col. Burnett. We pursued the road until we came to the opening, where we discovered the enemy, about three-quarters of a mile from us, positioned upon the brow of a hill rising above the plain. The Colonel immediately set about the disposition of his little force. Taylor's company he ordered to gain a clump of trees or brushwood. The field was studded all over with clumps of trees and bushes. Under the cover of the 'chaparral' to the right, Dyckman's company was ordered to deploy as skirmishers to the left, and advance unperceived and attack the enemy's right, while Hungerford's company was to advance upon the open plain and attack and charge in front. Arriving at the base of the hill, Hungerford charged

with his company up the hill and dislodged
the enemy, about eighty strong. However,
they fell back upon their main body, about
five hundred horse and one hundred and
twenty-five infantry. As soon as Captain
Hungerford had gained the summit they
opened a brisk fire upon him. He immediately withdrew his company just off the
summit of the hill, so as to protect his
brave men as much as possible. He then
ordered them to load kneeling, and rise up
so as to look over the hill, returning the
fire with alacrity and good effect. Captain
Dyckman, gaining an advantageous position,
opened a well-directed fire upon the enemy's
right flank, with execution, the Mexicans
making a movement off to their right, with
evident intention to cut off Captain Dyckman's company. Captain Hungerford, seeing
the apparent danger of the gallant Dyckman, made a counteracting movement to
thwart the supposed design of the Mexicans. The rancheros, being mounted, consequently moved faster than Hungerford's
infantry, but the movement had the effect
of causing the enemy to take a greater circuit than he intended, which brought him
outside of Captain Dyckman. He, however,

succeeded in outflanking us. But Captain Hungerford again opened his fire, this time by the front and rear rank alternately. The enemy having so far gained an advantage by nearly surrounding us, the Colonel, seeing this, ordered the recall previously agreed upon, when Captain Hungerford with his company joined the Colonel on the right. Captain Dyckman not answering the recall, fears were entertained for his safety. Thus affairs stood at the setting of the sun. Here an incident occurred worth recording, showing the coolness of man in time of the greatest danger. By this time the enemy had completed the chain and had entirely surrounded us. We were at their mercy. We knew not to what fate one of our companies was doomed. Col. Burnett, gazing at the last rays of the setting sun, as it tinged the heavens with its gold and silver beams, showing forth all the beauteous colors of the rainbow's hues, exclaimed in a calm and quite undisturbed tone, as if looking from his own balcony, 'What a beautiful sunset! Did you ever witness such a sight?' We afterwards formed around a clump of bushes, prepared to repel a charge. The enemy venturing within range of our

muskets, we opened a fire upon them by
platoons, which sent some six or eight of
their horses away minus their riders. They
did not appear very desirous of making a
further acquaintance, so they kept at a
respectful distance. Captain Dyckman at
this time joined us, he having sheltered his
company in another clump of bushes, while
we supposed him in the greatest peril. A
consultation was held as to further action,
Captain Hungerford, Captain Taylor, and
Captain Dyckman coinciding that we should
charge and break through the enemy's line
at his weakest point, which was where his
right had rested at the commencement of
the action, by this means to gain the main
wood on our left and cut him off from his
camp. Once in the wood, we were safe
from a charge of his horse; while with
this advantage, we could safely harass and
annoy him. The Colonel, however, after
ascertaining from the captains that their
men had no bread or water, two things
most essential to the soldier, he, with a
Jackson-like firmness, ordered three sides of
a square to be formed, leaving the rear of
the square open, with the understanding
that in case of a charge from the enemy,

to complete it by throwing back the second
platoon of Taylor's or Dyckman's companies. The square thus compassed, and with
these necessary precautions, we moved towards the camp, and triumphantly marched
off the field, without meeting with any
opposition, although we passed within a
short distance of the Mexicans, as they
were between ourselves and our camp. Col.
Burnett opposed the proposition of the
council of captains for the reason that the
men had no bread in their knapsacks nor
water in their canteens. We might have
done without bread, but water was much
needed, and without the latter our suffering
would have been intense; already it was
being felt among the soldiers; none but
those having experienced it can know the
great distress occasioned by the want of
water during the heat of an engagement.
Had Colonel Wynkoop followed the route
of his directions, we would have captured
the whole of the Mexican force; but for
some reason that I have not been able to
ascertain, he returned to camp instead, very
soon after separating from Col. Burnett,
leaving us at the mercy of an enemy not
bound by any of the obligatory rules of

civilized warfare, and showing, whenever
opportunity afforded, a savage barbarity
that rivaled the most uncivilized of the
Indian tribes on the American continent,
from which our little force narrowly
escaped. At the time of the occurrence,
the eyes of the whole American Union
were directed towards Vera Cruz, anxiously
awaiting news from that quarter, making
a mountain out of the smallest mole-hill,
and transforming a little skirmish into a
great and important battle. Had Col. Burnett made a report of the affair to the
Commanding General, we would have had
an early reputation, a reputation since
bought at the expense of many a brave
and gallant fellow, whose bones are now
bleaching among the heights of Cerro Gordo,
among the rocky pedregats of Contreras,
on the plains of Cherubusco, the hills and
swamps of Chapultepec, and the Garita de
Belen.

The batteries having been completed and
the siege batteries got into position, the cannonade commenced from the American lines
on the twenty-first of March, and continued
with but little or no cessation till the twenty-
seventh, when commissioners from the Mexi-

can authorities arrived at our camp, under a
flag of truce, to negotiate a capitulation of
the city and castle. The terms of the capitulation having been agreed upon and ratified
by the proper agents of the two Powers, the
city of Vera Cruz, with the famous and celebrated Castle of San Juan de Uloa, capitulated and was evacuated on the twenty-ninth
of March, the whole Mexican army laying
down their arms in the presence of the American troops, and being allowed to return to
their respective homes, the officers on their
parole. The Americans at once took possession of the city, which they found in a dis-
tressed state from the effects of the siege. It
was a horrible sight to behold the unburied
bodies. The buildings presented the picture
of an old city in ruins, rather than the com-
mercial emporium of a nation, their dilapi-
dated condition being the havoc made by the
shells thrown from our batteries, showing the
terrible result to the enemy of our superiority in the art and science of war. Our
troops immediately commenced putting the
city in proper order again, clearing out the
stones, mortar, and rubbish from the streets
and other public places. A few days of such
work gave the city a new and healthy appear

ance. The stores and public houses were
re-opened, and they soon resumed their accustomed business, being assured the proper
protection from the American authorities.
In the meantime, the troops were ordered
from their positions behind the sand-hills to
encamp on the beautiful level plains near
the city. This was a magnificent sight: an
army of about twelve thousand encamped
on a splendid plain, with numerous hills
overlooking the fields of snow-white tents,
each camp laid out in regular order, having
its streets and avenues, its parades, etc., all
presenting a picturesque and lovely scene.
Lying just off the beach, riding at anchor,
was the American squadron, the larger men-
of-war high out of the water, with their sides
bristling with bright pieces of armament, and
the broad pennant streaming from the main,
while the glorious 'Stars and Stripes' of
'happy land' were unfurled by the soft
breath of heaven from the peaks of large
and small craft, as if enjoying the hilarity
of the occasion, and adding to the brilliancy
of the spectacle. Such a sight of magnificent
splendor would warm the coldest heart and
almost make marble animate. This enjoyment was well received and duly appreciated,

after the privations and extreme sufferings experienced during the siege, the officers uniting in congratulations, renewing the acquaintance of former times, and forming new intimacies with the gentlemen representing the various States of our beloved Union gathered together in the service of their country.

"During a visit to town I took occasion to pay a visit to the castle. I cannot but express my astonishment at the impregnable appearance of the fortress, and yet to fall an easy conquest to brighten the already illustrious arms of the American troops! The castle is principally built of the coral rock, a soft material, with a heavy granite facing, the granite having been brought from the United States some time before the beginning of the war. The walls are very thick, the front wall well planned and strongly constructed. There are also numerous outworks of water batteries, adding greatly to the strength and defense of the principal work, the castle. The works were well-conditioned and in good fighting order, having a full and complete armament of arms of various caliber, and capable of sustaining a long and protracted if not a successful defense.

"On the eighth of April, the volunteer division (Patterson's) broke up their encampment and took up their line of march for the interior, preceded a few days by Gen. Twiggs' division of regulars. The first day's march was awful; the day was extremely hot, not a breath of air stirring the green foliage upon the trees. The road lay over deep, loose sand, ankle deep, for about six miles, and owing to the scanty means of transportation, the men were compelled to carry their heavy knapsacks, in addition to their haversacks, with four days' rations, besides arms and equipments and forty rounds of ammunition. Many of the men were compelled through excessive fatigue to lag along the road. We made only eight miles' march that day, and encamped, scattering along the road, near Monte Clavo, a beautiful hacienda belonging to Santa Anna. On the eleventh, we reached the Puenta National Bridge, a strongly fortified pass in a beautiful romantic situation, with two high, steep hills of rocks on either side. At the bottom of the baranca or gorge runs a beautiful river on the Sierra; at the left, as one enters the vale, stands a fort, commanding the approach from either direction. To the left, after crossing the bridge, is another of Santa Anna's lofty palaces. Gen. Twiggs had a pretty smart brush with the enemy at this place the day preceding our arrival.

"Nature had done much for the defense of the Puenta National, which the Mexicans abandoned after a few shots from Twiggs' artillery. We remained one night at this lovely spot of scenic beauty. The next day we followed the direction of our march. This was a hard march. The New York regiment furnished a guard of four companies to the artillery, my company being one of them. This guard was of course expected to keep up with the artillery, which came very hard on the poor fellows, so heavily laden with their trappings. We made but one halt during the march of seventeen miles, and no water to be found the whole distance. Their sufferings were intense, yet the poor fellows murmured not, bearing up under the fatigues like. beasts of burden rather than human beings. Really they are worthy descendants of their forefathers of '76. In the afternoon we encamped, or I should say bivouacked, on Plan del Rio, where

our gallant men refreshed themselves by
bathing in the stream running at the bottom
of the ravine. This is also a somewhat fortified pass. Gen. Twiggs here again had an
encounter with the Mexican troops the day
before our arrival. Gen. Twiggs had discovered the enemy some three miles distant, prepared to oppose our advance, being strongly
fortified and in full force on the heights of
Cerro Gordo. The General had made during
the day a reconnoissance of the enemy's position, and had gained much valuable information. He proposed to attack him the next
morning. Gen. Patterson, however, preferred
to await the coming up of the old war-horse,
Gen. Scott, from Vera Cruz. Nothing of importance occurred from the twelfth to the
sixteenth, when Scott arrived, much to the
gratification of all concerned. Reconnoitering
was continued during each day, and frequently the curiosity of the Yankees was
discovered by the artillerists of Santa Anna's
legion; they would make known the discovery by despatching a deadly missile of war
as messenger, but without any serious effect.

"General Scott, after having been put in
possession of all the information that was
obtained, formed his plans for the discom-

fiture of the braves of the Great Chieftain
of the New World. He proceeded at once to
put them into execution, and on the seventeenth commenced the movements necessary
to secure a good position. Roads were made
through the thick chaparral and over hills;
artillery was got into position; and every precaution was taken and all arrangements completed. Gen. Twiggs had a sharp fight on the
seventeenth, before he dislodged the enemy
from the advanced position upon the Sierra
Telegrafo, a hill immediately to the south of
Cerro Gordo, and within range of the guns of
the latter. This object was gained late in
the afternoon, with a small loss on our side;
that victory added greatly to the splendid
achievements that followed the next morning. As this point was the base of operations
against the strong works of the Mexicans
upon Cerro Gordo, our brigade (Shields') occupied a position near the base of this hill,
and during the night we dragged the heavy
artillery up the steep sides, and it operated
with terrible effect upon the enemy's lines.
It is astonishing how men will labor and
endure such hardships under an excitement
caused by the anticipation of a coming strife.
For the time being they seemed to be pos-

sessed of uncommon strength both of body
and mind. Shields' brigade bivouacked under
the hill, on the morning of the eighteenth
of April, a day so bright in the annals of
American history. It was ushered in by
the thundering peals of Mexican artillery, as
if saluting the first rays of the rising sun
and paying homage to the bright aurora
of an April morn. The grape and round-shot
swept thick and fast over our heads as we
lay under cover anxiously awaiting the order
to advance. Nothing can create a more fev-
erish excitement than lying inactive without
the view of a battle's range, hearing the
booming of the artillery and the sharp crack
of the rifles and musketry. We were not
kept long in suspense. The welcome word
came. 'Fall in! fall in!' was repeated by
the officers in rapid succession, and soon the
bristling bayonets of the brave volunteers
were reflecting in the soft rays of an April
sun. We filed off to the right, around the
base of the hill, and soon were exposed to the
terrific fire from the Mexican forts. Coming
in full view of Cerro Gordo, with our troops
already ascending it, only increased the desire
to become a participant in the coming struggle. But in this we were disappointed. Gen.

Shields being ordered to turn the enemy's left and gain position in his rear, we consequently crossed the ravine to the right through which the Mexicans were pouring a most destructive fire, and mounted the hill on the opposite side. As I reached the brow of the hill I turned to look back at my brave countrymen, as they continued to advance with steady and firm step. I then discovered that I was not the only one that looked upon that phalanx of chivalry, for the whole New York regiment were gazing upon the scene. At this moment the covering of the colors of the Fifth infantry was taken off, and the beloved emblem of the free took the morning breeze. As it was unfurled to the airy breath of heaven, the sons of the Empire State saluted with as three hearty cheers as ever came from the throats of men. Now, with a rapid pace, we resumed our route, passing through a narrow path by a flank. General Shields fell at the head of his brigade. Col. Baker, of the Illinois volunteers, being the next in rank, took command. About this time the heights of Cerro Gordo were taken, and the colors of the Fifth and Third infantry had taken the place of the tri-color of Mexico. A few minutes and the Mexican

army was in full flight, scattered in all directions. We gained the deserted camp of the
Mexicans. Here were sights too horrible to
behold. The shattered limbs of men and
beasts, the wounded and dead lying together,
horses and mules dead in the road, some running or rather limping away in all directions,
as if fearful that the enemy of their masters
was also theirs. We filed out into the road,
and waiting a few minutes for a couple of
pieces of artillery, we commenced the pursuit
of the flying Mexicans, who fled with the
greatest precipitancy before us. By this detour to the right our brigade gained the
advance of our army. We pursued the
enemy at a rapid pace for fourteen miles.
Breaking upon the plains of Encero, we
halted to await the coming up of the dragoons. Gen. Patterson, joining us with the
dragoons (he was previously sick, and we
were consequently placed under the command of Gen. Twiggs and in his division),
ordered a general halt and encampment for
the night. We encamped upon the plain,
and Gen. Patterson occupied Santa Anna's
hacienda of Encero, the third one of these
establishments that we had met from Vera
Cruz.

"The troops were allowed to shoot beef for the supply of the several camps. I suppose nearly a hundred head of cattle were shot to feed this army of invasion. They belonged, so I understand, to Santa Anna, but for which was paid, after the arrival of the army at Jalapa, the round sum of four thousand dollars, the money being handed over to a nephew of Santa Anna himself.

"The next day, the nineteenth, we entered the city of Jalapa. It stands partially upon a side hill, and presents a beautiful appearance when viewed from a short distance. It is a fine town, the climate being healthy and the temperature moderate. All the vegetable products of the tropics, as well as those of the northern climes, are here in abundance. Jalapa derives its name from jalap, a vegetable growing in the immediate vicinity. The troops, with the exception of the volunteers, occupied very comfortable quarters in the city. I will take this opportunity of giving publicity, as far as practicable, to the gross, negligent injustice done the volunteers by those having authority to ameliorate some of the sufferings of those brave, spirited patriots, who left their homes, family, business, all they held dear, to obey the call of

their country and sustain her honor and
glory. These gallant corps have been looked
upon with a disparaging eye and spoken of
with a slandering tongue. I will readily
admit that there are individual cases of out-
rageous depravity, but they are not confined
solely to the volunteers, who are not kept
under strict discipline. It cannot, therefore,
be reasonably expected that the volunteers
would be superior to the regulars in good
order and honesty.

"The volunteers were ordered to encamp
about three miles from the city, with only
three tents to a company, instead of the fifteen allowed for their accommodation. The
poor volunteers had to build for themselves
little brush houses to shelter themselves from
the pitiless storms of daily occurrence during
nearly three weeks. The suffering was terrible. It rained almost every night. None but
those who experienced or witnessed it can
depict the woeful condition of those brave
fellows.

"This is but one of the many instances
where the volunteers have been made to take
the unequal share of the privations and hardships of the campaign, while the regulars
have been snugly housed in good, comforta-

ble buildings. I have known times when the
officers in the volunteer service were crowded,
or rather jammed together, six or eight in a
room, while the officers in the regular army
were in the full possession and enjoyment
of splendid quarters, with an abundance of
room. Is it surprising that the volunteers
complain of this manifest partiality?

"The scenery around and about Jalapa is
of a magnificent grandeur, unsurpassed by
even the romantic scenery of the noble Hud-
son. The lovely Orizaba,— its snow-capped
peak towering in the clouds far above the
numerous hills and mountains surrounding,
— proudly stands a beacon of light to the
traveler for miles. The country around is
in a high state of cultivation, showing a
degree of prosperity not frequently met with
in Mexico.

"Gen. Worth continued his march as far as
Perote; the castle surrendered to him without firing a gun. This is a splendid work,
of great strength. It is situated upon a
plain, and about a mile from the city of
Perote. The city lies just under the mountains; it is not of much importance, and has
but few inhabitants, compared with the other
cities of the Republic.

"On the seventh of May we broke up our camp, to continue our march to the capital, glad to change our condition and leave the rainy season and all its attendant discomforts to the few Mexicans loitering about the vicinity.

"The volunteers, consisting of the New York and South Carolina regiments and the first regiment of Pennsylvania, under the command of Brigadier (now Major) General Quitman, reached Perote on the ninth. Gen. Worth, leaving the city and castle the same morning, left a small detachment here to await our arrival. We remained until the morning of the eleventh, when, leaving the Pennsylvanians to garrison the town and castle, we resumed our march. We encamped for the night at the hacienda San Antonio, upon the plains. The only thing worthy of note at this place is the well which supplies the hacienda with water. It is seven hundred feet in depth, and is well walled up, the water being raised by mules. It is the greatest artificial curiosity that I have yet seen.

"Nothing of import happened until we reached El Piñal, where we received intelligence from Gen. Worth that he anticipated an engagement the next day. Early next morning we struck our tents and resumed the march. About twelve o'clock, mid-day, hearing the firing of artillery, we moved on at a rapid pace. When nearing Amozoc, a small "pueblo" about seven miles from the city of Peubla, we discovered the enemy, about six thousand strong, evidently making his way toward us. We instantly formed our line of battle to receive him. He, seeing this preparation, changed his course, and left us on our right, apparently not caring to make the attack. This force was under the command of the redoubtable Santa Anna, who had left Peubla with the ostensible purpose of attacking us, as I learn from his dispatches to the Mexican War Minister. He returned to Puebla by a roundabout way. General Worth determined to attack the city the next morning. He made a disposition and left Amozoc during the night with his division, with orders for General Quitman to follow early the next morning. We were under arms at three o'clock, but receiving word from General Worth that he was about negotiating for the surrender of the city, we did not move until about seven o'clock, when we proceeded to enter and take possession of the city and fortifications. Santa Anna evacuated, leaving

a city of eighty thousand inhabitants, in addition to his army, to the occupancy of four
thousand American troops. We entered the
Grand Plaza at one o'clock, where we stacked
arms, and the soldiers, in the coolest possible
manner, lay down and went to sleep, until the
quartermasters had secured quarters for the
several corps. This will hardly be believed,
but it is none the less true. Fears of an out-
break were entertained by many of the higher
officers, and every precaution was taken for
its suppression, if any manifestation should
show itself. Matters were in this shape for
nearly two weeks, prior to the arrival of General Scott. A stampede was of nightly occurrence, but I suppose the object was to keep the
troops constantly vigilant, and on the alert.
Assassinations occurred almost daily; whenever a drunken soldier could be enticed to the
outskirts of the city, he was treacherously cut
down. While the American army occupied
Puebla, every effort was made by our Government to consummate a peace. The Mexican
authorities, however, always rejected the repeated offers of the olive branch.

"Puebla is built upon a plain, having on its
east a large hill, at the summit of which is
built a fort (Loretta), also a large church, like-

wise fortified. This hill is called Guadaloupe, and the works upon it command the town. There is a splendid promenade, known as the Alemada. At one end of the Alemada is erected a Temple of Liberty. The walks are handsomely laid out, having on either side splendid trees; between each tree numerous rosebushes and plants are growing, displaying the taste of a horticulturist, not often surpassed in the United States. The Alemada is en-closed by a beautiful, ornamented fence made of cement, a material peculiar to the country. There are also two theaters, a bull-ring, and a cock-pit, for the amusement of the citizens. The city of Puebla is by far the handsomest city that I have seen in this country, much superior to the city of Mexico in beauty; it is laid out regularly, and kept in perfect cleanli-ness. The inhabitants are more cultured, showing a refinement exceeding that of the capital.

"A short distance (about six miles) from Puebla is situated the ancient city of Cholula, celebrated in Cortez's time for the great human sacrifices, made upon the formed pyramid, which stands to the present day. Many officers of the army visited this spot on several occasions. It is indeed an interesting sight.

"On the 10th of August, General Twiggs' division, forming the advance, took up its march for the Mexican capital, followed on the succeeding day by General Quitman's division of volunteers, then Pillow's and Worth's in succession. Our route lay across the mountains, nothing of importance occurring in our division, or the others that I am aware of, until the twelfth, when the beautiful valley lay spread before us. The valley of Mexico is justly celebrated for its panoramic and scenic beauty and loveliness. We descended the mountains and entered the valley, encamping at the Hacienda de Buena Vista, just at the foot of the mountain, General Twiggs occupying a position at Ayotla from whence he pushed forward his reconnoissances, and discovered the enemy, very strongly fortified upon a hill in advance of him, prepared to oppose the passage of the American army. Generals Worth and Pillow occupied the old city of Chalco, situated off to the left of the main road, upon a lake of that name. These positions were respectively held until the fourteenth, when General Scott, not wishing to engage the enemy under such disadvantages (where he would, in all probability, suffer an immense loss, which he could ill afford),

changed his plans, and by a detour off to the
west, pursuing an old, broken-up road under
the mountain, and along the shores of the
lakes, avoided an action that would have cost
him one-fourth of his gallant army. On the
nineteenth, General Worth found a position in
front of the enemy's strong works at San
Antonio. General Pillow, with his division,
left San Augustine as General Quitman (?)
entered. Pillow advanced to meet the Mexicans, who were strongly fortified at Contreras,
under the command of the gallant General
Valencia. General Valencia's army was composed of troops from the north, and were said
to be the best in the Mexican service. About
mid-day, skirmishing began, between the
advanced guard of Pillow, and the light troops
of Valencia. The rifle regiments deployed
through the 'chaparral' and soon drove the
Mexican pickets back upon their works. Pillow continued to push forward his column, the
enemy opening upon him at long distance
with their heaviest caliber. Finally, a portion
of our light artillery found a position, a bad
one though, from which they could answer the
fire of Valencia. The ground between the
opposing forces was very rough, and much
broken up, being of a rocky, volcanic sub-

13

stance, with numerous chasms, making it
impossible for horse and impracticable for
artillery, except mountain howitzers. A part
of the infantry advanced over this 'pedregal' and assaulted the enemy's works in
front. General Smith, with his brigade, made
a movement off to the right to gain a small
village (San Geronimo, or en Senada). Gen.
Cadwallader also moved off to the right, taking more ground than Smith. These two
brigades made this movement for the purpose of preventing the junction of Santa
Anna, at the head of a large force, with
General Valencia. The brave and gallant
Colonel Riley had already gained the hamlet,
and received two repeated charges from the
enemy's cavalry, which he nobly repulsed
each time, the second time charging them in
turn, and driving them up the hill. General
Scott, who had come up a short time before,
in passing through San Augustine, saw the
desperate and doubtful conflict. He ordered
immediately Shields' brigade of volunteers
(consisting of the New York and South Carolina regiments) to support General Pillow's
division. These gallant fellows came up,
cheering lustily all along the road, elated at
the prospect of showing what they could do.

Passing General Scott, the pride of the American soldier, who stood upon a hill immediately in rear of the American lines, the veteran took off his hat in acknowledgment of a cheer from the volunteers, ordering them at the same time to gain a position upon the enemy's left.

"There are some who claim the laurels of Contreras, and others who are acknowledged the heroes; but to none but General Winfield Scott belongs the honor. He was the great master-spirit who guided and directed the glorious victory. The writer was himself upon the hill with General Scott, and knows, to his positive and certain knowledge, of the part taken by him, though the General, noble-spirited as he is, gives credit to Smith and Riley for the very excellent movements made by them during the night; but he, and no other, was the prompter of it all, and further, the writer is of opinion that had not General Scott arrived at that time to assume command, the American troops, for the first time in this campaign, would have been obliged to give way. General Pillow was in such a dilemma that it required an older and more experienced head to extricate him from the imminence of disgraceful defeat.

"Shields pushed forward his brigade across

the 'pedregal' (fording the ravines, the men
up to their waists) in the face of a most severe
and most destructive fire from the enemy's
batteries, gaining the Puebla de Encenada
about midnight his men lying down in the
mud about six inches deep. Just at dark it
came on to rain, and never was there a harder
rain.   Cold, wet, and hungry, they murmured
not, but in silence bore their privations and
sufferings, anxiously awaiting the first break
of day that was to bring them face to face
with the foe.

"About three o'clock in the morning, General Smith commenced a movement up the
ravine, running in the rear of the hill of Contreras.   By dawn, Colonel Riley had succeeded
in outflanking the enemy and getting in the
rear of him.   He advanced down upon the astonished Mexicans, like, as General Scott says,
'an avalanche from the mountains.'   The
enemy, not dreaming of such a possibility, had
made no preparations to protect his rear, and
before he could recover from his astonishment
the veteran Riley was in his works, and the
flower of the Mexican army put to flight, leaving their strong intrenchments.   Three hundred and sixty-five were taken prisoners by
Shields' brigade, who were well-positioned to

hold in check Santa Anna with his reinforcements, as well as to battle to the front, if the
occasion demanded. Among the prisoners,
taken by Shields, were several generals, colonels, majors, captains, and any number of subaltern officers. This battle was fought almost
entirely by infantry, artillery and cavalry not
being able to pass over the ' pedregal.'

"From Contreras, the Americans pursued
the retreating Mexicans, until the latter had
gained a still stronger position at Churubusco.
The rifle regiment was skirmishing along the
road. While our troops were passing through
the villages of San Angel and Coyocan, Generals Worth and Pillow were moving along
the San Augustine road, and General Twiggs
was upon the road from Coyocan, leading into
the city, forming a junction with the San
Augustine road, at the bridge of Churubusco.
Owing to the bad roads, and the short space of
time available, little or no information could
be gained by the reconnoitring of their position, nor could we learn anything of the
importance of their works. The rifles in
advance met, and drove in the light troops of
the enemy, and soon the roar of the artillery
was heard. General Shields with his brigade
was halted at Coyocan. Shields was ordered

to countermarch his brigade, and gain the
rear of the enemy's left flank, at the Hacienda
de Los Portales. The New York and South
Carolina Volunteers, composing Shields' brigade, breaking through the cornfields and over
ditches, came upon a level and open field, in
the center of which was a building used as a
barn, or grain storehouse. As soon as the
head of the line of the New Yorkers (marching by a flank) appeared upon the plain, the
Mexicans opened fire upon them. They, however, gained the rear of the buildings, and
commenced the formation of their line of
battle, throwing their left off obliquely, in
order to protect their men as much as possible.
Before the line was completely formed, the
order to charge was given. They charged,
and were compelled to retire under cover of
the building where they partially reformed,
charging again. They were for the second
time repulsed; the third charge, however,
proved successful. Previous to the last charge,
the Mexicans made a movement to flank
Shields' command, which happily was prevented by the gallant ninth, making a counteracting one. About this time the tête-de-pont
or bridge-head was taken. Shields gained the
road and pursued the flying enemy until

halted by Major-General Pillow. The convent of Churubusco, strongly and extensively forti- fied, was taken. This undoubtedly had great effect upon the operations at the bridge-head.

"A stream of considerable size, called Rio de Churubusco, runs through the hamlet, which made it difficult to pass without first gaining possession of the works at the bridge. After the capture of the church, and the fall of the tête-de-pont, followed by the final rout by Shields, Captain Kearney, with his dragoons, drove the enemy into their works at the bridge immediately before the city, himself and several of his command being wounded while so doing. The troops, at the very moment when the capital of Mexico was at their mercy, were halted, and an armistice was proposed in order to give the Mexicans a last opportunity to accept the liberal terms of peace, and thereby save themselves the dis- grace of another defeat, and the reduction of the capital of their country. The American troops were withdrawn to occupy the positions of Tacubya, Muscoac, San Angel, and San Augustine. During the continuance of the negotiations, the commissioners met at Tacu- bya. But after several days' sessions, General Scott being informed that Santa Anna was treacherously progressing the defenses of the city, in violation of the terms of the military convention, entered into and agreed upon by the two contending powers, he thought proper to give the requisite notice of the suspension of the armistice. On the sixth of September, he again assumed the offensive, and prepared for the speedy reduction of the city. On the morning of the eighth, General Worth was ordered to attack the enemy in his new position, at Molino del Rey. General Scott at the same time ordered up the divisions from San Augustine, San Angel, and Muscoac, and made preparations for investing the city.

"The battle of Molino Del Rey was a severely contested engagement, but after a combat of about two hours, the Mexican troops were compelled to give way before the invincible sons of Washington, though not without a severe loss having been sustained by each side. The occupation of Molino Del Rey proved to be of no importance whatever. On the eleventh, the several divisions received orders to take their positions: General Pillow near Molino, General Worth further across and on the road running to the north side of the hill of Chapultepec, General Quitman's division on the Tacubya road. Batteries were established there by Captain Hungerford, with two companies under direction of Lieutenant Smith of the engineers. Batteries were also established near Molino del Rey, under direction of Captain Hague, of the Ordnance, assisted by others. Early upon the morning of the twelfth, we commenced to cannonade the castle. The fire was returned with alacrity and spirit. The cannonading continued throughout the day, dismounting many of the enemy's guns, and making several breaches in the walls. Captain Hungerford asked permission of Generals Shields and Quitman, to retain command of his two companies, detached from the regiment, in order that the men might obtain some rest from their all-night labors. This was readily granted, accompanied with kind words for such thoughtful treatment of his men. However, always alert, he posted himself upon the flat roof of one of the buildings upon the edge of the town, from which point he could overlook the whole scene. Glass in hand, he watched the effect of every shot. Near the close of the day, he said to the officer next in command, "As sure as the sun rises to-morrow morning, we will be called upon to assault that hill, and I want you to be ready." Early on the morning of the thirteenth, the captain placed his two companies on the right, and across the road near the batteries, in order to be ready and in the front, when the order to advance should be given. He had not long to wait, for soon the movement began. Sweeping past the South Carolinians, the New York Regiment rushed forward to the assault. Just after leaving the road, and in crossing a field of well-grown barley, Lieutenant-Colonel Baxter fell, mortally wounded, and, the Major having been struck at about the same time, the Captain immediately sprang forward to the head of the line, assumed the command, and directed the movements of the regiment.

The intersecting space, i. e., between the road and the high wall surrounding the base of the hill, was obstructed by three deep ditches filled with water. Over this space he led his regiment. Reaching the wall, he directed the adjutant to break off ten men and see if there was not an opening, which he thought he had discovered the day before while watching from the house-top. Having rectified the regimental line, and the adjutant reporting the opening, he flanked the regiment, and, filing along the wall, entered the enclosure. While this was going on, the gallant band of South Carolinians, known as the Palmetto Regiment, were enlarging the breaches in the wall in order to afford themselves an opening. For the time and position thus gained, he was able to ascend the slope on the side opposite the city, and, reaching the brow of the hill, he halted for the discharge of two sixty-two pounders upon the rampart at the crest. Here it was that the gallant Dardonville planted the Excelsior flag of the Empire State. At this moment Major Burnham (having recovered from the shock he had sustained by his having been struck by the spent ball) came up and resumed the command. While we enter pell-mell over the wall and capture the West Point of the Aztec empire, the Mexicans retire before our bayonets, some precipitating themselves down the perpendicular side of the hill facing the city. In this moment of victory, Captain Hungerford himself gave the order to Color-Sergeant Riley:—"Haul down the Mexican flag, and run up ours, Sergeant." There was, however, difficulty in finding the passage or stairway leading to the flat roof of the building. The Sergeant, becoming impatient, ran the colors through a window in the second story and waved them in triumph; after which, finally finding the passage, the two colors of the New York and Voltigeur regiments met at the flagstaff. The one first raised is disputed, but when both were equally deserving, 'tis but little matter which was actually the first to be raised, and the honor can well be divided. The captain took prisoner Don Juan Carno, the engineer-in-chief, who had superintended the construction of all the defenses in and about the valley. These works were of such construction, and the positions for them so well chosen, as to excite the admiration and commendation of our general-in-chief, who said he had not seen better in Europe.

"About half an hour after the capture of the castle, General Scott rode into the open space in front, and seeing the young captain, who had already disposed of his prisoners, he called him to him, and complimented him before all the staff. The regiments shortly took up their march upon the city, the prisoners and wounded being quartered in rooms and properly cared for.

"While this was being done, Worth, upon the San Cosmo causeway, was moving forward, overcoming all obstacles and opposition. The ground and surroundings were such that the cavalry could not operate, much to their discontent, but they watched every move, and gloried in our success. Quitman, with his volunteers and the mounted rifles, dismounted, followed along the De Belen causeway, dodging from arch to arch, in steady advance. About midway, between the hill of Chapultepec and the Garita, a strong battery was encountered, flanked by similar ones off the road, which were soon captured, the cannoneers fleeing, and our own men following and entering the other and more formidable batteries and lines of breastworks at the gates, at the same time giving freely the point of the bayonet, driving the enemy, capturing their artillery, and gaining the gate of the city about one o'clock P. M.

The guns captured were turned upon the enemy, following them till a concentrated fire from three sources was brought to bear upon them, sweeping away every man, and killing Captain Drum and Lieutenant Benjamin.

Captain Hungerford, with his two companies, was ordered by General Quitman to skirmish inside of the gates and recover the guns left between the two forces. On the right was a long line of works, with several redoubts, extending to the gate of San Antonio. To the front, on the left of the

causeway, was situated a strong fort, called
the Citadel, and directly to the left of the gate
was a battery on the Paseo. In passing to
the front through the gateway, and while
crossing a small bridge, he sustained a fire
from these several directions, and, remarkable fact, not a man was injured, though the
clothing and canteens of many were struck.
Before the enemy could reload, the captain
had gained the arches of the aqueduct, running in the center of the causeway, advancing from arch to arch, driving the Mexicans
before him, till he had regained the guns then
on neutral ground, between the contending
forces; this accomplished, he returned to the
battery at the Garita, and reported. While
upon the platform of the captured battery,
and looking towards the city, a small party of
the enemy, occupying the roadway near the
citadel, were engaged in manœuvring a four-
pound cannon, and firing it. A ball from this
cannon struck a few yards in advance of the
captain, ricochetted, and, striking the apron of
the battery, rebounded, hitting the captain
between the shoulders.

"Had it struck him on its forward march,
the subsequent proceedings would have interested him no more, and he would have come

to a full stop, then and there. As it was, however, it did not place him even *hors de combat*, for he returned to his skirmishers, till recalled about half an hour after. Again, while occupying one of the arches of the aqueduct, two of his men fell, shot by the enemy's guns while their breasts were touching his shoulder blade; the same shock that struck them also killed a South Carolinian. It came from the mischievous little four-pounder, that had previously saluted the captain. How it got into the arch was discovered sometime after the taking of the city. The ball had struck one of the pillars of the gate, and glancing, it had been turned in the new direction with the fatal results already noted.

"Late in the afternoon, Worth had gained the San Cosmo Garita. During the night Santa Anna withdrew his troops from the city, and the civic authorities then surrendered it to General Quitman. This was in the early morning. Immediately after the surrender, we marched in, and occupied the Grand Plaza. At last all was over. The halls of the Montezumas were won, and the " Stars and Stripes," floating from the National Palace, was saluted by the thundering roars of our artillery, amid the cheers and wild huzzas of the victorious army.

"This ended the fighting part of the war. Some small affairs took place on the outside, but the object had been gained: and now to consummate a peace. Our troops occupied various positions in and about the valley, but within supporting distance of each other. Soon reinforcements arrived, which insured our safety, and our communications with 'Hail, Columbia' were again open. Now we would be able to receive news from our friends. We were for eight months cantoned in or near the city, having nothing to do but the ordinary duties of camp or garrison life, during which time the captain was for about two months in command of the regiment, the colonel and major being in New York wounded, and the lieutenant-colonel engaged in serving upon a High Court of Commission.

"Now you have a history of our doings since my last letter. You will notice that I have carefully avoided the use of the monosyllable '*I*,' though perhaps not more modest than the ordinary run of men. The use of that particular word is not very agreeable to me, hence its exclusion here. I have always preferred to let my actions and the official records speak for me.

"Hoping you will be able to gather the in-

tent of my descriptions, and wishing you the
best of health and prosperity.

"I remain,

"Your affectionate brother,

"D. E. HUNGERFORD."

The following letters were written on
paper bearing the seal and stamp of the city
of Mexico, captured by the United States
forces, and distributed among officers and
men as the legitimate spoils of victory. One
can well imagine with what eagerness this
paper was sought, telling on its face of the
glorious triumph of their arms, and enabling
them to send words of cheer and comfort to
their far-away homes. I am not surprised
that Colonel Hungerford has carefully preserved the record of those bygone days, which
to him and his family are fraught with interest
that no pen can do justice to. But the reader
will easily perceive, and readily enjoy, his
description of incident and country, given
with genuine good-nature and keen observation, and often with a depth of pathos, which
clearly mark the appreciative man.

I give the letters verbatim, feeling that to
alter would be to mar them. I may, however,
be excused for one general remark. Fear, he

15

appeared to have none, and, at times, he seems
to have allowed the poetry of his nature, even
among the horrors of war, to illustrate itself
by his vivid impressions of the beautiful
scenery about him.   A light heart enables one
to cast his burdens off, and, in his penned lines,
his amiability and cheerfulness of disposition
are often apparent.   One cannot fail to remark
the keen judgment and the breadth of view
displayed by the young volunteer officer,
which made him a true prophet of the coming
events.   But I will not anticipate.

His letter dated "National Palace and
Government House, City of Mexico, November tenth, 1847," and written to his brother,
says : "Being on guard, and not being able to
enjoy that repose so essential to the health
and better feeling of the human family, you
will pardon me when I say that, for want
of other employment, I while away a few
moments of a long, tedious night in scribbling
a few 'flib-flabs' for your entertainment.   The
opportunities for correspondence are not very
frequent, and, when an opportunity does come,
I generally find subject matter sufficient for
two or three letters to my better half ; but at
the same time I am not unmindful of the
claims of correspondence you have upon me.

"Since my landing upon the beach near Vera Cruz, on the tenth of March last, I have been an actor and participant in seven distinct and separate engagements, and have, thus far, escaped the leaden messenger of death, although at Churubusco, Chapultepec, and Garita de Belen, I was nearly sent into the presence of the Great Commander-in-Chief of the universe, without orders. At the latter place, on the thirteenth of September, I was ordered to the front in command of two companies, to skirmish and drive back the enemy. I was under a fire of four pieces of artillery, and about three hundred muskets, for one hour and a half to two hours, the enemy's artillery being placed in position of cross-fire. While performing this duty, I was struck in the back by a four-pound shot. Don't laugh, though the singularity of the shot made me laugh at the time. When it occurred, I was facing and looking at the gun that threw the shot, which, falling about fifteen paces in advance of me, glanced by me on my right, struck the work, rebounded, and struck me between the shoulder-blades. Soon after, I was ordered in, I took shelter in one of the arches of the aqueduct. I had not been there five minutes, before a round shot was sent in to the arch, killing two men, and severely wounding three others. The men who were killed were so near me that their breasts touched my back, as we stood under the arch. In another arch I had two men belonging to my company instantly killed by one ball, a four-pounder. Here my first lieutenant was so severely wounded, that he was disabled in consequence for some months. You may judge of my whereabouts, when I tell you that I lost, out of my company, at Churubusco, twenty men and one officer killed and wounded, and at Chapultepec, and the Garita de Belen, two officers and eleven men killed and wounded. I left Fort Hamilton, New York Harbor, with eighty-three men, besides four officers. I now number for duty fourteen men and two officers. One of the latter is a young officer, promoted from the ranks after our entrance into this city. Those whose bones bleach upon the plains of Mexico certainly deserve the appellation 'the gallant and brave,' while those who have already gone back to their homes, or soon will, carry with them the seal of having borne the brunt of battle, some with but an arm, others a leg, while others, again, carry in different parts of their body the leaden souvenirs which will always remind them of the twentieth of August, and the thirtieth of September, 1847.

"Since my tarry in this celebrated city of the Aztecs, I have discovered a great living curiosity in the person of a Mr. Samuel Jewett, a cousin. Only think, three thousand miles from home, and find a cousin. He is also from the State of New York, somewhere about Onondaga. He is married to a Mexican lady, and has a large family; this fact alone (I mean the large family) confirms the relationship. I frequently visit his house to while away an afternoon, and improve myself in the 'lingo' of the Mexicans, indeed, I have become so accustomed to speaking Spanish that I am fearful of losing my mother tongue altogether.

"We are at present doing nothing but guard duty, and spending the time in idleness. We will be so employed until the arrival of the expected reinforcements, when it is thought that our division, General Worth's, will be sent to Querctaro, a distance of about one hundred and fifty miles from here.

"I have not heard from home in four months; but, now that communications are established, I expect by this train two bushels

·and a half of letters, and a good-sized cartful of newspapers."

Again, on February fourteenth, 1848, he writes to his brother, in which he says, "If I do not write a long letter this time, you must pardon me, for I have had a great deal of official writing to get off by this mail, and I am very tired.

"I have no other battles to recount, since the last 'drubbing' they got before the gates of their capital. Señor Don Mexicano (?) evidently does not care about meeting us. By the bye, they got a "capital" flogging there, such a one as they will be likely to remember. A party of Texas rangers visited Orizaba, a short time since, in the hope of capturing Santa Anna, but they succeeded in capturing his regimentals only, he himself escaping by the aid of his cork leg; this unnatural appendage has made him as famous as the man in the song, Monsieur Herr Von Damn. There are various rumors of peace, none of which can be depended upon. A peace, at the present unsettled state, cannot be consummated, however devoutly wished for. Besides, it would be highly impolitic for our government to think of making a peace, until a firm and responsible government was established in the country.

There is no confidence to be placed in the thing
that they call a government : besides, the people
are not united, being almost in a state of insur-
rection within themselves. They must be made
to feel the full weight of the war, and let
them have time for proper reflection, become
united, establish a permanent government,
and then a peace can be made with safety.
At present, if a peace arrangement were to
be entered into, we would no sooner be out
of the country than they would commence
a border warfare, which would last for years,
and involve us over again in trouble and expense. It would then become necessary to
keep a large force upon our frontiers at an immense cost, whereas the resources are now
drawn from the enemy, to make him feel the
full burden of the war, which, in the course of
time, will bring him to his senses, and make
him sue from us, in turn, a peace, which he,
in his blindness, has refused. Who has ever
before heard of a conquering people, suing
and begging a peace? The thing is unparalleled in the historical records of the world.
The lenity shown these Mexicans by the
American Government is an example for European monarchies to follow. The liberal generosity extended to them has been mistaken as a

weakness in our resources. Why was not the
blow, so effectually struck at Vera Cruz, followed up? We there extended to them the
olive branch of peace, which they, in their mad
insanity, declined! Again, at Cerro Gordo,
the peace-offering was made, only to be
haughtily spurned. At Churubusco, also,
while our arms were shining forth in the
brilliancy of a victorious sun, our small but
sturdy column was withdrawn from the very
gates of their capital, to allow them to accept
the hand of peace. When the beautiful city of
Mexico was at our mercy, which we might
have entered without opposition, as they themselves acknowledged, but, hoping that their national pride would come to the assistance of
their understanding, and prompt them to save
their nationality ere their capital fell, here
again the demon of self-destruction swayed his
power. The termination you know. Our
troops took possession of their capital, their
armies scattered to the four winds of heaven,
their government broken, which they ineffectu-
ally tried to patch up at Querctaro. What remains to be done? Nothing but what I proposed in the above. To think of making a
peace with this remnant of a government
would be the maddest folly ; the one proposing

such a thing should be put in a lunatic asylum, out of harm's way.

"I am in very good health. This is a delightful climate, a continual spring. At present, the fruit trees are in full blossom, green vegetables in plenty the year round. The valley may well be called the paradise of the earth. On either side are steep and lofty mountains, forming a scene far surpassing the fanciful imagination of the artist, the basin of the valley, with its greensward, strongly contrasting with the snow-capped pinnacle of Popocatapetl. Here nature's loveliness has her empire, and reigns in majestic grandeur. I must stop, however, in the midst of such glowing beauty, for fear that I may turn your ideas from the wilds of Wisconsin to the lovely and fruitful valley of Mexico.

"Give my love to my friends."

The following report by the colonel of the regiment will be of interest as describing its part in the investment and capture of the city of Mexico. It will be noticed that the gallant captain comes in for his full share of the honors won on the field of battle. The similarity of the official report and the cap-

tain's own narrative, written hurriedly, is
worthy of mention.

" *To* Brigadier-General Shields :

"Official report of the part performed by
the first regiment United States Volunteers
of New York, in the investment and capture
of the City of Mexico.

"The Volunteer Brigade, commanded by
Brigadier-General Shields, to which my command belongs, left the city of Puebla on the
eighth, and encamped at Buena Vista on the
sixteenth, in full view of the country surrounding the city of Mexico, and arrived at
San Augustin, in position for investment, on
the nineteenth day of August, 1847. Generals
Pillow and Twiggs with the Third, and Worth's
division of regulars, left San Augustin on the
morning of the nineteenth, and, at three
o'clock, P. M., the New York and South Carolina regiments were ordered to their support,
under Brigadier-General Shields. The regiment marched immediately, leaving Major
Burnham with a force of about one hundred
men, consisting of company C, under command of Captain Barclay, Lieutenants Sher-
wood and Boyle, one detachment of thirty-five
men of different companies, and twelve sick.

The regiment pursued its way across the 'Pedregal,' a series of ledges of rocks and chasms, with great difficulty, and at the deep ravine, through which a torrent falls, some eight or ten lost their way, and returned to San Augustin. At midnight, we reached the village of San Geronimo, in a drenching rain. Every tent was occupied, and our troops, wet and weary, were obliged to stand under arms in the road until daylight, when the enemy's works in the immediate vicinity of the village were to be stormed by the second division of regulars. We then repaired to the church and other shelters in the neighborhood, by order of General Shields, to prepare our arms for action. As the sun arose, the cheers of the storming party were heard, and our men assembled to meet the legions of the enemy, who were retreating upon the fortifications, near the city of Mexico. We captured three hundred and thirty-six prisoners, and among them were one general, two colonels, and many subaltern officers, with at least two hundred stands of arms, lances, horses, etc.

"The regiment was then ordered to return to its former position at the church, from which small commands were sent to overtake straggling parties of the enemy, in which

they were particularly successful, under the
direction of Captain J. P. Taylor, and his first
lieutenant, A. W. Taylor. At about nine
o'clock, A. M., we received orders to advance
upon the city of Mexico, leaving company D,
and about fifty men of other companies that
had not yet returned from scouting, in charge
of the prisoners. We marched from the
village of San Geronimo, with about three
hundred officers and men. After passing
through San Angel, and halting for a short
time, the second division of regulars engaged
the enemy in front of Churubusco. We were
soon ordered to countermarch, and directed,
with other troops, to the right of the enemy,
and reach the rear of his formidable position.
The New York regiment was now upon the
right of the brigade. We followed the roadway for about a mile, crossed a ditch into low,
wet, grounds, pursued our way for about a
mile and a half more, through cornfields and
marshes, and reached the enemy's right and
rear at Los Portales; the whole, in consequence
of the character of the ground in which we
had passed, was very much extended, so that
a few minutes were lost in forming the
regiment to the front. During this time it
was discovered that the enemy's works were

flanked by an embankment, with a deep ditch
extending parallel to a roadway for more than
a mile in the rear, and to the hacienda of Los
Portales. This formidable breastwork and
hacienda were occupied by at least three
thousand infantry, besides large bodies of
cavalry. It was not until our line was formed
to charge this work that the enemy was discovered with large bodies of other troops
endeavoring to turn our left, but we had now
reached a point where we were receiving a
random fire from the enemy's line, at a
distance of about three hundred and fifty
yards. The order to charge was received with
cheers, and the regiment advanced to within
one hundred yards of the enemy's line, under
a most terrific fire, in which I was wounded
in the left leg by an escapette ball, compelling
me to turn over the command to Lieutenant-
Colonel Charles Baxter. The regiment as yet
being entirely unsupported, it was thought
advisable to retire until the South Carolina
regiment in our rear would come up and form
on our left, which that regiment did in most
gallant style. General Shields then ordered
the two regiments, or parts of regiments, to
charge on the enemy's line, which they did
most bravely up to the bayonets of the enemy,

breaking their line, crossing the ditch, and reaching the roadway, where we planted the standard of our state and nation. But this advantage was gained at a great loss. Out of less than three hundred officers and men who entered the field, one hundred and five were killed and wounded. A few were now sent back to see to the dead and wounded. The remnant of the two regiments was again ordered to advance upon the city of Mexico. In advancing, the enemy retired in pretty good order, until we were joined by a piece of artillery captured from the enemy, and commanded by Captain Ayres of the third regiment United States artillery, manned principally by volunteers. This piece was fired several times at the columns of cavalry, after which the enemy retreated in disorder. We were then halted, and ordered back to Los Portales.

" In the desperate engagement, where almost all were heroes, it was difficult to name those who most distinguished themselves, as all who were there may ever remember with pride, that they participated in one of the most daring charges ever made by Americans against an enemy. These were those in the command who were foremost and steadfast in

every movement, from whom I take occasion
to mention :

" Lieutenant-Colonel Charles H. Baxter, who
had two horses shot under him during the en-
gagement; Captains Garrett, Dyckman, Dan-
iel E. Hungerford, Abram Van Olinda, Morton
Fairchild, and Lieutenant Mayne Reid com-
manding Company B, who particularly distin-
guished himself; Jacob Griffin, Jr., Company
H; Charles F. Brower, commanding Company
F; J. Miller, commanding Company A; John
Rafferty, Company K; Charles S. Cooper,
Company A; Charles H. Innes, Company G;
James S. McCabe, Company K; J. Ward Henry,
Company E; James D. Potter, Company I; T.
W. Sweeney, Company A; Sergeant-Major
James L. O'Reiley, who fell, while gallantly
advancing in front of the colors; Color-Sergeant
Romaine, with the national colors, who, after
receiving a wound in the right arm, carried the
colors in the left, and it was not until he received the third and mortal wound; that the
colors fell. In falling, Corporal Lake, of the
colors, seized it, and was immediately shot
dead. Orderly Sergeant Doremus of Company
A again saved it from the ground, and carried
it throughout the engagement. The State
colors were gallantly carried by Sergeant

Rogers, Company I, during the battle. Orderly Sergeant Baxter of Company I, O. S. Fitzgerald of Company E, and O. S. Wilson of Company G, who, after being wounded, so that he could not use his musket, assisted Captain Ayres in directing the piece of artillery.

"Adjutant Robert A. Carter behaved gallantly throughout the engagement, and was sent at one time for medical assistance, and during his absence as well as throughout the day. . . .

"Captain J. F. Hutton, U. S. Commissary and Lieutenant George B. Hall, assistant quartermaster, assisted the commanding officer and rendered efficient services.

" It is with the highest pleasure that I recommend to your notice Assistant Surgeon Minor B. Halstead, acting surgeon of the regiment. His skill and activity can be alluded to by you with higher encomiums than my own. He was with the wounded prisoners in the morning, and with our wounded in the evening, and night and day ever since in our hospital, and in attending to the wounded of other corps.   He speaks in the highest terms of Dr. John G. McKibben, acting assistant surgeon, who rendered him efficient aid in the performance of his duties. To Dr. Swift, U. S. Army,

I would here return my most sincere thanks for his care and attention. It is with the deepest regret that I mention the death of Lieutenant Edgar Chandler, who fell early in the action, while fearlessly standing by his colors. In conclusion, I will say for my gallant regiment that it was the third occasion we served under the same commander, and with signal success.

"Signed, WARD B. BURNETT,

Colonel Commanding Regiment."

The following report by Lieutenant-Colonel James C. Burnham gives the official account of the part the regiment took in the battles of Chapultepec and De Belen. "First up the ditch, first up the enemy's works, and the first to place the national flag upon the conquered castle" tells the story of the valor of the First Regiment on the heights of Chapultepec. Captain Hungerford is well to the front, in the honor and glories of that day. One more roll of honor to bear his name.

"REPORT OF LIEUTENANT-COLONEL JAMES C.
BURNHAM.

"HEADQUARTERS FIRST REGIMENT U. S. VOLUNTEERS
OF NEW YORK.

"CITY OF MEXICO, September 16, 1847.
"TO CAPTAIN F. N. PAGE, *A. A. Adjutant-General,*

"SIR: I have the honor to make the following report of the part taken by the First Regiment U. S. Volunteers of New York, in the affairs of the twelfth and thirteenth inst. In the absence of Colonel Ward B. Burnett, who was still confined at the Hacienda Moscoac from a wound received on the twentieth ultimo at Los Portales, Lieutenant-Colonel Charles Baxter was in command of the regiment. The regiment, after furnishing the different details that had been ordered for a storming party, light battalion and batteries, was reduced to two hundred and eighty officers and men. We arrived at Tacubya on the morning of the twelfth inst., and were posted, until about eight o'clock on the morning of the thirteenth inst., on the right of the road from Tacubya to the city, and near Captain Drum's battery to protect said battery. About eight A.M., on the thirteenth, as the division filed past the gate on the Tacubya road, Colonel Baxter received orders to advance and storm the castle. After proceeding about half a mile, he was ordered by the general to file by the left by a ranch, through the cornfield. Here we were received by a shower of grape, canister, and musket balls, when Colonel Baxter fell, severely wounded, leading the charge. I immediately took command, and in ascending the hill, was struck by a spent ball, which disabled me for a few minutes. Notwithstanding the difficult nature of the ground, intersected as it was by numerous ditches, and swept by a galling fire from the enemy, the regiment which I have the honor to command, was the first up the ditch, first in the enemy's works, and the first to place the national flag upon the conquered castle. General Bravo, commanding the garrison, surrendered himself a prisoner of war to Charles B. Brower, commanding Company F. The Castle, having surrendered, I was ordered by the general to proceed with my command on the Tacubya road, and was halted at the aqueduct, where the men refilled their cartridge boxes. After a short rest, we advanced towards the Garita de Belen, where two skirmishing parties, under command of Captains Taylor and Hungerford, were detailed by order of General Quitman, and rendered essen-

tial services, in driving the enemy from the
batteries at the Garita. A working party was
also detailed to carry sand-bags, fill ditches,
and make a road under direction of Lieutenant Pinto, Company D. Captain Barclay was
then ordered to superintend the building of a
breastwork, and rendered me efficient aid.
As the second in command throughout the day,
the Acting Adjutant, Lieutenant Charles Innes,
having been wounded about this time, I appointed Lieutenant McCabe, of Company K, in
his place, and assigned Lieutenant Francis G.
Boyle in command of Company K.

"At dusk, a large working party was detailed
from the New York and Pennsylvania regiments, and placed under the command of Captain Fairchild, in order to erect a battery in
front of the Garita, as well as to strengthen our
position in other respects. At daylight, the
following morning, we marched with the rest
of the division into the Capital.

" I feel that it is due to Drs. Edwards and Mc
Shevey, of the Marine Corps, for their kind attention to our wounded during the absence of
our surgeon, Dr. M. B. Halstead, who was
ordered to remain in charge of the hospital at
Muscoac. Captain Hutton, commissary to the
regiment, was left in command at Muscoac, and

was active in forwarding supplies. Captain
Van Olinda was killed, gallantly leading his
company, and Lieutenant Mayne Reid severely
wounded at the head of his company at the
hill.

"In closing my report, I must do justice to
those gallant officers, by particular notice,
whose assistance to me both in the attack upon
Chapultepec, the advance on the city, added
greatly to the brilliant results of the day.
They were Captains Barclay, Taylor, Hungerford, Fairchild, and Pearson (the latter fell,
severely wounded early in the engagement);
Lieuts. Henry, whose gallantry deserves es-
pecial notice, Miller, McCabe, Innes, Brower,
Griffin, Green, Boyle, Scannell, Farnsworth,
Durning, and Doremus. A list of killed,
wounded, and missing in the storming of the
castle and the subsequent battle on the road to
Mexico is herewith annexed.

"I have the honor to be,
"Very respectfully,
"Your obedient servant,
"Signed.   "JAMES C. BURNHAM,
"Lieutenant-Colonel Commanding U. S. Regiment."

A sad duty for the colonel to perform was
making known to sorrowing wives, mothers,

and children the list of the dead and wounded in his company. Some had given all that man could give, life itself, in defense of country and flag. Let us hope for the fallen a kindly greeting on the eternal shore from the Great Comforter, and may they realize that "sweet is the welcome to the brave, who die thus for their native land," and forever fresh and green may their memory be kept in the nation's gratitude.

Messrs. Editors:

By publishing the following list of casualties occurring in Company G, First Regiment, New York Volunteers, you will confer a favor on many that are interested, who have not yet heard from their friends since they left for the seat of war.

Deaths.—Corporal James Abrecht, killed by Mexicans, Puebla, July 13, 1847. Privates John Benjamin died at Puebla, July 9. Peter E. Butcher died at Puebla, September. David Belt died at Vera Cruz, April 5. Bernard Cranmer, killed in battle, Churubusco, August 20. Robert Devoe, killed in battle, Churubusco, August 20. Joseph A. Dennis, Garita de Belen. Orrin Ellwood, died at the City of Mexico in November. Charles J. Hackler died at Puebla,

September. Thomas Ingram died at Moscoac.
September 11. Andrew Kline, killed in battle,
Churubusco, August 20. James Peck died at
sea, May. Charles C. Candall died at Puebla,
October. Alexander Rodney died of wound
received in battle, September 17. John Shaw,
killed in battle at Garita de Belen. Frank
Smith died in hospital at Perote, date unknown.
Thomas Topham died in hospital, Puebla,
August. Charles Wheeler died at Lobos Is-
land, February 27.

Wounded and otherwise disabled.— Captain
D. E. Hungerford, slightly. First Lieutenant
C. H. Innes, slightly, also at Garita de Belen, severely. First Sergeant John Wilson, wounded
at Churubusco, also at Chapultepec, slightly.
First Sergeant D. Montgomery, wounded at
Chapultepec, slightly. Corporal C. L. Thomp-
son, wounded at Garita de Belen, slightly.
Privates : N. Barnes, wounded at Churubusco,
slightly. E. Carr, wounded at Churubusco,
severely. C. Crapp, wounded at Churubusco,
severely. B. De Young, wounded at Churubusco, slightly. P. Farley, wounded at Churubusco, severely, lost right arm. A. G. Fiske,
twice wounded at Churubusco, severely. M.
Finney, wounded at Churubusco, severely, lost
right leg. William Hart, wounded at Churu-

busco severely, lost right leg. Thomas Healey, wounded at Garita de Belen, slightly. J. Mc-Kenney, wounded at the City of Mexico, severely. J. McGill, wounded at Churubusco, severely. John Smith, wounded at Churubusco, slightly. James Smith lost left arm. A. Laun, wounded at Churubusco, severely. Lott Swift, wounded at Churubusco, slightly. V. Van Slyke, wounded at Chapultepec, slightly. P. Berry, wounded at Churubusco, slightly. J. O. Donnell, taken prisoner by the enemy, March 10, 1847. He regained the company on September 16th, after the entrance into the city. He was beaten in such a manner, while prisoner, as to be disabled.

Yours respectfully,

D. E. HUNGERFORD,
Captain Commanding Company.

It is always more pleasant to award praise when it is not sought. Captain Hungerford has been always willing to let the records speak for him, and it is fitting to quote here a newspaper extract relative thereto from a Nevada journal.

[Extract from *Territorial Enterprise*, Saturday, December 10, 1864.]

AN ANCIENT DOCUMENT.

"A friend has shown us a proof slip taken in the office of the New York *Military Argus*,

directly after the Mexican War. It appears
that about the time the First Regiment, New
York Volunteers, returned, some did a large
amount of blowing about the glorious feats
performed by their valiant selves during the
war, much to the disgust of the really brave
men who marched with their country's flag;
so an official document, of which the slip before us is a proof, was published, giving a list
of officers of the First Regiment, who marched
with the army under the command of Major-
General Winfield Scott upon the City of
Mexico, the seventh, eighth, ninth, and tenth
of August, 1847, specifying where each
was employed upon the nineteenth and twentieth of August, and the eighth, twelfth, thirteenth, fourteenth of September, 1847. In this
roll of honor we find the names of two persons
now in this city, Messrs. Hungerford and Durning. According to this official record, Captain
D. E. Hungerford fought in the battles of
Contreras, San Geromino, Churubusco, Chapultepec, Garita de Belen, and the City of Mexico. Second Lieutenant Francis Durning
fought at the battle of Contreras, San Geromino,
Churubusco, Chapultepec, Garita de Belen, and
the City of Mexico."

While negotiations of peace were going on,

18

the gallant little army was resting on its arms
in the City of Mexico. Never in the history of
any nation were successes so continuous, and
so marvelous. Without the loss of a gun or a
flag, they had marched on their conquering
way, a distance of three hundred miles, from
Vera Cruz to the enemy's capital, with no
base of supplies, like Cæsar of old, burning
their bridges behind them. The enemy were
strongly intrenched, everything on their side,
their forces far outnumbering ours ; our troops
not understanding the language of the country
through which they were passing. With our
advance, every step was hazardous, every
height of importance capped by a strong citadel, the hills between blown over by hurri-
canes of sand, till, according to the captain's
own description, the bivouacs of the soldiers
resembled mounds of snow. But in the lexicon
of that army there was no such word as "fail."
The flag they carried must find a lodgment,
and wave victoriously over the Mexican
capital, if it took every man of them to do it,
and they were to find a grave beneath the
enemy's sandy hills. Did they succeed ? You,
I, America, the world know the story. It has
covered that little army with imperishable renown, and while one veteran remains, he

should have a claim on one and all of affectionate gratitude.

In the United States, enthusiastic celebrations were marking the joy of the people at the triumph of the nation's heroes, for such they had now become; and well may their praises be sung, for this, the third time in the history of the world, the spectacle was presented of a young republic so strong in its principles and the affections of its people, that, in the hour of its danger, it was able to furnish from every rank of its citizens, soldiers to whom the finest legions of Napoleon were not superior.

In the interim, while awaiting the signing of the treaty of peace, the army could at last enjoy a little well-earned repose. They relieved the monotony by various amusements. Though conquerors among the conquered, by their magnanimity of conduct, and the scrupulous regard shown for persons and property, the population was rendered less hostile to them than they expected. Balls were given in many places. All the theaters were open, and gambling games occupied most of the hotels and places of resort. Many excursions were made, by both officers and men, to the mines, and other places of interest in the vicinity.

The volcano of Popocatapetl and the pyramid of Cholula were often visited. In this way the time was passed; but the greatest joy was that they were now enabled to hear from the loved ones at home more frequently.

In the volunteer divisions many swords, spurs, etc., were presented by the different companies to the favorite officers. They were generally accepted. An attempt was made by the Captain's company to present him with a sword; but his strict ideas of what constituted proper military discipline would not permit him to accept it. When he learned that such a thing was in contemplation, he sent for his orderly sergeant, and asked him how the company was getting on, and what was that paper circulating among them? The sergeant after some hesitation replied that they were raising a subscription to present him with a sword. The sergeant was surprised at the answer the captain made him. Said he, "Go right back to the company, and stop that immediately. If I hear any more about it, I will put the whole company in the guard-house. They are neither to approve nor disapprove of my conduct." The captain rightly thought that it would seem ill to command the necessary discipline over his men, by the force of a gifted

sword. Nothing more was heard of the
sword after that; but the men saw that
their captain had illustrated most effectively
that duty for duty's sake, and not for the commendation of others, should guide the true
soldier, whether he be found in the ranks, or
wearing the epaulettes of the officer. This
incident only increased the popularity of the
captain among his men. Indeed, they had
many times to experience his watchfulness and
fatherly care over them; they knew he had no
likes or dislikes for them, except that he loved
the good soldier, and hated, loathed the bad
one. One little fact, among many that might
be cited, will show how his thoughtfulness and
keen regard for their interests endeared him
to them. The sum of twenty-one dollars was
allowed each member of the company for his
equipment of clothes, etc., and it was disbursed
through the captain of the company. It was expected, or rather the army contractors expected,
that the soldiers would promptly expend all of
that money in the purchase of the necessary
articles. But the contractors were not going to
squeeze every cent out of Captain Hungerford's
men, if the captain could prevent it, so he
promptly explained to the men that only the uni-
form and one or two other things were required

to be standard, the remainder could come from
their own store of clothes. The consequence
was that the contractors did not get all the
money from Captain Hungerford's company,
owing to the vigilance of the captain, but, on
the other hand, when the army had entered the
city of Vera Cruz the captain was enabled to
return to every man in his company a part of
the twenty-one dollars, accompanied by the
full statement of the number and price of each
article drawn. It was a great surprise to them,
as they had never expected to receive a penny
of it, but their captain was thinking of them
and guarding their interests more than they had
anticipated.

Returning to the incident of the sword, the
captain had declined a similar presentation
from his friends before leaving New York, saying he had not yet won such a distinguished
honor, but that if he lived to return, and his
conduct had been such as to merit their esteem,
he would be only too proud to receive such a
testimonial from his fellow-citizens. Until
that time, however, he could not feel justified
in being the recipient of an expectant approbation. "As I behave, so reward me," he said.
"'Well done, faithful servant' is sufficient
reward for me, which I doubt not, if deserv-

ing, you will award." To such sentiments he has always most strenuously adhered, keeping up the character of an officer and a disciplinarian, while with the warmest of hearts, looking to the interest and well-being of his men, at the same time maintaining the dignity of the commander.

But to return to Mexico. An election having been held, and a new and more responsible government having been established, with whom we could with safety negotiate, the treaty of "Guadaloupe Hidalgo" was signed. Soon after its ratification the various divisions received their instructions from the War Department for evacuating the country, which was effected in a most orderly and considerate manner, thus ending a campaign of wonderful successes, without a single defeat or reverse, fighting against a vastly superior number, behind fortifications placed in most favorable positions for defense, fortifications pronounced by our engineer officers to be equal to any in Europe.

The Mexican Engineer-in-chief had received his English education in an educational establishment in Bond street, New York, from which he graduated with distinguished honors. The Faculty of the school, after the war, gave

a banquet in honor of Captain Hungerford, in
recognition of the humane treatment to the
gallant enemy whom he had taken prisoner at
Chapultepec. They further testified their appreciation of his soldierly and manly conduct,
by presenting him with many letters of intro-
duction and recommendation to numerous
high officials and distinguished persons in
Cuba and Mexico, should he have occasion to
visit those countries.

This banquet will ever be a pleasing souve-
nir in the captain's memory.

The First Regiment of Volunteers was received in New York on its return with every
demonstration of joy and gratitude. Its fame
had preceded its coming. After its brilliant
record during the war, and in deference to the
united wish of the people of the city and State,
it was deemed that a public and appropriate
reception under the direction of the municipal
authorities should be tendered them on their
arrival in the city as a testimonial of the estimation entertained by their fellow-citizens of
the gallant bearing of the regiment, shown in
those most brilliant triumphs of American arms,
which marked their victorious march through
Mexico, especially at the battle of Churubusco
and the storming of Chapultepec, at both of

which places it displayed a courage and a heroism which justly distinguished it as one of the bravest regiments of the whole army.

The common council held several meetings, and made the necessary arrangements for the reception. They but expressed the feelings of every one in the unanimous resolution passed in which they said that it became a great and magnanimous people, while rejoicing in the restoration and blessings of peace, to be mindful also of those whose personal sacrifices, privations, and valor won a boon so grateful to humanity. Every man comprising our small army in Mexico was expected to do his duty, and it appears that the individual conduct, fortitude, and bravery of our own volunteers fully sustained the expectations of their fellow-citizens, elevating the standard and military standard of their country at home and abroad, deserving alike the gratitude and benediction of a free people. They therefore thought that the city of New York — not unmindful of the merit and services of those brave men who volunteered to represent her in the army of our common country upon the soil of Mexico — should welcome their country, families, and friends, with grateful acknowledgments for the faithful and brilliant manner in which they

have fulfilled their duties in nobly sustaining
our honor and flag on the battlefields of Mexico, in their moderation in victory, in their humanity to the sick and wounded of the enemy,
as well as their irrepressible energy and valor
in action.

The regiment having arrived at Fort Hamilton from Vera Cruz, the twenty-seventh of
July was designated as the day of their reception. On the morning of that day the common
council, accompanied by many distinguished
visitors, proceeded in a steamboat to Fort
Hamilton, where the regiment embarked in
the presence of a large crowd that had assembled to witness their departure, and amid the
booming of the artillery of the fort. As the
boat neared the city, and swept past the battery, it was greeted by the discharge of cannon,
and the citizen soldierly and a vast multitude
of the people assembled there to welcome the
return of those men after their participation
in some of the most brilliant triumphs of
American valor. It was, indeed, a grand welcome to the returning heroes. Arrived at
Castle Garden, the highest honor they could
receive, a national salute thundered forth its
greeting; and as they marched ashore, "Home,
sweet Home" was played by the band, while

the immense gathering gave vent to their feelings in deafening and long-continued cheering.

His honor, Mayor Havemeyer, then addressed the regiment, welcoming them back with grateful heart and a pride of their gallant deeds animating their fellow-citizens. Colonel Burnett fittingly and modestly replied, after which the regiment re-formed and marched through the city. All the available military organizations in the State were called out, and many volunteer companies took part in the parade. The reception that the gallant and patriotic First New York received, as they marched through the various streets, was all that the most sanguine heart of them could have desired. Bunting was flying everywhere, and the whole city seemed to be in the streets to do them honor. Thousands had come from the neighboring towns to mingle their applause and huzzas of welcome to returned heroes. The tattered flags, torn uniforms of officers and men, and the many gaps in their ranks told a tale that touched the hearts of those thousands of inhabitants and strangers that densely crowded the streets, filled the windows and balconies, and lined the tops of the houses and public buildings along the route of the

procession. Everywhere they were received
by the heartiest and most enthusiastic demonstrations of joy at their return, and admiration
of their bravery. When the procession was
over, they marched back to Castle Garden,
which was filled to the doors by the military,
eminent citizens and strangers and others.
Here the mayor and the several committees
were waiting to receive them. The national
and regimental colors and two guide flags
were presented to the mayor, followed by another, a flag given to the regiment by General
Scott after the battle of the City of Mexico.
This flag had been made by the ladies of
Mexico. Appropriate and feeling speeches
accompanied the presentations. After this
part of the ceremony, the medals, which were
voted by the common council to be bestowed
on officers and men, were presented. This
concluded the reception. The regiment, re-
forming, embarked, and accompanied by many
distinguished officers and citizens, landed at
the fort, where leave was taken of them. Thus
ended a day never to be forgotten by the gallant participants, nor by a single one of those
thousands who assembled from all parts to
honor those to whom the country owed so
much. New York has seen many days of

public joy and demonstration, but never in the memory of those who have survived that occasion has there ever been an event of such a touching character, and marked by such unbounded enthusiasm penetrating every rank of the community. Old and young, rich and poor, had that day united in a spontaneous and unparalleled welcome to the country's heroes. Truly it can be said, at least on this occasion, that republics are not ungrateful, for ours, by the enthusiastic joy with which its people received its citizen-soldiers, was neither ungrateful to, nor unmindful of, those brave men who had risked their all for their country, offering up their lives on the altar of pure patriotism. The twenty-seventh of July will forever remain a lustrous day in the annals of the great commonwealth of the Empire State.

CHAPTER IV.

AFTER the ceremonies of reception and the return to the fort, the Captain commenced his preparations for mustering out of the service of the United States Government. Through his attention to details, and fidelity in the care of what was entrusted to him, he was able to make out his muster roll and final reports, accounting accurately for each man and his account, and for all property received during a two years' service, in the short space of time of two hours and a half. Many captains whose arrival at the fort preceded his by twelve days, were retarded by from three to fifteen days, owing to the additional time required for the settlement of their account. This shows how well the Captain had profited by his study of the army regulations, while he was stationed at the fort.

His final accounting with the government having been duly audited and found correct, he was enabled to receive his pay, and an additional three months' extra allowance, more than two months before any other officer in the regiment.

This speaks most favorably for his promptness and accuracy. In fact, it became necessary for Congress to pass an amnesty act, exonerating volunteer officers from further liability and accountability, while doing service in the War with Mexico. But the Captain, as we have seen, had no need to take advantage of the amnesty. Moneys, camp and garrison equipage, ordnance stores, in a word everything, even to the last flint of a musket, were all rigidly accounted for by him.

The citizens of his ward, desirous of honoring him for his gallant services, called a meeting, with the object of presenting him with a suitable testimonial. One of the committee appointed by the meeting had the indelicacy to call on the Captain, and asked him what he would like to have. The Captain replied that he had merely done his duty like so many others, but as they had already

decided to convey to him in that manner
the expression of their sentiments, he could
not refuse to accept their testimonial. Since
he was asked as to his choice of the object,
he would take the liberty of suggesting a
sword, epaulets, or pair of spurs, or anything that would bear the appropriate military signification. The committee, however,
held that a watch would be of more utility,
seeing that the war had ceased. The Captain naturally did not debate the subject
with them.

They purchased a very valuable watch,
had suitable inscriptions engraved thereon,
and made preparations for a splendid banquet, but on the day before the presentation
was to come off, the Captain took the boat for
Albany, and he does not know to this day
what became of that banquet, at which the
principal figure would have been missing.

If the gift had been a sword, or anything
pertaining to the military service, the Captain would have been most happy to receive
it, but having already a costly watch to
remind him of the passing moments, he felt
no necessity to have two. Though he did
not choose to accept the watch, he, nevertheless, was highly appreciative of the kind

wishes and sentiments of the citizens of his
ward, which prompted them to honor him
in that way.

His business connection having suffered
during his absence in the army, on his return many of his friends interested themselves to have him appointed to a position
in the Custom House. This was not difficult to do, owing to the gallant record
of the Captain. His name was second on
the list, and he was about being named for the
office. This, however, did not meet with the
Captain's approbation, and as soon as the matter was brought to his attention, he took immediate steps to have his name erased, saying
that he did not do service in Mexico to obtain
a political office, and he did not wish any one
to have the chance of accusing him of being
a Democrat for the bread and butter he ate.
This incident only illustrates those that have
preceded it. His principles did not allow
him to accept the honorable and profitable employment that was offered him, because it conflicted with his high standard of
honor, so, notwithstanding the sacrifices its
refusal entailed, he would not yield to the
entreaties of his friends.

About this time the country was fired by

20

the news of the discovery of gold in California.
New York, like other cities, was excited and
stirred up by the marvelous tales told of the
new El Dorado. Captain Hungerford was
casting about for some opportunity for the
development of his energies. Now a field
presented itself. It appealed forcibly to his
adventuresome disposition, besides the hope
of securing the pecuniary rewards. California was three thousand miles away, at the
other end of the continent, but he did not
hesitate an instant. He quickly made the
necessary arrangements, bid good-bye to his
wife and family, and like other brave-hearted
and courageous men, he pushed out from
New York, and set his face toward the land
of gold. He arrived at Vera Cruz the middle of February, 1849, at twelve o'clock, mid-
day. In three hours the quick-moving Captain
had left the walls of the city behind him, on
his way to the Capital, which he finally
reached without molestation. An incident
took place on the route which showed his
coolness and courage. He had been informed
that ladrones or robbers infested the road.
At Jalapa, the Captain was pointed out the
chief of the band, but, instead of displaying
any fear of the famous bandit, the Captain

walked right up to him and notified him that he was starting out on the road that night, and if he were going to attack him he would be ready to meet him. The desperado of great renown was dumbfounded, but made no reply, thinking probably that he would have too warm a reception from that particular party. So the Captain and his friends, owing to his daring, were allowed to pursue their way in peace, being spared the usual fate of many others.

They remained three days at the Capital, the Captain renewing acquaintances, purchasing horses, and preparing to proceed on the long journey to the Pacific coast. Again taking up the march, the adventuresome band arrived at Guadalajara, there making another halt of three days to rest his men and animals; setting out again, refreshed and eager, he finally arrived at Mazatlan, on the Pacific coast. There he purchased a small schooner, of about forty tons. He had determined to go by sea from that point to San Francisco. In the harbor was the English frigate *Inconstance*, whose gallant captain was Sir Charles Courtney, a true Briton admirer of pluck and daring. The adventuresome Captain received a royal welcome from him, and

was the recipient of many courtesies at his
hands. He visited the ship quite often, and
was allowed the privilege of copying maps and
charts of the coasts. Besides, other kind as-
sistances were rendered him. The genuine
hospitality extended him by Captain Courtney
was the most pleasing remembrance of the
whole trip, and is always borne in grateful
memory by him.

Captain Hungerford was occupied for two
weeks in fitting out the frail little bark. His
knowledge of sailoring and navigating was of
the most meagre description, but he readily
adapted it to the work at hand. At Mazatlan
the Captain found twenty-seven Americans,
gold-seekers like himself, who had reached
there, but were unable to proceed further,
being absolutely destitute. They had come
from the Southern States, through New Mexico
and Texas; they too had tramped many a
mile. Joyfully the two adventuresome bands
greeted each other. But what was to be done?
The Captain's resources were slender, the boat
already crowded, and he had the greatest
difficulty in looking after his own men. But
his heart was touched at the distress of his
countrymen. He could not leave them behind;
so, notwithstanding the sacrifice, he generously

agreed to take them on board, and whatever extra expense was incurred they could settle when they arrived at San Francisco.

Putting to sea in their little craft, they were greeted with hearty cheers and "bon voyage" from the gallant tars of the "*Inconstance*," led by their captain, the sailors having manned the rigging, to wish the brave hearts a God-speed. The cheers were heartily returned from the deck of the schooner, and waving adieu they boldly set sail for the golden shores of California. But the winds were not propitious. After a tedious twenty days of calm in the Gulf of Cortes, now known as Gulf of California, they reached San José del Cabo, near Cape San Lucas. Here they took aboard fresh supplies of water, meat, and vegetables, and again started out. Reaching the cape he put out to sea for eighty or a hundred miles; returning, he would find the same rock of the cape to meet their anxious gaze. The little boat, having a round or egg-shelled bottom, and no keel, could only hold her own with the fresh, northwest winds which prevailed, blowing down along the coast. What an agonizing delay to those adventuresome spirits, burning with the desire to reach the El Dorado — twenty-one

days of this fruitless endeavor! At last he
put in at San José del Cabo, the point he
started from, where he abandoned the
schooner. A consultation was then held; the
result was that the Captain, selecting ten
trusty men, determined to finish the hazardous
journey by land, though he knew he would
have to travel fourteen hundred miles through
an unknown country, beset with dangers
and swarming with hostiles. But men of his
stamp do not count perils, so they fearlessly
pushed forward. The others remained on
board, and going back to Mazatlan, they
sold the schooner, obtained passage on a
steamer which had come round Cape Horn,
and arrived at San Francisco some time in advance of their more adventuresome comrades.
The Captain and his followers left San José in
April, and from the day of starting out all was
hardship and privation. Had it not been for
the grim resolution and indefatigable energy
of the Captain, more than one would have
fallen by the way overcome by fatigue and
sufferings. For four days they were without
food, three days without water. Gnawing
hunger, burning thirst, and intense physical
exertions were their lot, yet they pressed on.
For sixteen days they rode through a sandy

desert, from habitation to habitation, without
shelter or food for man or beast. To this
day the Captain remembers the experience
with a shudder. He does not think that in
all God's terrestrial domain there is a spot
of country so desolate and so barren as that
which they passed through on that never-to-
be-forgotten sixteen-days' ride. Only the
determined character of the Anglo-Saxon
could have surmounted such obstacles and
sufferings. At El Rosario, a small hamlet,
they secured sufficient to keep body and soul
together; from there they dragged on footsore
and weary, till, coming to a small settlement,
they saw a sight which gladdened and thrilled
their hearts to the core. The American flag
waving in the breeze greeted those exhausted
but strong-hearted pioneers from afar. And
that starry banner was flying over territory
which their valor and heroism had made all
their own. No storm-tossed mariner on a tem-
pestuous sea ever beheld the long-watched-
for beacon light with more heartfelt joy than
did those brave men, when they gazed upon
the national emblem of their country, in that
far away hamlet. Surely, the words of the
poet found no response in the breasts of
those weary travelers, when he said,—

> "Breathes there a man with soul so dead,
> Who never to himself has said,
> This is my own, my native land?"

San Diego was the name of the place, and a garrison of three companies of U. S. infantry was stationed there. Here the Captain found his friend and former companion in arms, Lieutenant Tom Sweeney (now Brig-Gen. Thomas W. Sweeney, a one-armed veteran on the retired list of the U. S. Army), formerly of his regiment, and who had been transferred to the regular army. From him the Captain and his followers received every attention and assistance, in their dire and pitiable condition.

Now the hardships were over; from thence to San Francisco all was without incident, till he entered the Plaza, Portsmouth Square, the second of July, 1849. To reach there he had made a journey of six months and three days; he had undergone sufferings, privations, and hardships. But now all was forgotten. He had retained what he had started out with—a strong heart, unflinching courage, and unbounded energy. These were the qualities that would be bound to tell. One without them had no place nor right in that community.

CHAPTER V.

THE gold fever had drawn from every class. Among those sturdy pioneers were lawyers, doctors, men of family note and education. Most of them, indeed all of them, had no fixed purpose, except to reach the land of promise. All were willing to set aside the prejudices of caste and education, in their endeavor to obtain what passes current everywhere, and is the open sesame to the world's friendship. In consequence, the professional man could often be seen at the most humble occupation, feeling that he suffered no degradation from the contagion of honest labor. There was no waiting for something to turn up. Every one went to work at the first opportunity offered, content to remain in a temporary position, until time and circumstances would justify a suitable change. Mere labor-

21

ers received fabulous rates of pay, and even by
digging dirt, a man could in a short time
accumulate a considerable sum. Idlers have
no place in our system of society, and, in the
early days of California, there were assuredly
no drones in that hive of busy bees. The
American character adapts itself readily to
time and place, and the phenomenal development of the Pacific coast, unparalleled in the
history of civilization, is the most striking
example of it.

There has been so much written on the
early days of California, and the stirring
incidents have been related and commented
upon so fully, that it would be superfluous to
go over the ground here, though the history of
that time will never be without interest to the
manhood and youth of our country, and
always thrilling in the memory of the actual
participants.

There were no wharves then in San Francisco, and all freights coming into that port
were discharged by means of lighters. Captain
Hungerford was not long in finding something
to do. He was offered the position of superin-
tendent of three or four bateaux to do the
lightering of several large vessels. He accepted, and his salary was fixed at twenty

dollars per day. The men received an ounce of gold, or sixteen dollars a day, for their labor. At that time, indeed, the laborer was worthy of his hire, and needed no "protection."

From lightering the Captain became a merchant, and, under the firm name of Simon & Co., he conducted a general store on Clark's Point, then a hill, just under Telegraph Hill, now the junction of Broadway and Sansome streets.

The winter of 1849–50 was one of the hardest known in the history of California. The town being built mostly of canvas houses was ill fitted to withstand the severity of that season; the heavy winds, rains, and storms, often leveling the insecure habitations and places of business. Those sturdy pioneers who may still be living will readily remember the mud lakes in the street. On Montgomery, from Pacific and Washington streets, the sidewalks were built up with sacks of beans and cases of tobacco, two and a half feet in height. Many crossings of the principal streets were made of corduroy and plank, placed on short piling. The visitor of to-day, and the people of San Francisco of the present generation, little know of the suffering and deprivation of those times, that tried men's soles and boots, worth one hundred and fifty dollars a pair.

The heavy rains had caused a great deal of damage, and it was the Captain's misfortune to be one of the sufferers. The frail structure wherein his business was conducted had become undermined by the floods, and the owner, not thinking it worth while to repair it, since it was to be demolished the following spring, the Captain compromised by relinquishing his lease. Winter having come, and business being suspended on account of lack of communication with the mines, the Captain closed up his affairs, having amassed a considerable sum as the result of his energy and hard work. Now he was stricken down. Pneumonia had followed a severe cold, and dysentery set in with it. All through the winter, and late into the spring, he struggled with these grim enemies, but his grit and determination carried him through, as they had done before. While still convalescent, thin and emaciated, but with all the vim of his former self, he started for the mines. Again the raging element was against him. The flood which swept Sacramento City carried with it his stock-in-trade, with which he was trying to reach the mines. However, nothing daunted, he continued his course on to Marysville, thence to Forster's Bar, on the

Yuba River. Here he met with many ups and downs. He engaged in various trades and occupations, carrying on butchering, black-smithing, mining, auctioneer, law; anything that was honest and would prove profitable, everything going on at the same time. He employed a large number of men, and any one at all capable was generally taken in and given a chance at Hungerford's. He was, in theatrical parlance, a "general utility" man, always on the stage and able to respond to every call. During the summer he was robbed by Jim Stewart, a notorious character, who afterwards suffered for his many misdeeds, being hanged by the Vigilance Committee at San Francisco. The Captain sustained a loss of nearly five thousand dollars, a portion of which, however, he subsequently recovered.

Another winter was passed amid the snow and inclemencies of the bleak Sierra Nevadas. In the spring of '51 he pushed on further up the Yuba to the Forks, now known as Downie-ville County, seat of Sierra County. Here he formed a partnership with Dr. C. D. Aiken, and commenced the drug business, the Doctor practising his profession, and the Captain, under his guidance, attending to the commer-cial affairs of the firm. For five years the

copartnership lasted. During this time he
had learned thoroughly the drug business,
and, having the advantage of the Doctor's
practice, and the County Hospital close by, he
was also enabled to acquire a training in the
medical profession. He was an industrious,
hard student; many a midnight taper he
burned, poring over his books. But for him,
like all other successful men, what was worth
doing at all was worth doing well, and, in all
his undertakings through life, he applied
himself with a zeal and perseverance that
compelled success.

Civil pursuits, however, did not wean the
Captain from his military tastes. The old
love was not extinguished. During this time
he organized the "Sierra Guards," a military
organization belonging to the State Militia.
This action on the Captain's part roused the
patriotism and military ardor of the people,
and helped to turn a part of their attention
from the wild pursuit of sordid gain. Four
other companies were raised in the county,
forming the Sierra Battalion, of which he was
elected, and commissioned, Major Commanding.
Now he was in his element; he devoted all his
energies to his command, and soon himself
and men had won quite a reputation for drill-

UNITED STATES OF AMERICA.

STATE OF CALIFORNIA.

By ~~John Bigler~~ Governor, and Commander-in-Chief of the Militia.

Know Ye, That reposing special trust and confidence in the Fidelity, Integrity and Patriotism of *Daniel E. Newgaford*

I, *John Bigler* Governor of the State of California, and Commander-in-Chief of the Militia thereof, and in the name and by the authority of the People of said State, do hereby appoint and Commission the said *Daniel E. Newgaford* as *Captain* of the *Sierra Guards* to take rank as such from the ____ of ____

In Testimony Whereof, I have caused the Great Seal of the State to be hereunto affixed.

Witness my hand, at the City of *Sacramento*, on the ____ day of ____ A. D. 185_ and of the Independence of the United States of America Seventy-*_____* years

John Bigler

By the Governor :

Secretary of State.

ing and efficiency of organization. Indeed, his popularity was such that, in 1855, the Sierra Guards presented him with a magnificent sword. The following description of the occasion is taken from a newspaper of the day.

"On Monday, the eighth inst., Col. R. H. Taylor, on behalf of the Sierra Guards, presented a magnificent gold-hilted dress sword to Major Daniel E. Hungerford, their chief officer, as a testimonial of respect for a soldier who distinguished himself in the War with Mexico, as well as their appreciation of a gentleman who needed not such distinction to ensure the friendship and respect of his fellow-citizens and associates.

"The sword, a most elegant and costly specimen of workmanship, bears on the scabbard the following inscription:

MAJOR DANIEL E. HUNGERFORD,
From the Sierra Guards,
January 8, 1855.

Vera Cruz,
  Cerro Gordo,
    Contreras,
      Chapultepec,
        Garita de Belen.
"Our Volunteers were there."

"It was expected that Harlow B. Cossett would make the presentation, inasmuch as he

was mainly instrumental in getting up this
most deserved and appropriate present; but,
owing to Mr. Cossett's legal engagements that
day, the sword was presented by Col. Taylor,
after a very appropriate extempore address, in
which he spoke eloquently of the distinguished
services of New York's sons, not only in Mexico, but on other fields of strife. We regret
that our limited space will not permit a full
report of his remarks, but we must content
ourselves and our readers by quoting only the
closing words of the address; he said:

"'This blade is of true steel; and in the day
of trial, hereafter as before, be true as steel to
your friends and to your country. The blade
is bright, so were your own brave deeds upon
the battle-fields of Mexico, in behalf of that
proud banner of our Republic. It is bright, so
is the recollection of your services in the
hearts of your comrades in arms, and of those
who this day surround you. It is bright, so
may your pathway be through this life, where-
ever the star of your destiny may guide you.
The hilt of this good sword is bound with
silver, firmly bound; may it be long years before "the silver cord" of your life may be
loosened, "or the pitcher broken at the foun-
tain, or the wheel broken at the cistern"; the

scabbard is gilded with the glow of the most precious of metals; so may your own deeds untarnished glow with golden light, while you shall remain on this terrestrial camping-ground, and, when at last you shall march forward at the great roll-call hereafter, may your field of duty be in a land whose golden brilliancy shall be undimmed for ever." Major Hungerford replied as follows:

"'Col. Taylor, and Gentlemen of the Sierra Guards: It is with pleasure and pride that I receive this beautiful memento of your appro-bation, though I fear that, in this instance, the merit has been over-rated. Be that as it may, your kindness of to-day will be by me remem-bered with gratitude, and it shall, if opportu-nity ever presents, be my incentive to such conduct as may be more deserving of such a mark of your consideration.

"'The inscription engraved upon the scab-bard of your testimonial brings vividly to my mind scenes in which it was my good fortune to be a humble participant, the result of which. I leave to your kind indulgence, and the pages of our country's history. What wonder is it that our arms are brilliant with gallant deeds, when such reward awaits the soldier's return? I accept this splendid sword from the Sierra

22

Guards, and here, in the presence of this as-
semblage, I dedicate it to the service of my
country, subject to its calls, whether it be on a
foreign shore, defending her rights, punishing
her wrongs, or upon our soil, repelling an invading foe, or, worst of all that can befall a
nation, a civil strife, threatening her nationality, — to any and all of which I most sacredly
volunteer its good steel, trusting in the God of
Battles for strength to wield its' bright blade
in the cause of liberty and the rights of man,
justice, and the honor of my country.'

" The Guards made a fine appearance that
day. It would be hard to find a finer looking
little company anywhere; the company was
formed at the instance of Major Hungerford,
and very apt scholars have they been of a very
accomplished instructor."

That sword, presented thirty-five years ago
in a presentation speech well worthy of being
remembered, and of his remembrance, was, in
the Major's well-chosen words, dedicated to the
service of his country, at home and abroad,
and his career has been an echoing fulfillment
of the promises made there, that no tarnish
should ever rest upon its bright blade. The
true soldier, the cultivated man, the good husband, the kindly father,— well may his family

UNITED STATES OF AMERICA.

State of California.

By _____ Governor, and Commander-in-chief of the Militia, and Patriotism of _____

KNOW YE, That reposing special trust and confidence in the Fidelity, Integrity and Patriotism of _____ I, _____ Governor of the State of California, and Commander-in-chief of the Militia thereof, and in the name and by the authority of the People of said State, do hereby Appoint and Commission the said _____ as _____ to take rank as such from the date hereof. _____

IN TESTIMONY WHEREOF, I have caused the Great Seal of the State to be hereunto affixed. *Witness* my hand at the City of Sacramento, on the _____ day of _____ A. D. 1856, and of the Independence of the United States of America the _____

By the Governor.

Attest. _____

Quarter Master and Adjutant General.

_____
Secretary of State.

and descendants cherish and revere his well-marked life.

The reader will not fail to remark the foresight and penetration of the gallant Major, when he says in his words of acceptance: "or worst of all that can befall a nation, a civil strife, threatening her nationality." The sound of the rumblings, which betokened the upheaval that was so soon after to come upon our fair land, had been heard by the young officer, when they had not reached the ears of veterans and gray-headed statesmen. The shot at Sumter found in him no waverer. Long before he had resolved that, when war came, which he clearly saw would come, the army that bore the "Stars and Stripes" at its head would be the army on whose muster rolls the name of Daniel E. Hungerford would appear.

During this year his family joined him, and the joys and sweets of domestic bliss were his to cheer him in his labors. But he was to be again tried; a fire broke out; the devouring flames consumed everything, and sturdy hearts saw their all vanish in the pitiless smoke of a great conflagration. Of that bustling town hardly a stone upon a stone was left. But there were no weeping and sitting on the ruins

for that community. Ere the smoking embers
had ceased to burn the sound of the hammer
and buzz of the saw were heard, and, with the
slender materials at hand, larger and more
substantial homes were built, and soon the
sun shone on happy homes and contented people. The Captain and his Doctor partner were
foremost in the work of "reconstruction." In
such disaster and sufferings they felt their
time, energy, and assistance belonged to their
fellow-men. The gratitude of those they befriended was their rich reward. The Captain
hired a large building on the outskirts of the
city, fitted it up, and gave accommodation to
many homeless people; and, though fabulous
prices would have been gladly paid to obtain
shelter, he would not accept any compensation
whatever, except an insignificant sum from
each, just enough to cover the hire of the
building, which it was impossible from his
own means to defray.

War, fire, and flood had now sorely proved
the Captain, though in all his misfortunes he
had never failed to lend a helping hand to his
fellow-creatures in distress. The Captain, or
Major, as we must call him now, and his kind-
hearted wife, unostentatiously did many acts
of kindness and charity, which endeared them

to the people of the town. Unselfish deeds always bring their own reward, and this reflection has consoled them when some of those they befriended were forgetful in their gratitude.

Reverses only make more persevering the courageous heart; and in spite of all his troubles and difficulties, which would have discouraged many a man of sterner stuff, the Major spurred on in his endeavors, feeling that the "tide in the affairs of men" would soon take a more favorable turn.

The Territory of Utah, particularly that portion which bordered upon California, known as Washoe, had been reported to be a rich mineral district. Tales were told of the wonderful finds, and, as in every new discovery, it was thought to be richer than any preceding it. Many flocked to the region. The Major, always on the alert and quick-acting, heard the news, and, in the spirit of adventure, and the hope of bettering his condition, set out for Virginia City. Arriving there, he found the town in a state of great excitement. The day before, intelligence had been received of the horrible massacre on the Carson River, May, 1860. Men, women, and children were gathered in the streets, and terror and conster-

nation were depicted on every face. Many
thought that the Indians would swoop down
and butcher every one in cold blood, as they
had done with their fellow-citizens at Carson
River. All business was stopped, and nothing
was talked about or discussed but the threatened Indian attacks. Those who have never
lived in those early mining towns cannot form
any appreciate idea of the daily dread of the
people, constantly living in the fear of burning and massacre by the bloodthirsty savages.

Meetings were held at Virginia City, Carson, Gold Hill, and Silver City by the excited
citizens to take means for defense. What was
to be done? There were few, if any, arms; and
men without weapons could be little or no use
against the Indians. It was known, however,
that the Major had arrived, and it was also
known that he, being in command of the Sierra
Battalion, had under his control, just across
the borders of the State and Territory, arms
and ammunitions. A committee was, therefore,
appointed to wait on him, and ask him to furnish arms, etc., for their protection, and to fit
out an expedition to fight the Indians. The
Major, while fully recognizing the gravity and
peril of the situation, replied to the citizens
that he was an officer of the State of Califor-

nia; the arms, etc., under his control were the
property of the State of California, and it was
not in his discretion to take them beyond the
State limits; to do so would constitute an un-
authorized invasion of the Territory of Utah,
belonging to the United States. Every argument was used to induce him to permit the
arms to be brought over, but without avail.
They offered to indemnify in any amount, in
any liability, but the Major could not see his
duty clear to accept. Never in his life before
was there such a conflict in his mind between
duty and human sympathy. There was not
one of that committee whose heart was torn
like his own by the thought of the massacre of
their fellow-citizens. The mutilated bodies
were being brought in to weeping wives and
children, and frenzied men were clamoring
for vengeance against the miscreants strolling
up Mount Davidson. He thought over the
. terrible situation. "Our citizens are being
killed, property destroyed, no immediate relief
or protection. The only succor is in my
hands." After deep and earnest thought he
concluded as follows: "Gen. Jackson took the
responsibility at New Orleans; so will I now,
and to the people I leave my justification."
Thus decided, he acted without delay. He im-

mediately sent the following despatch to Dr. E. G. Bryant, of his staff:

"VIRGINIA CITY, May 13, 1860.
"To E. G. BRYANT, *Downieville :*

"Send me immediately all the arms and ammunitions of the National Guard. Telegraph Lieut. Hall at Forest City to send all the rifles in his possession. Send to Goodyear's Bar, to Captain Kinniff, to send me all his rifles. Forward as soon as possible. Big fight with the Indians. The whites defeated. Send me your heavy sabre. Spear, Meredith, and Baldwin killed.

"Signed,   MAJOR D. E. HUNGERFORD."

Happily, an hour after sending the foregoing despatch the Major received the following from the Governor of California:

"SAN FRANCISCO, May 13, 1860.
"To MAJOR HUNGERFORD :

"*Sir*, You will please collect such arms and ammunition as you can find in Downieville, and forward them, by express or otherwise, to the scene of action in Carson Valley.

"Respectfully, your obedient servant,
"JOHN G. DOWNEY."

The Major received this with great joy. He was now relieved of all responsibility, and he entered heart and soul in the preparation for avenging the massacre. Men of his ardor and energy, coupled with military knowledge, were of vital necessity to the terrified settlers at that direful time.

The citizens held a meeting that evening. T. D. Johns was chosen as commander to defend the city; and he appointed the Major as Adjutant. Without a moment's delay, the latter commenced to organize the forces into companies. Everything was in disorder; chaos reigned supreme. The inhabitants were panic-stricken. The occasion demanded a man of the character and ability of the Major to restore order and give assurance to the terrorized citizens. Unceasingly he worked night and day, until gradually a feeling of confidence and security began to take the place of fear and distrust. The Major, having been informed of the action of the good people of Sierra County, many of whom were acting as escort to the arms which had been telegraphed for, despatched a messenger to them with instructions to organize into four companies at the first halting place, and that he would meet them en route, before they reached Virginia City. This was done. The Major met the party eight miles from the city, assumed the command, and on the following day entered Virginia City under arms, and in full military order. The inhabitants received them with open arms, wild with joy. They greeted their rescuers with deafening cheers. The anx-

23

iously-awaited aid had come; now their
brothers would be avenged. Here the Major
reorganized the battalion, as they had only
undertaken to escort the arms and stores as
far as Virginia City. Captain Creed Haymond's company also joined him at this time.
Three companies of United States troops having been ordered from San Francisco, under
Captain Stewart, with instructions to report
and coöperate with the military organization
that should be found in the territory, and
Major Hungerford's being the only organized
military body, Captain Stewart reported to
him. The Major, Captain Stewart, and Captain John, held a consultation and agreed upon
a plan of campaign. Col. Jack Hayes, of
Texas Rangers celebrity, arriving at Virginia
City while preparations were going on, the
excited citizens clamored for his services. A
braver man than Jack Hayes never lived. He
had won his reputation by many sanguinary
encounters with the redskins. Given a handful of men he would often defeat and slay
three and four times that number of Indians.
He never had any experience in regular
military organization, and so was not capable
of, nor did he claim ability to, handle and
direct large bodies of men. But the people

insisted on his appointment, and he was placed at the head of the expedition. Major Hungerford wished to retain command of his Sierra Battalion, his own pupils, in whom he naturally had more confidence, feeling that he could thus render more effective service in fighting the redskins alone. The result of the expedition justified the wisdom of the Major's desire. However, with his consent, reluctantly given, it was finally merged into the Utah Regiment, Col. Hayes commanding. Col. Ed. Saunders was elected Lieutenant-Colonel, and Charles Fairfax, Adjutant; Hungerford being, of course, the Major. Col. Hayes, before being elected, had agreed to follow the plan proposed by Hungerford, Stewart, and John, which was to attack by the front (Carson River), while a movement would be made in the direction of Honey Lake, and thus entrap the whole Indian force between Pyramid and Mud Lake. Col. Hayes, however, thought best not to adhere to his first determination; so he moved to the Carson River, and there encamped for three days. From his encampment on the Carson, he moved forward in the supposed direction of the hostiles, who, it seems, kept themselves well informed with regard to his movements, retiring as often as it suited their purpose to do. They finally made a determined stand at a narrow pass through which the trail ran. Here the first battle, known as Williams' ranch, occurred. It was of a most irregular character, without order or command ; but this cannot be said of the Sierra Battalion. It was kept well in hand by Major Daniel E. Hungerford, who, besides leading in the thickest of the fight, was able by his manœuvre to save the day. Were it not for the discipline of his men, and his tactical manœuvering, they would have lost the camp, and every man in the command would have been massacred. The well-conceived plan of young Winnemuca, the intelligent chief of the Pay Utahs, had been perceived by the Major, who immediately, by making the movement which checked him, saved all.

The following is taken from the *Alta California*, describing it :

" At one time they (the Indians) showed a disposition to outflank our men, a platoon of them riding along the sand ridges up the river bordering the camp, but Major Hungerford checked this movement by sending out a force, which stopped their advance in that direction." This is correct, except that Major Hungerford, instead of sending out a force, commanded and accompanied the movement himself. Col. Hayes, recognizing the danger, and seeing the dispositions of the Major, rode across the field to where he was, and congratulated him then and there upon his good generalship and promptness.

The battle terminated in favor of the whites, but it was not of a decisive nature. The Indians withdrew to the Truckee River. The Regulars were not in this battle, not joining the forces till the following day.

As the lesson of this engagement, Col. Hayes, perceiving the loose and unsatisfactory character of the organization, and seeing that discipline, if not so necessary in guerilla warfare or Indian encounters, was absolutely essential to the success of operations on a large scale, separated the command into two divisions, Lieut.-Col. Saunders commanding the mounted force, and Major Hungerford the infantry, composed of three companies of Regulars, the Sierra Battalions, and companies of hastily-formed volunteers from the mining camps, Col. Hayes being Commander-in-chief. The next day, the now reorganized forces marched to the Truckee River and succeeded in turning the position held by the Indians. On the day preceding the morning of the

second of June, our scouts reported the
Indians occupying the heights and crags
commanding our line of march. Their position could not have been better chosen. At
the intelligence brought in by the scouts, all
was uproar and excitement; the camp was in
a ferment; the horsemen running for their
horses, etc. The Infantry, commanded by
Major Hungerford, were soon under arms,
and proceeded to attack the enemy, who
were strongly posted on the hillside, and
sheltered behind rocks. The fortifications
were simple, but almost impregnable, composed, as they were, of two large rocks, a
short distance apart, placed on each boulder.
Another rock was put between, resting on
the top of the two others, thus forming a kind
of arch, and the loophole made between being
used by the Indians to fire through. Standing
behind the large boulders, and firing through
the opening, their heads were the only parts
of the body exposed. Apparently secure, the
redskins awaited the attack of the whites.
Major Hungerford, however, spoiled all their
carefully laid calculations by moving off to
the right, flanking the enemy, and causing
him to abandon his position. By the Major's
movement, they were forced to fight in the

open. There the chances of success would
be more even ; but, Indian-like, they did not
prefer this style of warfare; so they retreated
in the direction of Pyramid and Mud Lakes.
Though hotly pushed, they succeeded in escaping, owing to their knowledge of the country.
The whites pushed forward to Pyramid Lake,
where they found the Indian villages deserted.
Here they encamped for the night. Col.
Hayes had sent out five men as scouts, as an
advance. Following soon after himself, at the
head of his mounted force, he came upon their
dead and naked bodies, which told one more
story of Indian atrocity and the ambuscade by
which they perished. The Indians had retired
to their mountain fastnesses ; not a trace of
them was to be seen. Fearing the vengeance
of the whites, they had either hid themselves
in their ravines and mountains, of which they
alone knew the secret, or had moved away
from the region. Thus ended the Indian war
in Washoe. The Volunteers returned to Virginia City and other camps, where they were
disbanded. The Regulars remained at Pyramid Lake, and established an intrenched camp
(Haven), which they occupied for a considerable time. They afterwards fell back upon
higher ground, and built Fort Churchill.

Major Hungerford returned to Downieville,
organized a prospecting party, and again
returned to the vicinity of Pyramid Lake.
Here he found the bodies of one hundred and
thirty-three dead Indians, slain by the avenging settlers in the battle at that place. He
built a small fort which he called Fort
Defiance, which is standing to-day, and again
commenced prospecting operations. After
some weeks of labor he went back to Downieville, carrying with him on his back the whole
distance the remains of his friend, William S.
Spear, one of the party, killed in the first
expedition, known as the Ormsby Massacre.
The Major could not allow the bones of one
who was so dear to him to bleach on the field;
so he determined, notwithstanding the danger
and difficulty of the task, to restore them to
his sorrowing wife and family. The expedition in which the brave Spear lost his life, was
sent out after the murders at Williams' Ranch.
Hastily formed, and without proper organization or discipline, they were no match for the
wily enemy. Coming up with the Indians at
Truckee River, the latter furiously attacked
and defeated them, slaying eighty-three out
of the total force of one hundred and fifteen;
a massacre indeed!

After the dispersal of the Indians by Col.
Hayes' force, the Infantry, which, as stated,
was commanded by Major Hungerford, the
settlers were free for some time from the fear
of Indian attacks. Of the part taken by the
Major, the following quotation from a paper
of the day speaks:

"Major Daniel E. Hungerford arrived from
the Pyramid Lake Expedition last week. We
have been informed by private letters from
the camps that, in command of the Sierra Battalion, Major Hungerford won the highest admiration of the officers and all the men, by his
knowledge of military affairs and assiduous
instruction of the volunteers. Considering the
brave and distinguished service which this
brave and good-hearted gentleman has rendered in the war with Mexico, the country
has treated him shabbily. While trivial and
worthless persons have been promoted, this
man, whose brave conduct was especially and
publicly acknowledged in the commanding
officer's official despatches, is not thought of
when important places are filled by men in-
ferior to himself. Major Hungerford is a
soldier by nature, education, and experience
in the most important battles of the Mexican
War. Military service is his proper vocation,

24

and no man on the Coast is more capable of extensive usefulness, or better deserves the consideration of his fellow-countrymen."

Apropos of Pyramid Lake, it was for some time thought that Fremont was the first to explore it. The distinction really belongs to Major Hungerford, as the clipping from a California paper of April 8, 1865, clearly shows.

"PYRAMID LAKE. ITS ORIGINAL EXPLORERS.— The *Virginia Enterprize*, alluding to recent explorations among the islands of Pyramid Lake, in the State of Nevada, falls into error. It says that no boat had previously navigated the Lake, and that no craft except Fremont's tub-rafts had been before seen on its waters or reached the island. This is a mistake, as we shall proceed to prove.

"In July, 1860, Major D. E. Hungerford, then of Downieville, later of the Army of the Potomac, and now of this city, organized a prospecting party and went to Pyramid Lake. On arrival there they constructed two canoes, lashed them together, and thus reached the island at the head of the Lake. The names of the party of thirteen, a record of the expedition, and date of the event were placed in two bottles, one of which was buried in the rocks at the place of landing, and the other at the highest point of the island, where they also erected an American flag, constructed of their shirts. A celebration was held, and George M. Beach, Esq., of this city made a speech. On their return to the mainland they filled the canoes with stones and sunk them. The collective name of the party was 'The Pyramid Lake Pioneer Mining Company,' chiefly belonging to Downieville."

The following is a copy of the honorable discharge of the Major from the regiment. He was the last in service. Indeed, when the companies returned to Virginia City all were disbanded except his own command. He, fearing that trouble and rioting might result from the sudden disorganization of so many armed men, had taken the precaution to retain his command and discipline. This proved to be a necessary step, for he was afterwards obliged to restore order and stop the looting which was being carried on by some of the soldiery. His forethought and prudence were highly appreciated and deeply felt by the citizens, many of whose property and lives he was the means of saving. Always expectant and looking ahead, he clearly foresaw what would come about from the relaxing of discipline and military rule:

HEADQUARTERS UTAH REGIMENT OF VOLUNTEERS,
VIRGINIA CITY, U. T., June 10, 1860.

To DANIEL E. HUNGERFORD,

Major Utah Regiment of Volunteers.

DEAR SIR, — The Utah Regiment of Volunteers under
my command is hereby disbanded, and you are, therefore,
honorably discharged from the service as Major of the
Regiment. Your accounts will be forwarded to the War
Department with the accounts of the regiments in general.

I have the honor to be, your obedient servant,

JOHN C. HAYS,
Col. Commanding Utah Regt. Vol.

(Attest)   CHARLES S. FAIRFAX, *Adjutant.*

The official report of the Major to the Governor of the State of California is here given.
In the difficult and trying rôle the Major had
to play, few could have acquitted themselves
with more honor and patriotism. No self-lau-
dation, but praise and commendation for
others he freely gives.

HEADQUARTERS SIERRA BATTALION, C. M.,
DOWNIEVILLE, June 26, 1860.

To JOHN G. DOWNEY,

Governor and Commander-in-Chief of California.

DEAR SIR, — I have the honor to report, in obedience to
your despatch of the thirteenth of May, 1860, directing me
to collect such arms and ammunition as I could find in
Downieville, and forward them by express, or otherwise, to
the scene of action in Carson Valley; being myself at the
time in Virginia City, I telegraphed to Surgeon E. G. Bryant to forward the arms, accoutrements, etc., of the National

Guard, Captain John E. Ager, and the arms, accoutrements, etc., of the Goodyear Rifles, Captain B. Kinniff, which were received and turned over to B. L. Lippincott, Quartermaster of the Utah Regiment of Volunteers (receipts for which are herewith enclosed). Not having instructions as to the disposition of the arms, etc., upon their arrival I considered myself as bound in discretion to turn them over to a military organization, to the end that they might be used for the best protection of the inhabitants of Utah Territory, and I trust that my acts may receive the approbation of your Excellency. The hurried manner in which all business connected with the fitting out of the expedition against the Indians was done, must be my excuse for not having received more satisfactory vouchers for the arms, accoutrements, etc., property of the State of California. I am compelled also to cite in further extenuation the great excitement existing, as well as the difficulty of finding persons occupying situations who were acquainted with that peculiar line of public business.

It is with pleasure that I inform your Excellency of the patriotism of the citizens of Downieville, who promptly responded to the call of their fellow-countrymen in Utah for assistance, and by private subscriptions raised the means of subsistence and transportation for the one hundred and thirty-five good citizens who volunteered to escort the arms, accoutrements, etc., free of expense to the State, many of whom volunteered again for the campaign. These were organized into three companies, under Captains E. J. Smith, John B. Reed, and F. F. Patterson, and subsequently joined by Captain Creed Haymond's Company of Sierra Greys, the whole forming the Sierra Battalion, under my command, and subsequently a part of the Utah Regiment of Volunteers, under the command of Colonel John C. Hays, remaining with, and taking part in, the military operations, until discharged on the tenth of June, 1860.

In September, 1854, I organized in this (Sierra) County the Sierra Guards, and have continued in the service of the State since. In 1856 I was commissioned as Major of the First Battalion, Second Brigade, Fourth Division, California Militia, and, having now seen some of the companies put to the more practical use, I beg leave most respectfully to tender this my resignation as Major in the service of California, to take effect July the first, 1860.

I have the honor to be your Excellency's most humble servant,

D. E. HUNGERFORD,
Major Commanding Sierra Battalion.

The Major thought proper to withdraw his resignation, as clouds were beginning to darken in other parts of the country, and he wished to have his hand on a sword hilt that could be quickly drawn. The Governor, replying, acknowledges the efficient service the Major has rendered, and expresses his appreciation of the aid that he gave to the citizens of the neighboring Territory.

STATE OF CALIFORNIA, EXECUTIVE DEPARTMENT, }
SACRAMENTO, June 28, 1861. }

D. E. HUNGERFORD,
Major Sierra Battalion, C. M.

DEAR SIR,— Your communication of the twenty-fourth inst. is received. Officers of your battalion have been commissioned, and the requisitions filled out with the best arms now in the service.

I am pleased that you have found it compatible with your private affairs to withdraw your resignation, as I should dislike exceedingly to lose your services at a time when they may be needed. You can rest assured that anything I can do to advance the efficiency of the Sierra Battalion will be done, as I will not soon forget their promptness when called upon to render aid to our neighbors in Nevada Territory.

Very respectfully your obedient servant,

JOHN G. DOWNEY.

THE Republic was to pass through such an ordeal as no other government had ever undergone — this time, not on a foreign soil, but in its own land, where rivers of blood would flow, and four long years of fratricidal strife would wage, before the "Stars and Stripes" would wave in triumph from every part of the Nation's domain, North, South, East, and West.

Dark, ominous clouds were appearing on the horizon of our national destiny. They had not been seen by all, or if seen, were generally regarded as a nimbus that the golden sun of pure patriotism would soon dispel. But thoughtful men — they were not many — knew the terrible storm would have to break. Major Hungerford, as we have seen in the preceding chapter, six years before the awful conflict began to rage, had pierced futurity by his

clear perception of the true import of what
was passing about him. Perhaps already during the Indian campaign he had seen in his
mind's eye the conflicts of those mighty armies
in a few years rushing together on a vaster
field. It is not appropriate in these pages to
discuss the causes which led to that great war.
They are well-known, and nothing would be
gained by their repetition here. The pages of
history are open to all, and therein one can
read.

When Lee laid down his sword to Grant at
Appomattox, hatred and strife should have
been laid down with it, and peace and recon-
ciliation taken up. The secessionists of to-day
are those who, by voice or pen, commit the
heinous crime of hindering or impeding the
blessed work of good-will and fraternal union.
Our misguided brethren of the South—whose
valorous deeds in a cause they thought just
shine with the glorious feats of arms of the
heroes of the North, forming part of our common heritage, the heroism of the American
soldier—have been, as we all know, conquered
by the sword they took up. Now that the
beaten foe has accepted the result, their country overrun, their property destroyed, and
many of them ruined and impoverished, can

we not afford to be generous and extend the
outstretched hand in fraternal friendship?
The stars which glitter in the firmament of
our National banner now gleam with no fad-
ing light. Blood and treasure have made them
of a never-ending brilliancy, and when the
roll-call of those States of these United States
is called, there is to-day no faint wavering response, as before the shot of Sumter was fired;
but, instead, a thundering answer of "present,"
which is heard to the furthermost corners of
the earth.

Major Hungerford in these dark days was
at Downieville. Like every other true patriot
he was waiting in anxious suspense, hoping
that our statesmen would devise some means
to avert the pending strife. But such was not
in the power of man. The lowering clouds
had to burst. And when once the national
flag had been fired upon, from that moment
there was but one side on which a loyal soul
could stand.

The Major, in his far-away home in the
Sierra Nevada, beyond the reach of railroad
or telegraph, was watching the operations with
his accustomed perspicuity and foresight.
When the pony express brought in the news
of the disaster at Bull Run, he was one of the

first to get it. He then knew the war was
really on. To help preserve the flag and
Union was his first duty. No other had any
claim on him. "The civil strife threatening
her nationality" was now at hand. Returning
home that evening he said to his brave little
wife, "I am going to Washington to join the
army;" but, far from being dismayed, she
replied, "I am not astonished, I expected it."
This Spartan wife and mother did not try to
induce him to remain; she knew his country
demanded his services, and she would not
keep him, notwithstanding the sacrifices she
would be compelled to make.

In two days the Major was off for the seat
of war, his sword, his baggage, and a God-
speed from his wife and children to cheer him
on his journey. It was the Major's intention
to go direct to Washington and offer his services to the President, asking him to assign
him wherever he was the most needed.

Arrived at San Francisco he embarked the
next day on the Pacific Mail steamer for New
York, via Panama. On board, he met fifteen
U. S. Army officers, among whom were Major
Robert Allen, Major Grierson, Captains Win-
field Scott Hancock, Mason, and Myers,
Lieutenants Grigg, Alexander, Ingram, and

others, from all of whom the Major received
every courtesy and consideration. Several of
these officers were his comrades in the Mexican war. After a pleasant passage of twenty-
three days, he reached New York, and, before
stepping ashore, he was offered the appointment of Lieutenant-Colonel of the Thirty-
Sixth New York Volunteers, which was immediately accepted, the Major receiving the warm
congratulations of his fellow-passengers, foremost among whom was his good friend Hancock, afterwards Major-General, whose friendship he retained till the last day of the General's life.

The pony express had carried across the
continent the names of the passengers aboard
the steamer; hence the Major's arrival was
anticipated, his gallant record being well
known. A command was at once made for
him, which, as related, was tendered him
before he left the steamer.

In forty-eight hours from landing he had
started for Washington, to join his regiment.
The night before his departure (Sept. 18, 1861),
writing to his wife, he says: "I arrived here
on the fifteenth. I was met on board the
steamer by a Lieutenant of the Thirty-Sixth
Regiment (Col. C. H. Innes) with the proffer of

the Lieut.-Colonelcy of the regiment. You
may judge of my surprise. The regiment is
now in Washington, and I shall leave to-day to
join it. I accept this, and hope for promotion.
The army appointments have been all made.
The chances of war are unknown. We may
never meet again. A soldier stakes his life,
and he can fall at any time; but if the sacrifice
must be, why, then, the hope of meeting in a
better world." When the Lieutenant-Colonel
reached Washington, after reporting to the proper authorities, he immediately set to work, dis-
ciplining his command and exerting himself to
the utmost in the discharge of his duties. He
marked out for himself the high standard of
conduct which he always followed, and he
knew no other law than duty, conscientiously
performed, come what would. While at the
camp, in writing to his wife, under date of
Oct. 7, 1861, he says, " You will perceive that I
have not changed my locality yet, nor do I
know when we will be moved from here. We
are constantly at work preparing for the field.
Since I joined the regiment I have been gratified to see a very great and marked improve-
ment in the regiment. Without wishing to
flatter myself I can truthfully say (this to you
alone) that I am popular among military men,

and particularly am I considered by my
commanding generals and others. I have
marked out for my course a strict discipline,
not only over myself, but I hold others equally
rigid. It has never been my policy to expect
more from others than I do from myself. I
may in the end make some enemies, but that
necessarily follows the conscientious performance of any public duty. I find I am gaining
considerable reputation. As an instance of
this, to-day our regiment was inspected by the
Assistant Inspector-General of General McClellan's staff, whom neither I nor any of the regiment knew, yet he seemed to know all about
my military career and capacity. This would
go to show that I am spoken of in high military circles. Also, I am making the acquaintance of distinguished public men, and I hope
by a proper course of conduct to profit by such
acquaintance."

"Since my coming here, I have been rather
unfortunate. First I had dysentery, then a
tremendous boil, having ridden fifteen hours
without dismounting. When I got rid of that,
I sprained my knee, and strained the muscles
of the leg, from which I am at present suffering. I have, notwithstanding the Surgeon's
and General's advice, kept constantly on duty.

The People of the State of New-York:

BY THE GRACE OF GOD FREE AND INDEPENDENT

To _____ Daniel B. Hungerford _____ Greeting.

We, reposing special trust and confidence, as well in your patriotism, conduct and loyalty, as in your integrity and readiness to do us good and faithful service. Have in accordance with the provisions of the act of the Legislature, passed April 16. 1861, entitled "An Act to enhance the embodying and equipment of a Volunteer Militia, and Troops for the public defense." appointed you constituted and by these Presents, do appoint and constitute you the said Daniel B. Hungerford

_____ Lieutenant-Colonel _____ in the 8th Regiment N.Y.S. Volunteers.

to rank as such from _____ August 5th _____ 186___

You are therefore to observe and follow such orders and directions as you shall from time to time receive from your Commander-in-Chief of the Military Force of our said State, or any other your Superior Officer according to the Rules and Discipline of War, and hold the said Office in the manner specified in and by the Constitution and Laws of our said State and of the United States, in pursuance of the trust reposed in you, and for so long shall be your COMMISSION

In Testimony Whereof, We have caused _____ of our Military Secretary as to have affixed the Seal of the State, at our city of Albany, at Albany, to these presents and signed the same, and caused the Great Seal of the State to be hereunto affixed, the _____ day of _____ in the year of our Lord one thousand eight hundred and sixty

EDWIN D. MORGAN, Governor of the State of New-York, and Commander-in-Chief of the Military and Naval Forces of the same.

Passed at the Adjutant General's Office

Tho. Hillhouse
Adjutant General

E.D. Morgan

I have received my commission, which dates from Aug. 5, 1861."

The next letter is dated November 4, 1861. In it the Lieut.-Colonel speaks with proper pride of his appointment on a Board of Military Examiners. He has not yet recovered from his injuries, but he is impatient to get to the front where the fighting is going on. He says, " Here, as at my last writing, expecting orders every day to move to the front. I wrote you in my last of the accident I had met with by the fall of my horse. I have not yet recovered, in fact, I am suffering as much as I did the day after the injury. The boils have all disappeared; were it not for that unfortunate fall, I would be in the enjoyment of very good health. I learned to-day, through Brig.-Gen. Couch, that I was held in esteem at Division (Gen. Buell's) Headquarters, and also at General Headquarters (Gen. McClellan's). In proof of their estimation, I have been detailed by General McClellan as one of the Board of Military Examiners, to examine the volunteer officers as to their competency, and fitness in moral and military capacity. This I consider a very high compliment to me and my qualifications, inasmuch as I was not aware that General Headquarters knew of the existence of such an individual as your humble servant. I regret that my regiment is not with the advance, and I fear that we may be continued in the vicinity of Washington all winter. In that case, my chances of advancement look rather slim. If I could only have one or two good fights, or even respectable skirmishes, I think I would be all right. For the last two days and nights we have had a terrific rain-storm, which I fear may have caused a failure of the great naval expedition; of that, however, I am not at liberty to speak. On the first of the month we were mustered for payment, but we will not receive any money for a week or two yet. If we do not move from this place until after the men are paid off there will be a high old time, for soldiers and sailors will have their regular spree."

The following official documents refer to the Board of Examiners mentioned by the Lieut.-Colonel in his letter:

HEADQUARTERS ARMY OF THE POTOMAC, ⎫
WASHINGTON, Oct. 21, 1861. ⎬

SPECIAL ORDERS ⎱
No. 110. ⎰ EXTRACT.

20. Under the authority of the 10th section of the act of July 22, 1861, a Military Board, to consist of the following-named officers, will meet at such place in Buell's Division

as its commander may designate, at 10 o'clock A. M. on Wednesday, the 23d inst., or as soon thereafter as is practicable, to examine into the capacity, qualifications, propriety of conduct, and efficiency of all officers of volunteers serving in said Division who may be brought before the Board.

Detail for the Board.

Brig.-Gen. D. N. Couch, Volunteer Service.

Col. Gilman Marston, 2d New Hampshire Vols.

Lieut.-Col. H. L. Potter, 2d Regiment Excelsior Brigade, N. Y. Vols.

The Junior member will record the proceedings.

By command of Major-Gen. McCLELLAN.

[Signed]   S. WILLIAMS,

Asst. Adj.-General.

[OFFICIAL.]

DIVISION HEADQUARTERS, Oct. 23, 1861.

J. M. WRIGHT,

Assistant Adj.-General.

Gen. COUCH.

HEADQUARTERS ARMY OF THE POTOMAC, }
WASHINGTON, Oct. 31, 1861. }

SPECIAL ORDERS }
  No. 124. }   EXTRACT.

14. Lieut.-Col. Daniel E. Hungerford, 36th New York Volunteers, and Lieut.-Col. Jeffers M. Decken, 10th Massachusetts Volunteers, are detailed as members of the Military Board, appointed by paragraph 20 of Special Orders No. 110 of the 21st inst., in the place of Col. Gilman Marston, 2d New Hampshire Volunteers, and Lieut.-Col. H. L. Potter, 2d

Regiment Excelsior Brigade, New York Volunteers, who
are relieved from the operation of said order.

By command of Major-Gen. McClellan.

[Signed]   S. Williams,

Assistant Adj.-General.

[Official.]

Division Headquarters, Nov. 1, 1861.

J. M. Wright,

Assistant Adj.-General.

Gen. Couch.

Headquarters 1st Division, 4th Corps d'Armée,
Brightwood, D. C., March 19, 1862.

Special Orders
No. 26.

4. The Military Board, first convened by virtue of Special Orders No. 110, Par. 20, Headquarters Army of the
Potomac, afterwards amended by Special Orders 124, Par.
161, same source, of which Brig.-Gen. D. N. Couch is President, is hereby ordered at these Headquarters at 10 o'clock
A. M. to-morrow, March 20th.

By order of Brig.-Gen. D. N. Couch.

O. Edwards,

Assistant Adj.-General.

Lieut.-Col. D. E. Hungerford,

36th N. Y. Vols., through Cols. Briggs and Innes.

The next letter is to his brother, and is
dated Nov. 9, 1861, still at Camp Brightwood,
D. C., Headquarters 36th Regt. N. Y. Vols.

These communications, written at the time,
and in the close intimacy of brotherly friend-

ship, truly reveal the character of the man. The sentiments therein expressed are indeed noble. They show the true patriot doing his whole duty, as well as a willing heart and hand allow. The Union demanded his full and entire allegiance, and he gave it freely.

He writes: "I left my home in the mountains of California on the sixteenth day of last August for the purpose of coming to Washington to offer my poor services to my country in these trying times, when she most needs the services of her true and loyal sons. I came here without knowing what part or position I should play in the grand drama. It little troubled me whether I was an officer or a private, so long as I played the patriotic part.

"On my arrival at New York the fifteenth of September, before I had landed from the ship, the position of Lieut.-Colonel of the 36th New York Regiment of Volunteers was offered me, which I at once accepted, anxious to be of use in any capacity to the government that my fathers and myself had, on other occasions, fought for.

"I remained in New York but two days, and then hastened to join my regiment, already in the field, who were, with one exception (the Colonel was my First Lieutenant in Mexico),

entire strangers to me. On the eighteenth of
September I joined my regiment, and found
all the officers anticipating my arrival, they
greeting me as an old and familiar friend. I
immediately entered upon my duties, and have
so continued up to this date, with a willing-
ness, zeal, and devotion that I feel confident
the immortal spirit of our father approves of.
Oh, I feel sometimes that that same spirit of
our noble parent looks smilingly upon the acts
of his youngest born, and approves of his self-
sacrifice in assisting to maintain the best government ever instituted by the hands of man.
I am not a Republican, and I did not vote for
Abraham Lincoln, but he is the President of
the United States, the Chief Magistrate of my
country, and as an honest American citizen,
loving his country's institutions, I am bound to
sustain him and his administration. In so doing I lose none of my rights as a citizen. On
the contrary, I am sustaining the principles of
true republicanism.

"I regret as much as any one can this war,
but it is upon us; we must not stop to inquire
who or what was the cause of it, or at whose
door, *if any*, the fault must be laid. It is our
duty — as we love our country, as we love the
principles of self-government — to fight it out,

if we have to shed the last drop of blood in our bodies to do it.

"My regiment is at present encamped about three miles from Washington. We are in daily expectation of orders to make an offensive movement. Whenever the order reaches us, I feel it will be responded to with steady and willing hearts; whosever lot it is to fall, future generations will bless the sacrifice.

"I left my family in Downieville, Cal. Whether I shall ever meet them again is not in the power of man to foretell. Write them a few words of encouragement, though encouragement my brave little wife does not need. So long as she knows her husband is doing right and serving his country, she is prepared for any sacrifice, and without a murmur."

On Dec. 5, 1861, he writes, this time to his wife. Though immersed in his own special duties, he had not failed to keep himself thoroughly informed of the military movements being made. His judgment of the actual situation and his ability to forecast many of the future operations of the forces, are quite remarkable, and well worthy of being noted here. There were but few at that time who had such a clear idea of events and their significance as this volunteer officer.

He says: " I am pretty sure that we are to
remain here for the winter. I don't believe
that there will be any important movements
of our army in Virginia. I think the army
will occupy its present position until the opening of the spring. There will be, however,
some expeditions, both military and naval,
sent along the southern coasts during the
winter. If any of the enemy's troops are withdrawn from Virginia, our troops may, under
those circumstances, be advanced to occupy the
localities vacated; but it appears to be the settled policy of the authorities not to attack the
enemy in their strong positions at Manassas,
while in Kentucky, Missouri, and the Southwestern States to vigorously prosecute the
war, at the same time to make attacks along
the coast, and thus effectually besiege the in-
surgents; then, in the spring, when roads are
in fit condition, to advance in this direction.
We are in sufficient force and combination to
resist any advance of the enemy in our established lines of defense. By this means we dis-
tract him from the southwestern and coast
movements, and while he is weakened by the
exhaustion of his resources and the discour-
agement and consequent loss of discipline, I
should not be surprised, before the spring set
in, to find them partially disorganized.

"Our success along the coast encourages the Union element in the disloyal States. It may tend to a speedy peace, perhaps, without the great sacrifice of life which will necessarily follow the meeting of those two great armies. God grant it may so prove!"

The following letter from the Governor of California was received by the Lieutenant-Colonel, about then, in acknowledgment of his resignation, which he had sent in when he joined the Union forces:

STATE OF CALIFORNIA, EXECUTIVE DEPARTMENT, }
SACRAMENTO, Dec. 13, 1861. }

Lieut.-Col. D. E. HUNGERFORD,
36th New York Vol., Washington City.

COLONEL,—I am in receipt of your letter of the 12th ultimo, tendering your resignation as Major of the Sierra Battalion, California Militia, and incidentally apprising me of your holding command as Lieut.-Colonel in one of the New York regiments in active service.

While I regret your absence from this State, which may yet need your services, I am pleased to congratulate you upon the present honorable position you have attained among the gallant soldiers of the great Republic.

Wishing you health and distinction,

I am very respectfully your obedient servant,

JOHN G. DOWNEY.

The medical knowledge that the Lieut.-Colonel had acquired in California served him well now. He writes of his assisting the sur-

geon in the vaccination of the men. Solicitous
of the welfare of his command, he did all in
his power for their protection and well-being.

Of proven capacity himself, he readily saw
the incompetence of others, and he clearly perceived the real ill that the splendid Army of
the Potomac was suffering from — politics and
favoritism in the appointment of its generals.

December 29, 1861, he writes as follows:

" I have been assisting our Surgeon, Dr.
Edward B. Dalton, all day to-day vaccinating
the regiment. There has been considerable
small-pox in and about Washington, but it has
not spread as yet to any extent in the army.
God grant that it may not!

" I am very much inclined to the opinion
that this brigade to which I am attached will
not set the Potomac on fire while under the
present general (Couch). I don't think that
he enjoys the greatest confidence of the General-in-Chief, and every day lessens my esteem
for him as a military leader. I do not
believe that he will ever breakfast off of more
than a dozen Secessionists at any one meal.
Col. Innes is a candidate for Brigadier-General,
and, in the event of his success, I will probably
be the Colonel of the Thirty-sixth.

" What a plague civil-political soldiers are!

The country has been sufficiently punished with them already. Political generals, political colonels, do., do., do., down the list until it completely runs in the ground. No wonder that our army has met such reverses. I hope that such appointments are about played out."

CHAPTER VII.

CHRISTMAS came and went, and the New Year broke upon a vast army preparing and straining every nerve to be revenged for the Union defeat at Manassas. The rejoicings of holiday time would not come again to many thousands of that gallant host, calmly awaiting the shock of mighty battles, and expecting so soon to hear the word of command that would hurl them against their brother foe. But the cheering words from home and friends, and the proud consciousness that each was doing his part in the noble work that would preserve the Union, and win the blessings of future generations for their sacrifices, made them bear up under their privations and look hopefully to the future. Many of those sleeping on the tented fields and undergoing the hardships incident to a winter's campaign, had left their luxurious homes to battle for the defense of the country; but, whether from the lap of luxury or the poorest hovel, every one felt he had an equal interest in the sublime task. The flag belonged to them all; it sheltered and protected the humblest and greatest, therefore each joined in rallying to uphold the symbol.

Lieut.-Col. Hungerford was occupied during all this time by the ordinary duties of camp life, keeping *au courant* with the military situation, and foreseeing many of the movements which afterwards took place. Always expectant, he determined to have his command ready for action when the time came. In his letter of Feb. 7, 1862, he gives a grotesque description of his method of securing discipline. If he did not allow the grass to grow under the feet of his men, he certainly did not let the herb assume any undue proportions under his own. Ever on the alert, no one can accuse him of taking his duties lightly, or, so to speak, sleeping at his post. The career of the Thirty-sixth throughout the war gives the best proof of the efficacy of the treatment adopted by the vigilant commander, which, by way of illustration, we give the subjoined letter descriptive:

" My whole attention is given to the regi-

ment. I don't allow them much time for nonsense, and I think I am right in so doing. At
seven o'clock, target practice and drill ; and at
half-past ten, drill and target practice, until
'roast beef'; at half past twelve, battalion
drill and firing until 'retreat'; all in addition
to their other duties, which prevents the cultivation of the herb known as grass to assume
the power of vitality under the soles of their
shoes. I have now one of the most orderly
regiments in the service, thanks to my fatherly
care in providing for the wants of delinquents,
and the kindly assistance of two courts
martial. They have tasted of the fruit of
their folly, and they don't appear to like it
much. I first tried moral suasion. That
proved a humbug, quack remedy. Then I
prescribed 'extra duty.' The patients didn't
appear to improve much under the treatment.
I then resorted to the old, empirical practice of
guard-house. The patients seemed to revive
and improve so much as to induce the hope of
success. But they in a short space of time
relapsed, when I discarded all the homeopathic
doctrines and resorted to the allopathic, which
treatment has worked with almost magical
effect, so much so that I am determined to follow this mode of treatment in all cases of a

refractory character that may come under my
care.

"For news, that is '*non est in swampo.*'
Idleness reigns supreme throughout our lines.
No skirmishes, no grand movements, no dreadful marches (thank God!), nor what is more
pleasant, no countermarches, like Bull Run,
for instance."

On the eighth the Lieutenant-Colonel in-
forms his family that a relative will shortly be
under his command, but he gives fair warning
that the said relative must do his full duty,
and expect no favors from him. He did not
believe in having two rules to go by, even if a
member of his own family was to be benefited
thereby.

I would call attention to what he says in
regard to the campaigns that were to be
carried on. He seems to have divined the
general plan of operations afterwards followed,
and not only was his prediction correct in this
instance; but, as the reader will see, in his
other letters he was equally prophetic. He
writes:

"I was visited to-day by a nephew, a son of
my sister. He is at present a Corporal in the
Eight Cavalry, New York Volunteers, but will
shortly be transferred to my regiment as Sec-

ond Lieutenant, and if he doesn't behave, I'll
soon get rid of him. I am determined not to
let the ties of blood interfere with the proper
discharge of my official duties. The plot
thickens. Gen. Grant has taken Fort Henry
in Tennessee, and taken possession of the
Memphis & Ohio Railroad, near that point,
thus cutting off the enemy's communications
and supplies with the great ports of Arkansas,
Mississippi, and Alabama. It is no doubt
intended that Burnside, with his forces, should
extend along North Carolina, in the rear of the
rebel forces in Virginia, forming a continuous
chain, connecting with Buell's forces in Kentucky and Tennessee, which will effectually
shut off the rebel supplies from South Carolina, Georgia, and the contiguous States.
While these manœuvres are being executed
other expeditions, both naval and land, will
engage the enemy's attention, and, if the
enemy does not keep a sharp lookout, he will
be caught in the McClellan rat-trap. The
next two months will be full of events and
glorious achievements. What disposition is to
be made of your humble servant, I don't know.
I can only hope for the best, *i. e.*, that Providence and the powers that be will so arrange
it as to give a fellow a chance to snuff the

sulphurous volume as it rises from the battlefield, and not keep us here guarding the sand and mud heaps that surround the capital of this fair land, which, by way of military compliment, they call forts. *Nous verrons.* It is now after ' taps' and the camp is as silent as the stillness of death. Nine o'clock, and one would not suppose that nearly a thousand stout hearts are beating in the immediate vicinity, the owners of which by a short roll of the drum would almost instantly be arrayed in battle attire, ready to meet the foe of their common country. Such is the order of discipline, though somewhat tedious and troublesome to attain, it is gratifying to know that out of chaos I have established order and discipline, the first great principles to be inculcated in an army."

Again on February 16th, he foretells the taking of Savannah, which, two years later, fell, also Fort Donelson, which capitulated the next day.

The other parts of his letter are not uninteresting reading. The surgeons come in for legitimate criticism. They were about the only people that were fattening at that time. One can well understand the impatience of the Lieutenant-Colonel to be at the scene of

action, while such glorious victories were being
won. Coming from the far-away town of
Downieville, high up in the Sierra Nevadas,
he wished for something more than preparing
for fights which were so slow in coming.

"We are having glorious news now, clean-
ing the rebels out in every direction, at
Roanoke Island and Fort Henry. The enemy
have also evacuated their stronghold at Bow-
ling Green, Kentucky, and to-morrow I expect
to hear of the fall of Fort Donelson on the
Cumberland River. We will meet with a very
severe loss there, I expect, but I feel confident
our forces will carry it. Next comes Nash-
ville in that section, then Columbus, while
Burnside in North Carolina will be playing the
dickens in Rebeldom, and Sherman will be
advancing upon either Savannah or Charleston
in South Carolina, some minor operations
going on along the Florida coast, and the
Grand Army of the Potomac stands ready to
pounce upon the enemy in Virginia as soon as
they weaken their lines to reinforce or succor
any of the threatened points. Thus affairs
stand in critical excitement. Before this
reaches you great battles will have been
fought, and a consequent rattling among the
dry bones of sinners on both sides. Many a

one will have run his race, and a great many
made unable to run, for want of the proper
understandings (legs), and another great number will fail to reach the golden opportunity
for want of proper arms. Well, it will give the
lazy surgeons something to do. They have
been having jolly times long enough, while we
poor — have been exposed to the inclemencies of all kinds of weather, doing guard duty,
etc. Let's have a fight, by all means, if for no
other laudable purpose than giving the doctors
something to do."

Another prediction has come true. Donelson has fallen. The escape of Floyd excites
his ire, as it did that of every other honest
man. Referring to the first battle of Bull
Run he recalls a fact which is not often mentioned by the many that condemn in such a
wholesale manner the defeat of the Union
forces. Battery after battery was lost to the
rebels during that engagement, yet seldom
have the Northerners received credit for their
heroism on that day. He also rightly character-
izes as "gammon" the foolish talk of South-
erners as to the greater bravery of their troops.
I say some, as the sensible and really brave
men on their side, vastly in the majority,
never gave way to such foolish assertions.

28

North and South are equals in bravery and
heroism. The noble qualities which distinguished the American soldier were not seen in
those from a section only. North, South,
East, and West had all their share in the glorious quota.

"As I predicted yesterday, we have the
news of the capture of Fort Donelson. Generals Johnson and Buckner and fifteen thousand prisoners are ours. That infernal scoun-
drel, John B. Floyd, escaped disguised. What
a pity! It is said that he stole away. This
afternoon there has been considerable saluting
from several of the forts surrounding the capital, and to-morrow morning, at sunrise, I send
forth our twenty-four pounders on Fort Massachusetts, the thundering peals of jubilant rejoicing in thirty-four guns. Everybody is
pleased and in good humor, except an occa-
sional regret at the escape of Floyd. The par-
ticulars of the battles have not yet reached us,
but I fear a heavy loss on both sides. The
enemy was well-positioned, having in addition
to Fort Donelson several subordinate forts,
batteries, and intrenchments, with a force for
their defense above the military percentum.
It is given as a ratio, six assailants to one as-
sailed, when fortified. They had more than

that, and consequently the advantage, and notwithstanding their chivalrous notion that the Southern people are vastly superior, they have not proven themselves equal to the Northern troops on Roanoke Island, Fort Henry, Fort Donelson, or, indeed, any of the important battles. Even at Bull Run they were nearly, if not quite, equal in number to the Union forces, yet they lost battery after battery until the stampede caused by cowardly Congressmen and ignorant teamsters. Their vaunted superiority is all 'gammon.' God Almighty did not put all the brave men in the Southern States, I think he left some outside; it may, however, have been a mistake."

"I expect to hear of the taking either of Charleston or Savannah by Burnside or Sherman, perhaps by Butler. There will be pretty exciting times shortly, and it grieves me that I am stuck in this camp, going through the mimicries of soldiering without any of the realities and glories. Some troops must occupy this position, though, and I am unfortunate enough to be one of the poor — -. It is too bad, after coming all the way from the mountains of California to get into a fight, to be compelled to gratify my ambition in the expenditure of gunpowder, celebrating other people's victories. I might have done as much at home with the Downieville artillery. *Volo non valeo.* I am willing, but unable. I am afraid that I shall perforce be compelled to return home a whole man, without even a little scratch to show that I have been a participant in the great struggle for the preservation of the Union."

February twenty-sixth finds him a busy man. He tells the special duties he has been detailed upon, from which it would appear that, as he states himself, his superiors do not find him deficient in his capabilities. Enthusiast in his profession, he takes great pride in every new advancement.

Again his surmises are correct. Virginia was to be the base of operations, though at that particular time the order for the movement was countermanded.

"I am doing an extensive business just now in Division Headquarters and Adjutant-General's Headquarters, answering letters, making reports, and writing to you at the same time.

.   .   .   .

"There is every probability of our taking the field very soon. Artillery regiments have been sent, and relieved us of the charge of the forts on the line, which leaves us free to be

used, and we are preparing for a movement
somewhere, which way, of course, we are not
yet advised; but I strongly suspect Virginia
will be our destination. The only regret I feel
is that we have not another Brigadier-General.
I have no confidence in General Couch. I
don't think him composed of the right material; while he has unlimited confidence in me,
I am sorry that the confidence is not at all re-
ciprocal. However, it may turn out for the
best, as it may give me greater scope to take
responsibilities on the battle-fields if we ever
get there. I have had a magnificent drill to-
day, passage of defile, retiring, forming squares,
and changes of front while firing. I challenge
any regiment in the service, regular or volunteer, to surpass it. The difference in the discipline and drill in this regiment is almost
magical. It has so changed since I have had
it. My whole time has been devoted to it. I
have not been outside of our immediate camp
except when field-officer of the day for two
months, night or day. If I could retain the
command for two months longer I would bring
it up to the standard of the regular army, a
great thing to say and accomplish with any
volunteer regiment; but I would succeed or
be willing to hazard my commission upon it.

I expect that I will have to relinquish the command to Col. Innes next week. His court-martial will probably be adjourned *sine die*, and I am already detailed upon another court. They keep me constantly employed, but I would rather be left alone with my regiment a while longer, for by its efficiency I win my honors; but there are other qualifications besides drilling and fighting that constitute the thorough soldier, which, by the way, it would appear they think me not deficient in. I have been considerably complimented by being detailed upon particular services of importance, among which the Military Board of Examiners, then Inspector, then President of Board of Commissioners, and now upon a high military court. You may be sure that I would not be called upon to hold such positions unless my superiors knew that I had the proper qualifications. However, I would prefer something more substantial. I should modestly suggest promotion. God help us! A battle or so might help a poor fellow. Big men get killed sometimes as well as little ones, and there is no telling who may be called for."

In this letter we have him recording the pleasing manifestation of his men, which testified to the esteem in which they held him, notwithstanding the tight rein he had always drawn.

The secret of governing men is enforcing precept by example, and, as the Lieutenant-Colonel took every care to do his own duty thoroughly, it was all the more easy to enforce discipline among his subordinates.

His commission, the honored evidence of his military service, was his one thought. He held it most dear, and the safety of that precious paper was his great solicitude. He bids his wife guard it as his most sacred treasure.

Feb. 27, 1862, he writes:

"I have just learned that orders are now in preparation for my regiment to be at the cars in Washington by daylight to-morrow morning. I have just given some necessary instructions to carry out the anticipated order. While waiting am momentarily expecting the order. I am unable to even guess our destination; may be able to form an opinion to-morrow. I send herewith my commission for fear of accident. We have to leave everything behind for the present, taking only what we can carry about, and on our persons."

"Please take care of it, as you know how proud I am of all my commissions. There is no paper in the world as dear to me as my commissions in the service of my country.

"We have just had our evening parade, and have published the order for marching, which was enthusiastically received by the men, and, although Col. Innes was present, the men proposed three cheers for the Lieutenant-Colonel, which were given with a will. I did not think the men would be very willing to cheer me, as I have drawn the rope pretty tight, while the Colonel has been very easy with them. It shows that the men can appreciate the necessity of discipline. I have not sought their good opinion. Little difference it makes to me whether they approve of my course or not. I do my duty; they must do theirs. If they don't, it is my place to compel them. I have the reputation of a severe disciplinarian, but I would rather that than be thought easy-going. Baby soldiering is not to my style. We are not advised as to any intended movements, nor have we any curiosity to learn. We are here as soldiers ready to obey orders, not speculate or question upon them, so long as there is authority to support us."

"If I had orders from competent authority to unhinge the gates of hell, I would endeavor to execute and carry them out. That is the spirit in which I act."

"I am pleased to know, however, that the men are soldiers enough to see that discipline must be maintained. I regret, though, that the Colonel was present when the men cheered me, as it may have wounded him for the moment, though, of course, it will not affect our friendship in the least. He is aware that he and I are working together for a common object. The better discipline there is in the regiment the better it will be for all concerned. His ideas of discipline are different from mine. I am an advocate of a firm hand, without fear or partiality, holding every man to his duty. The Colonel thinks as good results can be had by being easy-going. There is where we agree to disagree. Our personal relations, though, have been and will continue to be of the most pleasant character."

However, the hope of winning laurels was to be deferred, — another disappointment, keenly felt by officers and men ; but "sweet are the uses of adversity." The delay enabled the paymaster to discharge his indebtedness, and Lieut.-Col. Hungerford being one of those whose means were not abundant, and who had the obligation of wife and children to maintain, was not averse to receive from the Treasury what had now become due to him.

29

February 27th, in the evening, he indites
the following lines:

"Another 'stampede.' Just as I began to
indulge in the hope of winning laurels the order for our march at three o'clock A. M. to-morrow was countermanded. It appears from
rumor that General Banks had crossed the
upper Potomac and had been repulsed, and
that our Division was to have supported him;
other than this your informant knows nothing
of the cause of the alarm. It is a great disappointment to both officers and men, who were
eager for the fray. Everything has quieted
down, and stillness again reigns with uninter-
rupted sway. The sweet harmony of peace
we are in hopes will soon be broken. Everything tends to, or appears to, forebode a forward movement of our Division. How long
this 'bungling' will cause delay I cannot tell.
We were gradually preparing for such an
event and were almost prepared when the confounded news broke in upon us. Am glad it
has turned out as it has, for it will enable us
to go on with our regular muster to-morrow."

Washington's birthday, 1862, found the vast
army awaiting the signal to move against the
rebel host. The ancestors of both sides had
fought in a common cause against a common

enemy; that day saw one-half of the nation endeavoring to destroy what their forefathers had struggled to establish. Well might the combatants contemplate and pause in reflection on the anniversary of the birth of the immortal Father of their country. But if those reflections made fatter those battling under the rebel standard, it strengthened the hearts and hands of the heroes enlisted under the "Stars and Stripes." Let us hope that the spirit of the great departed had, on that day, no cognizance of the scenes being enacted in the land he loved so well. The following letter, breathing sentiments well befitting the day, was written by the Lieutenant-Colonel:

"One hundred and thirty years ago to-day the great and good Washington was born. Oh, with what indignant scorn must he look down in spiritual vision upon a portion of his recreant countrymen at this day in arms arrayed in unholy war against that which cost so much treasure and blood to establish, instead of following him in his precepts and example and heeding his wise admonitions. We find ourselves antagonistic, brother to brother; how illy are we repaying the loving-kindness and anxious solicitude of the great *pater patriæ*, Washington, a name to be honored among men until the end of time.

"The one hundred and thirtieth anniversary of the birth of Washington has been most generally celebrated throughout the Union armies, cities, and towns. Various have been the amusements in the different camps, redolent with jubilant joy; salutes have been fired from the numerous forts along our lines, the reverberations passing hill and dale, until the echoes returned like the distant roar of heaven's mighty artillery, and Providence seemingly smiles her kind approbation upon us and bids us hope. Heaven grant that, ere another year is added to the account of time, our country may be relieved from its present distress and trouble, and that peace, plenty, and happiness will have again resumed their proper sway, and reign among us, and that, upon the return of another anniversary, a whole and united people may join in their thanksgivings to God for the great and beneficent gift bestowed upon humanity in the person of our great Washington, whose teachings, examples, and great virtues can only be emulated, not excelled."

The vacillation in the political course of Martin Van Buren had no charm; on the contrary, it excited his complete disgust. Having a firm character himself, consistent and true to his principles, formed after mature consideration, he loathed wavering, and detested ingratitude.

He understood soldiering in its proper sense, and knowing that there are not or ought not to be, any luxuries on the battlefield, he did very little repining for them, as is seen by what he wrote at the time:

"I am indeed flattered by your kindness in placing my photograph by the side of the illustrious old 'Hero of the Hermitage'; but excuse me if I fail to see the compliment in being placed by the side of the renegade Martin Van Buren, a man, after having been nurtured, fostered, and made great by his party, and when that party most needed his services (1848) to willfully, and with malice in his blackened heart, abandon and desert those friends that had raised him from the picayune and pettifogging lawyer of Albany to the highest office in the gift of the people. I cannot feel complimented or flattered by being placed in the same gallery with that ungrateful wretch. I would advise you to kick either one of us out of doors. Two such can have no affinity. While I would, with honor, strive to emulate the example of 'Old Hickory,' I, with equal honor, scorn the apostatizing ingrate of Kinderhook.

"If the confounded mud would only dry up, we might have something cheering to do; no doubt an advance movement, and a lively spree with the enemy, for a change from the dull monotony of a quiet camp life. There is too much sameness about our present style to suit me. You manifest a great desire to send me something to make me comfortable. Lord bless your dear, kind hearts! I have too much comfort now, more than I desire; that is just what I am complaining about. Who ever heard of soldiers having nice, comfortable quarters, and comfortable beds to sleep in, and living upon nice turkey and chicken? Pshaw! This is all holiday soldiering. Give me my blanket, the cold ground for a bed, the heavens above for a shelter, a piece of fat pork or bacon and a hard biscuit, and a chance at the enemy once in a while. Then I will think I am soldiering. To thunder with this Miss Nancy arrangement, lumbering up our trains with all such baggage! The old fellows of '76 didn't have such traps encumbering them and delaying their progress for weeks and months. I would not give a snap for soldiers, who could not be out in the pure air of heaven, and subsist without carrying along with them a fashionable hotel with their French cook. The gallant Illinoisians are not bothered with such nonsense. I have seen them at Vera Cruz, and Cerro Gordo, where they were lucky if they had a single blanket and a hunk of fat pork. But Lord, how they did fight! I wish I was out West among them now. Didn't they go in at Forts Henry and Donelson? They are of the right stuff."

His letter written under date of March 7, 1862, is in a jocular vein, but still shows that he was awaiting the call to action with no quaking heart, even though the result might be for him a desolate widow and weeping children ; but such was the chance of war, he thought, and he had to abide by it.

Here, again, events justified his judgment. A few weeks after how many Union soldiers had fallen! Sad prophecy for poor, bereaved families.

"I am thankful for your kind wishes that I might have a fight or two, as well as your kindly expressed desire that I might not be wounded or killed. The former I don't mind so much, if slight, but I have no particular desire to have the distinguished honor of the latter. However, of that I must take the soldier's chance. There is no telling what might happen ; there is more or less very

careless shooting done in all armies, and I
don't know that the rebels are an exception.
I am pleased to learn that of the two evils you
have chosen the lesser, retaining me in your
presence to the exclusion of that black-hearted,
ungrateful wretch, Van Buren. I feel, as you
say, 'some better.' 'Old Hickory' is good
enough for me, besides your own true, honest
faces turned occasionally upon me. Again, I
feel called upon to acknowledge your kind
remembrance of me, when sympathizing with
me, making my rounds at the dead hour of the
night. Have you ever seen a live hour of the
night? I have, and a right lively hour, too. I
think you are right in your opinion that there
will be more blood spilled. The worst has not
yet been. A few weeks more, perhaps days,
and there will be more widows and orphans in
the land.

" I have not read McClellan's dream, as you
ask. I never knew he had been dreaming.
When? That is the question. Not since the
Rebellion broke out, for he has not been asleep,
as the rebels will learn to their cost, presently.
He has been too much occupied in fattening
up his great serpent, the 'Anaconda', to trust
himself in the embrace of Morpheus.

" If Brother Zeth thinks I am doing nothing, he is quite mistaken. I am busy from the time I get up until ten o'clock with the affairs of the regiment, then I go to court martial, of which I am a member, and sit there until three o'clock, then return to camp and drill my regiment until half-past four o'clock; then comes evening parade, after which one would suppose that I ought to be pretty well tired out; but there is no peace for the wicked. I am subjected to more hard work with all the incidental annoyances, until after taps, nine o'clock, officers and men laying all the business, complaints, and troubles before me, after which I am so tired, confused, and worried that I find consolation in writing, scribbling, and scrawling these few unintelligible lines to you."

The regiment at last received the order to march, and gladly all obeyed. But more disappointments were on hand. Ordered back from Virginia to Camp Brightwood, after a march that not one of them will ever forget, they arrived weary and sick, but not disheartened. Who can doubt the bad effects of such false movements?

He writes, March 17th:

"We returned here on Saturday night, or rather, Sunday morning, having left Virginia

at eight o'clock on Saturday night; after one
of the most dreadful marches through mud up
to our knees, we arrived — or a portion of us,
at least, some not having got in yet, — on
Sunday morning, about daybreak. It had
been raining for two days, though to call
it rain is a libel. It poured. I thought that
I had seen rough weather, but it is all a
mistake. I have seen nothing, but sunshine
before. To attempt a description would
puzzle the brain of Fenimore Cooper, so I
will not undertake the task. Suffices to
say, that we all got as wet as mortal man
was ever wet before, and as muddy as poor
human beings well could be. And then,
traveling all night in that comfortable condition, and lying down in wet clothes and
blankets — that is what you call the stern
realities of campaigning. All that was
necessary to fill up the beau ideal was a
bullet hole through the body, to complete
the picture of the horrors of war. Cæsar's
dispatch was "*Veni, vidi, vici.*" I came, I
saw, I conquered; but we can exclaim,
that we went, we didn't see the enemy, and
we turned around, and came back to our
camp, tired, muddy, wet, and hungry. Thus
ended that brilliant (?) campaign, long to

be remembered by all who were unfortunate enough to be among the number."

Once more hopes raised and dashed to the ground. Another order to march countermanded. Really, indeed, these men were sorely tried, with all these delays.

He writes (March 18th), describing the feelings of the men at these ill-advised directions:

"Confound the luck! The order for our march to-morrow morning at seven o'clock is countermanded. It is too bad to be fooled about in this way, first dragged into Virginia through the mud, and kept there several days, without the necessary camp equipage, and then brought back again through the mud and rain in a night as dark as pitch, and just as we were beginning to feel all right again, to be brought with the hope of leaving to-morrow, sure, then to have that hope taken away, looks too much like trifling with us."

CHAPTER VIII.

Embarking of Regiment — On the Peninsula — Camp
Winfield Scott — Account of the Affair of the Vermont Regiment at Warwick Creek — Corroboration
by the Comte de Paris — The Thirty-Sixth holds the
Left — Fight with the "Teaser" — Reporting valuable Information.

FINALLY, the time has come to measure
strength with the enemy. Actual fighting was to take the place of drilling. Men
and officers felt that at last the trial was
at hand. Burning to emulate the Western
armies in their glorious victories, they were
impatient to do their share in the crushing
out of the Rebellion, and, if the battles of
that campaign did not have the decisive
results that were looked for, who can say
that the bravery and gallantry displayed
by the Army of the Potomac during those
conflicts were ever excelled?

He writes (March 24th):

"We will probably embark on Wednesday, to — God only knows where, but to
Virginia is my humble opinion. I only

hope that we won't be long on board transports. I am a pretty good sailor on dry land, but a very poor soldier at sea. I'll tell you how you may know where I am. It won't be long before the newspapers tell you where General Keyes is, then you will know that I am 'somewhar thar,' or 'tharabouts.' Do not expect to hear from me often. I shall be in hubbub and excitement of more moment than writing letters. We expect a severe struggle, but who can doubt the result? That we will whip the rebels is our firm conviction, but some of us will not be able to answer to our names at roll call, after the struggle is over. But such is war, and every one must take his chance, doing his duty to himself, his friends, his country, and his God. If it should be my fate to seal my devotion with my life, I hope you will reserve a green spot in your memory for one who most truly loved his country, for his country's cause."

At last, on the Peninsula, historic ground, where a century before the last act in the drama of National Independence was played, now another act in another drama. The supreme test of Republican government was to hold the scene. The clamor of the

people was satisfied. The Army of the
Potomac, after innumerable difficulties, was
marching on to Richmond. The battles of
McClellan's campaign were to bring out
once more, and show to the world, the
mettle of the American soldier.

April 8, '62, he says : " We left Camp
Brightwood, on the twenty - fourth ultimo,
embarking at Washington, and disembarking at the old town of Hampton, near
Fortress Monroe, and proceeding to Camp
C. W. Smith, where we remained three days.
On the fourth, we left our heavy baggage
in camp under a sufficient guard, and took
up our line of march for Yorktown, expecting to meet with considerable dispute at a
place called Young's Mills, where the enemy had a continuous line of works; but for
some reason best known to themselves, they
abandoned them on our approach, without
firing a gun. From all appearances they
had occupied the positions all winter with
a considerable force. They had constructed
comfortable quarters. To-night will be the
third night that we sleep here. Yesterday
and the day before there was some skirmishing; we have taken several prisoners,
and gained a deal of information, both as

regards the enemy's position and strength
and the topography of the country. About
three miles to our front is a creek ; upon
the opposite bank, extending at (it is supposed) a distance of three or four miles,
are the rebel batteries. Our pickets and
the rebels exchanged frequent shots across,
while we were engaged in repairing the
works and making new ones. We expect to
make the attack the day after to-morrow.
The enemy frequently fired upon our fatigue and reconnoitering with shell, to which
our parties pay little attention, but continue
their task with astonishing coolness. We
have been for the past five days on a
very short allowance of provisions, but, as
to that, we are being relieved. I have had
but the half of a blanket, and a horse-
blanket at that, for five nights, our baggage trains having failed to connect ; and
three days out of the five it rained like
the deluge to assist us in our trouble ; but,
notwithstanding all that, we have not a
sick man on the list. This shows what
the boys will do and stand when they
have a chance."

"What is being done by the other *corps
d' armée*, I do not know, but suppose each

is playing its alloted part. We are full of
confidence, and a few days will tell which
army is the best."

On April 19th, writing from Camp Winfield Scott, near Yorktown, Va., he says:

"Yesterday morning we changed our
position about a mile closer to Warwick
River. We are within reach of the enemy's guns, but he has not discovered us,
the thick woods concealing us from his
view. Our works have been progressing
slowly ; the roads are miserable, but are
improving, the weather having been, for
the past two or three days, more favorable. The day before yesterday, one of the
Vermont regiments lost about eighty men,
killed and wounded. They charged across
a creek and swamp, and succeeded in gaining the enemy's advanced work (rifle pit),
holding it for more than an hour and a
half; but they were compelled to abandon
it for the want of proper support. While
in the act of retiring, the rebels opened upon
them from their upper works, causing the
loss they sustained. General Smith is much
censured for ordering the assault, and then
not supporting it properly. He will probably be placed under arrest, and, from what

I can learn, there appears to be just ground for censuring him. Our artillery keeps firing at intervals during the day, as I suppose, for the double purpose of distracting the enemy's attention from our working parties, and of ascertaining their calibre and position.

"Rain is falling, and I am afraid that the roads will be horrible again by to-morrow. The ground is low and marshy, and most of our roads being newly made, a little rain renders them almost impassable. The bad roads in California are nowhere in comparison with these. All of our stores, supplies, and artillery have to be brought over these roads, and when two or three thousand heavy wagons have passed over them, I assure you they are not much improved. We will not be prepared to commence final operations before the latter part of next week. It is reported in camp that the enemy sent over a flag of truce to-day, asking permission to bury their dead, which shows their loss thus far must greatly exceed ours. I can give you no description of their position or works, for I do not leave my own brigade, fearing that, in my absence, my regiment might be called upon

31

to change position. I have, however, been several times in front, while officer of the day, and will probably be so again to-morrow; but I can see only a small part of their extensive line of defense. I have already written you of the enemy's taking a pop at me while visiting my guards. Since then, I have not been in any particular danger. Your kind advice for me to take care of myself reminds me of the woman who cautioned her son not to go near the water until he had learned to swim. I am afraid if I should follow your suggestion that it would not redound to my honor, nor be creditable to my family. I do not expect to be rash or desperately daring, nor do I care simply to do my duty. I would not give a fig for a million soldiers who would do only their duty and no more. Circumstances very frequently require that one's duty must be exceeded ; these circumstances with me, however, have not yet been made apparent. When they present themselves, it is time enough to act as their necessities would appear to demand."

What he states in the preceding letter is fully corroborated by the Comte de Paris. In his "History of the Civil War," Vol. II, the

Comte says: "On the sixteenth of April, towards four o'clock in the afternoon, four companies of the Third Vermont, supported by the fire of twenty-two cannon, which had already dismantled two of the three guns in the enemy's work, bravely rushed to the assault of that work. The Federals bravely crossing Warwick Creek with great boldness, below the dam, took possession of the breastworks which commanded it, after an engagement in which they put to flight two regiments of the enemy — the Fifteenth North Carolina and the Sixteenth Georgia. The most difficult part of the task was accomplished, a foothold having been obtained on the other side of the creek; all that remained to be done was to take advantage of the surprise of the enemy to push regiment after regiment as rapidly as possible across the ford to pass beyond the breastworks, to take possession of the redoubts, and thus to pierce the enemy's line; but the generals of various grades who had organized this demonstration had failed to agree beforehand as to the importance it was to assume, and much precious time was lost. For an hour the foremost assailants exhausted themselves without receiving any other reinforcements

than five or six hundred men of the Fourth
or Sixth Vermont. The enemy took advantage of this delay to mass all his available
forces upon the point menaced ; that is to
say, more than two divisions. The small
body of Federal troops could not attack the
redoubt, where the Confederates were increas-
ing in number at every instant ; but they
made a stubborn defense in the breastworks
they had conquered. Being finally over-
whelmed by numbers they were obliged to
retire and recross the river. This unfortunate affair produced a sad impression on
the minds of the soldiers who had seen their
comrades sacrified without any orders being
given to go to their assistance."

In the next letter from Camp Winfield
Scott, near Yorktown, May 1, 1862, it is easily
seen the opinion held of the Thirty-sixth
by General Keyes, when he ordered this
regiment to hold the extreme left. The
Lieutenant-Colonel complains, though, that
he cannot be in the thick of the fight, and
so is rather disappointed. He describes the
situation.

"I wrote you about the 'stampede' we
had on that dreadful night, the second day
after we were ordered to Young's Mills,

which is the extreme left of General Mc-
Clellan's Grand Army of the Potomac. The
Thirty-sixth has the honor of holding this
position. It is at the mouth of the Warwick River, on the James. We have a
battery of four Parrott guns, supported by
companies from my regiment. On the
twenty-eighth, the rebel gunboat *Teazer*,
and a companion, paid us a visit at the
battery, where I was in command. They
threw us fifteen shell, and three solid shot,
which did us no harm, being too high. I
did not answer them, as my battery was
too light to inflict any injury, and I did
not want to expose my weakness. I prepared, however, to dispute any attempt at
landing. General Keyes complimented me
for my forethought, and, as he expressed it,
coolness in receiving the enemy's fire, without returning it, he being fearful that we
had returned it, and thus exposed our
calibre. I asked to be supplied with two
heavy guns, but, up to the present, they
are not forthcoming. Had I had them at
the proper time, I should have sunk the
Teazer, and put a stop to her annoyance.
For the past week I have had a rather
hard experience of it, being in the saddle

eighteen out of the twenty-four hours per
day. Last night I had the first good sleep
in a long time.

"It is said that our besieging works are
progressing about Yorktown, but how, God
only knows. I have heard and read of
things being done, but — that's all. I am
considerably disgusted with these great,
ignorant, blundering, idle, petty, political,
intriguing, homeopathic generals and preach-
ing colonels. •

"We have the intelligence of the taking
of New Orleans. It will be some time
before you hear of a similar result at Yorktown, and if such a thing should be easily
done, you may expect to hear of General
McDowell's being defeated, which would
not surprise me in the least. The enemy
are doing something upon their right, which
would indicate the withdrawal of considerable part of their force. For what purpose
is of course surmise, but I should judge
that it may be for the purpose of reinforc-
ing Johnson or Jackson, and giving battle
to McDowell or Banks, with the intention
of leaving Yorktown. They need a victory
at any cost, particularly now, in order to
give them prestige. Time alone can give

us the knowledge of what their movements are intended for. I have reported this already, but yet there is no attempt to frustrate or prevent them.

"My business is to prevent the enemy landing and turning our left flank. The position I hold is a very honorable one, but there is not much glory to be won. I am afraid it is not very probable that the enemy will attempt a landing. We only wish he would; it would give us something to do besides watching that he doesn't."

Lieutenant-Colonel Hungerford on April 30th reported to division headquarters, the substance of that to which reference is made in his letter of May 1, 1862. As he predicted, Shields and Banks were defeated and Yorktown was evacuated. Ye', although the preparations for evacuations were reported at the time, this important and most valuable information was not acted upon: no advantage whatever was taken of his discovery. Did it ever reach the ears of General McClellan? If not, why not? Who is to blame? No historian has ever made mention of this, but it is here placed on record to show the vigilance of this volunteer officer, and the incompetence of one,

or some, of the so-called generals of the
Army of the Potomac. On this point, the
Comte de Paris, in his second volume of
the "History of the Civil War" says:
"This movement (the evacuation) had been
determined upon since the thirtieth of April
at a council of war held in Yorktown by
Jefferson Davis, Lee, Johnson, and McGru-
der." It had been, therefore, reported by
Lieutenant-Colonel Hungerford the exact
day it had been decided upon. Our army
knew then of the first preparation of the
Confederates, and that on the very day the
movement began.

In writing, May fifth, the Lieutenant-
Colonel again speaks of the information
he reported:

"I have already written you that my
regiment is occupying on the extreme left
of the Army of the Potomac, also of the
shelling I received from the rebel gunboat
Teazer. General McClellan ordered an immediate advance this morning, he having ascertained for himself that the enemy
were evacuating Yorktown. I had reported
this on the thirtieth of April, but no notice
was taken of it. The light cavalry and
light batteries were sent in pursuit of the

fugitives. This morning considerable firing
has been heard in the direction of Yorktown and apparently upon the York River.
Situated as my regiment is, we can only
surmise what it is that our gunboats are
shelling out the rebel batteries above and
opposite Yorktown. I am left in a fix with
my regiment. This movement of the rebels,
and pursuit by our army, leaves us at
Young's Mills as a guard to keep open our
land communication, while the army pushes
forward to win glory. I know that it is
very necessary for some one to be along
the line of communication, but, as I have
said before, it is very hard that it should
be my luck to be that one."

In a letter from Camp Bottom Bridge,
Va., May 22d, he describes his important operations on the preceding day. It is evident
that it matters but little to him whether he
obtained any recognition for his services.
To do his duty, and let the rest take care
of itself without the aid of newspaper or
other puffing, was his idea of a soldier's conduct.

"Yesterday I was placed in command of
about a thousand men to support a reconnaissance. Crossing the Chickahominy, at the

32

bridge recently destroyed by the rebels, I
pursued a by-road for nearly two miles ;
the road, for the greater part of the way,
passing through a dense wood, suddenly
converging upon an open field, where, in
front of and facing the road, I discovered
the enemy's pickets. I drove them into the
opposite woods, when the enemy opened
upon me, with shell from a small howitzer,
and with their carbines. They, fortunately
firing high, did no damage; but they were
not so fortunate, as we unsaddled four of
them. I should have pursued them still further, but I did not wish to disobey orders ;
as it was, I exceeded my instructions; but
the happy termination of the affair covered
all criminality.

"The reconnaissance was satisfactory, and
valuable information gained. The ground I
obtained was held during the night; and,
this morning, we commenced some field
works to sustain the position. This being
my first chance, I determined to take a little
extra responsibility ; and, although perfectly
satisfactory to all concerned, it will not be
made much of. I am afraid it will not be
blazoned through the columns of the newspapers. However, that makes no difference ;

I am used to it, and can stand it. It doesn't
lessen my zeal in the least.

"As for what will happen in the vicinity
of Richmond I can form no idea. There are
all kinds of rumors here; if we have a battle at all, it will be a terrible one; but, after
the evacuation of such places as Yorktown
and Williamsburg, it is impossible to say
what they will do. We may be before Richmond two, three, or four weeks, without
anything like a battle being fought. If we
find the enemy strongly fortified, and will
make a stand, we will then no doubt commence a regular siege. These things cannot
be accomplished in a moment. They require
time. It takes time to reconnoitre, establish
batteries, get up supplies, and do a thousand other things that the public don't understand. 'On to Richmond,' is easily said,
but not so very easy to carry into execution."

This action of his in crossing the bridge
was, however, too important and too meri-
torious to be passed over without notice. A
New York pictorial publication, in giving an
account of the affair, says: "On the twenty-
first of May, 1862, Lieutenant-Colonel Hungerford crossed the Chickahominy in com-

mand of about fifteen hundred men at Bottom Bridge, and had a brisk skirmish with the enemy. They held their ground until relieved on the morning of the twenty-second." A picture of the troops crossing the bridge accompanies the account. In his letter it is apparent how clearly and accurately he gauged the situation of the army, and what would result, all of which really did come to pass.

CHAPTER IX.

On the thirtieth of May, Lieutenant-Colonel Hungerford, always watchful and keen-
sighted, was on duty, as field officer of the
day. That day he reported to Generals Devens and Couch that the rebel General Longstreet, with his division, had passed down
between White Oak Swamp and the James
River. This was information of the most
valuable kind; and he, knowing full well its
importance, and feeling that some move of
the enemy was in contemplation, delivered
the information in person to General Couch.
By reference to the Comte de Paris's work
on the Civil War, Vol. II, it is there stated
that "on the thirtieth the necessary instructions were given the Confederate Com-

mander Johnson for the battle of Fair Oaks."
It would appear, however, that his vigilance
was once more to go without reward. The
information never went any further, and no
attempt was made to frustrate whatever
may have been Longstreet's design. On the
following day Longstreet retraced his steps
and surprised Casey at the head of the
swamp. Sweeping his pickets before him,
the rebel hordes fell on the Unionists and
ruthlessly cut them down; although the latter fought like tigers, they could not con-
tend against the overnumbering thousands.
This brought on the battle of Fair Oaks.
General McClellan did not even know that
a battle was raging, and the booming of the
cannon was the first intimation he had of
it; but, if the report of the field officer of
the day had been forwarded to his headquarters, as it should have been, it would
have obviated his telegram to General Keyes
during the battle next day, inquiring what
"all that firing was for?"

The Lieutenant-Colonel had done his full
duty in reporting to his division headquarters. Had he gone further he would
have violated military etiquette, but he
little thought at the time it would never

get beyond there. It may well be asked
on whom shall the blame fall for not
communicating the information to General
McClellan's headquarters? There can be
but one answer,—surely on General Couch.
How much the difficulty of General Mc-
Clellan's command of the Army of the
Potomac was increased by incidents similar
to the one just related, but few know.

In this battle the Thirty-sixth New York
Volunteers were ordered to the front to
occupy some unfinished rifle pits on the
right of the Williamsburg road. Only three
of the companies could be sheltered; the
remaining seven companies were all exposed, lying upon the ground in line of
battle, that being the second line. The first
line was hotly engaged, all the overshot
reaching them. During the engagement
General Keyes came in rear of the Thirty-
sixth and, dismounting, threw himself upon
the ground saying in a loud tone which
was heard by almost everybody, "This is
my favorite line, and I want you to hold
it to the last." Encouraged by the confidence thus placed in them the gallant
Thirty-sixth cried out, "We will, General,"
in a tone that fully showed their grim

determination to do it or die. Upon his
retiring, one of the soldiers of the Thirty-
sixth found a despatch, which he had
dropped. It being open, the contents were
seen to be "What is all that firing for?"
and signed "McClellan." It was given to
Colonel Innes, who was commanding the
brigade, Lieutenant-Colonel Hungerford being in command of the regiment.

The battle raged all day, both sides
fighting with desperation and frenzy. About
three o'clock the enemy appeared on the
right front, passing through an extensive
clump of fallen timber. Two regiments
were in line of battle on a cross road, and
a little in the right and rear of the position
held by the Thirty-sixth. A light battery
of six Napoleons had previously been posted
higher on a rising ground, and was firing
over the Thirty-sixth. Lieutenant-Colonel
Hungerford, seeing the rebels advancing,
with his three right companies, the only
ones he could use unless a change of front
was made, and confident that he could beat
back the enemy, and himself full of ardor
for the struggle, he turned round, expecting
to see the six Napoleons belching forth and
the two regiments already mentioned con-

tributing their support; but he saw neither.
They had vanished. "Some one had blun-
dered." Another mistake to be added to
the long roll. Dumbstruck, he had to see
the rebels advancing until they had flanked
the Thirty-sixth, and gained the ground
from which the two regiments had been
withdrawn. He, however, continued to fight
against the fearful odds, his well-trained
men dealing a destructive fire to their outnumbering opponents. In the meantime,
Hungerford sent his adjutant to General
Keyes, to report that his flank was turned,
and to ask for instructions. The adjutant,
returning, brought the order to retire, which
was done in perfect order; and, in going a
distance of about one thousand yards, he
fired three effective volleys from his regimental line, to show that the Thirty-sixth
were still there, even if ordered to retire.
In falling back on a wood, he discovered
General Peck with two or three of his staff,
to whom he reported, as follows:

"I have the honor to report the Thirty-
sixth New York Volunteers well in hand,
and I ask for orders." General Peck was
greatly agitated, and he excitedly answered,
"I have no orders to give, I have had my

horse shot under me." Lieutenant-Colonel
Hungerford, surprised at the reply, and
hardly understanding the fact of a General
having no orders to give under such circumstances, again asked for orders, saying,
"General, give me an order of some kind,"
to which the latter replied, "You must do
the best you can, I have had my horse
shot under me." "You said that before,
General. I propose to fall back on the saw-
mill opening, and there make a stand," was
the Lieutenant-Colonel's response. Hastily
he returned to his regiment. Arriving
there, he saw on the road masses of stragglers. Ordering immediately his right company across the road, he blocked it and
allowed none but the wounded to pass.
There in the heat of battle, and in almost
less time than it takes to record it, he
organized the stragglers, appointed officers,
and, instead of a flying mob, there were in
a few minutes fifteen hundred formed men
in line. Soon after, General Phil. Kearney
and General Peck came up, the latter more
tranquil, as he had secured a horse.
Lieutenant-Colonel Hungerford reported this
time to General Kearney (he being the
senior) as having collected fifteen hundred

men, and again asked for orders. But he was disappointed again, for General Kearney ordered him to retire to the second line of intrenchments, having gathered three regimental colors. These men were distributed along and through the line of intrenchments, by order of Colonel Innes. General Peck does the gallant Lieutenant-Colonel a great injustice, in his report of the day's work. The General claims to have collected himself fifteen hundred stragglers from various regiments, but the fact is that he did not collect a man. It was Lieutenant-Colonel Hungerford that did it, and the stragglers were from Peck's own brigade, the general who had his horse shot under him, and who had no orders to give. The memory of General Peck may be at fault, but even making full allowance for the excited state of mind he was in, it should not have been very difficult to remember to whom the honor and credit were justly due, instead of attributing it to his own self, who was engaged in catching a horse, and not organizing stragglers.

The battle of Fair Oaks, bloody and indecisive, nevertheless led to important results. Though but a few thousands were

engaged on each side, it had, notwithstanding, the proportions of a great battle. Some
parts of the field were won and lost three
times. From every section of the battle-
ground came accounts of great bravery and
heroism ; and if, as the Confederates say,
some of their generals, by not arriving at
the time, or not arriving at all, compromised
the success of their operations, surely the
Federals have a right to say, that the inaction of half their army had prevented them
from turning it into a great victory for the
Union arms ; but a discussion of the battles,
though interesting, is not apropos here ; it
is to follow the Thirty-sixth, and the part
that Lieutenant-Colonel Hungerford took, that
these lines are concerned with.

The Comte de Paris, in treating of the
losses on both sides, says :

"The heaviest losses on both sides were
sustained around Seven Pines ; those of
Longstreet and Hill amounted to more than
three thousand, those of Keyes to three thousand one hundred and twenty men." Can
stronger testimony be quoted? The Thirty-
sixth was one of the few regiments that did
not throw their ammunition away in inac-
curate firing. The Lieutenant-Colonel had

drilled them too well for that. He was always impressing on his men that each cartridge fired was worth exactly six cents, and to waste any was certainly a crime. Indeed they had taken his lesson so much to heart that in the actual fighting their bloody work showed how well they had profited by it. Two days after the battle, when he visited the scene of his part of the fight in order to ascertain how his men had fired, he knew they had done well, but he was astonished to see such a remarkable result. He examined carefully the entire area in the range of firing which was thickly wooded, and he could find only three shot marks on the trees above a man's height, while the trunks were notched all over by the chippings caused by the bullets. This certainly gave abundant proof of the execution caused by the fire of his men. Besides, there were still lying on the ground twenty-seven unburied bodies of the killed rebels. They had not yet been carried off the field. The average casualties being five wounded to one killed, what must have been the loss sustained from the deadly aim of the Thirty-sixth? Well might the Comte de Paris state that the severest fighting was at the point occupied by the Thirty-sixth about Seven Pines.

After the battle of Fair Oaks, bad
weather set in. General McClellan's plan of
advancing step by step, and fighting if necessary to gain those steps, was still the
general plan of operations. But to move required good weather. Thousands of men,
artillery trains, etc., cannot be set in motion
like pieces on a chess-board. At last everything was ready. Though exposed to swamp
and typhoid fever, and a prey to the deadly
climate, the men had confidence in their
commander, and were not discouraged. In
the next battle they were to meet a reorganized army, strengthened by fresh combatants,
under a new commander (Lee), assisted by
the idol of the Confederacy and the terror
of the North, Stonewall Jackson. Stewart,
the famous cavalry leader, at the head of a
column, had made a movement against the
Union forces with the idea of gaining information and befogging the mind of the Union
commander with regard to the ultimate
plans of Lee. In both he succeeded, though
his attack was beaten off in consequence of
his having attacked a railroad train. The
occupants spread the news, with the effect
of sending the Union cavalry in pursuit,

forcing his retreat. McClellan, being deceived as to the real size of the force holding Richmond, was settled in his conviction that the Confederate Capital would have to be taken by a slow siege. The battle of Oak Grove on the twenty-fifth of June, a minor engagement fought with the purpose of securing a more favorable position for his left wing, (for he was preparing to extend it,) made him feel that some move of great importance was contemplated by the Confederates. Their feeble defense of Oak Grove made him suspicious. He determined to feel the enemy with his left; but Lee, upon that very day, had agreed with Jackson to attack McClellan's right. The latter had deceived the Federals as to the destination of his troops. They thought he would attack Fremont. No one supposed that the right flank of the army of the Potomac was the point to be struck at; but, just before the attack was made, McClellan had divined his intentions. Jackson had escaped the three Union armies. One more failure McClellan had to shoulder and make the best of; but he did not falter. He met it by the force of his military genius, and strategic ability.

Gaines's Mill was fought; though taken
at a disadvantage. McClellan was not surprised. Keyes, in whose division Lieutenant-Colonel Hungerford was, occupied the
vicinity of Bottom's Bridge, and the road
which crosses the swamp near its entrance.
The Lieutenant-Colonel did not lead his
men, being field officer of the day, but they
again distinguished themselves; though at
Malvern Hill when under him, they were to
win greater glory, by making one of the
most gallant charges of the war. The Lieutenant-Colonel, as field officer of the day during Gaines's Mill, was here, there, and everywhere, receiving and giving orders, and in
general doing everything that one in his position could do. If he was not at the head
of his men, he had the proud satisfaction of
knowing that they were all fighting with
ardor and bravery.

After Gaines's Mill it was McClellan's turn
to deceive the Confederates. The preparations for the retreat were so quietly made,
and masked so effectually, that the enemy
were not aware of the movement, nor did
they suspect that it was the James that Mc-
Clellan was falling back upon. This design of McClellan's they had not fathomed.

When they did discover the retreat, they determined to follow and give battle. On the thirtieth of June, Frazier's Farm and Glendale were fought. In the latter, the rebels were superior in force, but in both engagements the rebels were beaten back. Lee was being outwitted by McClellan. The masterly retreat was saving the army of the Potomac. The Thirty-sixth took their full share in these battles, and added to their reputation; but at Malvern Hill they were to win their greatest renown. This battle was fought on July first, the Unionists being posted on the slope of the hill. The Comte de Paris, in giving the disposition of troops, says that the bridge at Carter's Mill, which spans a small stream called Western Run, and the approaches to Haxall's, where a large number of roads converge, were intrusted to Keyes's Corps. He had made a good selection for that important post, as they had shown themselves fighters that would hold out to the last. The same historian (the Comte de Paris), in describing the battle, records the capture of the flags of the Fourteenth Alabama by the Thirty-sixth New York, the most gallant feat performed at Malvern Hill. He says:

34

"Howe had been waiting for the Confederates at a short distance. The latter, being received by a terrific fire, halted, when a charge of the One Hundred and Second completed the repulse at one side, while on the other the Thirty-sixth New York carried off the flags of the Fourteenth Alabama."

The following clipping from a California paper gives a detailed description of this daring piece of gallantry :

"A GALLANT CHARGE."

"At the battle of Malvern Hill, the last of the seven days' fight before Richmond, the Thirty-sixth New York Regiment was posted upon the right flank of Major West's batteries. About half-past three in the afternoon, a rebel regiment came out of the wood and formed their line of battle. The color-sergeant stepped out about ten paces to the front, and planted the colors of his regiment, as in the days of ancient chivalry, challenging the foe to take them. The gallant Thirty-sixth made a change of front, delivered a volley, charged bayonets, drove the enemy back into the woods, and captured the rebel flags. This gallant exploit was witnessed by twenty thousand Federal troops, who made the air resound with their cheers and huzzas. The colors represented the Fourteenth Alabama Regiment. The Thirty-sixth was the last regiment to give way before the rebels, on the first day of the battle of Fair Oaks, stubbornly disputing the ground, while retreating before an overwhelming force, until reaching a favorable position, when they held the victorious rebels in check."

The following official reports of the part
taken by the Thirty - sixth New York in
those engagements reflect much credit on
the gallantry, bravery, and coolness shown
by the Colonel. The reader will see that
the Thirty-sixth and their dashing officers
had their full share in the fighting and renown :

[Official Report.]

"HEADQUARTERS 36TH REGT., N. Y. VOLS.

"INTRENCHED CAMP, June 5, 1862.

"*To Lieutenant* BYRON PORTER, A.A.-G.

"SIR :

"I have the honor to report, for the information
of the brigade commander, the part taken by the regiment under my command in the battle of the thirty-first
of May. Almost simultaneously with the first discharge
of arms in our front, about ten o'clock A. M., I received
orders to move with my regiment to the front, to the
support of Captain Flood's battery, who had taken up a
position on the right of the Richmond stage road. I at
once proceeded to the right and front of the battery,
and occupied a portion of the rifle-pits in course of
erection there, and held that position until about six
o'clock P. M. when I was ordered to fall back, as the
enemy had turned our right flank in large force. At
this time, General Devens having been disabled, I assumed command of the brigade, and the command of
the regiment devolved upon Lieutenant-Colonel Hungerford, who led it off in good order near Battery
Couch by my orders. All of the officers and men of

my command behaved with the utmost coolness and bravery. I make particular mention of Lieutenant-Colonel D. E. Hungerford, who exhibited great coolness, bravery, and judgment, in the skillful handling of the regiment after having the command; Major J. Rainey; Surgeon E. B. Dalton; Captain James J. Walsh; Lieutenant D. E. Murphy, and Sergeant-Major Charles P. Lindsey. Enclosed please find a list of the killed, wounded, and missing.

"I have the honor to be

"Most respectfully yours,

(Signed)   "CHAS. H. INNES,

"*Colonel 36th Regt., New York Vols.*"

"HEADQUARTERS 3D BRIGADE, 4TH CORPS,

"INTRENCHED CAMP, June 5, 1862.

"*Captain* FRANCIS A. WALKER, A.A.-G.

"SIR :

"I have the honor to report, for the information of the general commanding the division, the part taken by the brigade under my command in the battle of the 31st of May and the 1st of June. Subsequent to the disabling of General Charles Devens, which happened about 6 P.M. at that time, having received an order (the enemy having turned our flank in large force) to fall back, I at once ordered the Thirty-Sixth New York Volunteers (which was the last regiment in the rifle-pits) to fall back to the intrenched camp and take a position there; at the same time I despatched an orderly with the same instructions for the Tenth Massachusetts Volunteers, who soon arrived in good order, under the command of Captain Orzo Miller; at the same time three companies of the Seventh Massachusetts Volunteers, three of the Tenth Massachusetts, and two companies of the Thirty-Sixth fell into line, having been out on picket duty, and Captain Flood's battery, who at once came into battery. Having disposed of this force, I at once turned my attention to the arrest of all stragglers, and disposed of them to good advantage in the rifle-pits, according to the similarity of arms. At this time General Keyes arrived on the ground, and I informed him of the disposition I had made of the forces there. It proving satisfactory to him, he ordered me to take charge of all the stragglers that might pass through there. Shortly after Colonel Hayman of the Thirty-Seventh New York Volunteers marched in, and I communicated my instructions to him, and stated that it was very necessary to have a strong picket thrown out, that I could not do it without weakening very materially my position. He at once placed himself and regiment at my disposal, and picketed our left flank and front. About half an hour before day the whole command was formed in line, ready for action. The Seventh Massachusetts having been temporarily detached for service on the right, with the general commanding the division, I am unable to report the part taken by them, but feel assured they have done great credit to themselves. Too great praise cannot be rendered to Brigade-Surgeon Charles O'Leary, and Surgeons E. B. Dalton, Thirty-Sixth New York Volunteers, and C. W. Chamberlain, Tenth Massachusetts Volunteers, for their devoted attentions to the wounded. I desire to call to the special notice of the general commanding Captain Orzo Miller, who commanded the Tenth Massachusetts Volunteers after Col. Briggs had been severely wounded.

He led his regiment in gallant style, and only left the
field when ordered to fall back at dark, which he did
in good order. Colonel D. E. Hungerford and Major
James A. Roney behaved with great gallantry and coolness throughout the engagement. Massachusetts and
New York have cause to be proud of these regiments.

"I have the honor to be

"Yours respectfully,

"CHAS. H. INNES,

"*Commanding Third Brigade, Couch's Division, Fourth Corps.*

CHAPTER X.

IN all the Lieutenant-Colonel's letters it is
seen how thoroughly he kept himself
informed of the movements of the forces,
and the accuracy by which he foretold
many of the movements which were afterwards made. For one of his perception
and discernment, it is not surprising that
he was able to perceive what would escape
the eye of the ordinary observer of the
situation. During all the operations of the
Army of the Potomac, he had his attention
fixed on the Western armies. He saw what
few did, that a vital blow could be struck
at the Confederacy by an attack through
Texas, the citadel of rebellion. Keeping his
own counsel, the matter was quietly sub-

mitted to the authorities at Washington,
and was favorably considered by them.
They may have seen the importance of the
movement, but it was through the Lieutenant-Colonel that it was first formally
brought to their attention. After Malvern
Hill, the plan having received the official
sanction, he felt that the moment had come,
the time was ripe.

During the operations of the Army of
the Potomac he was not unmindful of the
importance of the Pacific coast, and the
danger that it was in from the secession
element. 'Tis true that California was a
loyal state, none more so, but it is also a
fact that there were not a few in that
state whose hearts did not beat warmly for
the Union cause. Colonel Hungerford had
personal cognizance of this, indeed, he had
been even solicited, while in California, not
to go to Washington to enter the Union
army; but to remain, and a high command
in the Confederate service would be given
him. Needless to say, the offer was spurned
by him. "Gentlemen," he replied to them,
"you insult me by such an offer. My honor
and patriotism alike demand that the flag
of my country is the one for which I

should draw my sword. I have already fought twice under it. My father in 1812, and my grandfather in the Revolution, have, it is my proud boast to say, shed their blood in its defense. It is not in the character of one of the Hungerford race to raise his hand in rebellion against his own flag."

This feeling and patriotic response was well calculated to impress those traitorous souls. Indeed, had the offer been made in a different manner, he would have denounced them in their true colors, but coming as it did honor forbade him that course.

From the banks of the Chickahominy he conceived the idea of invading Texas by way of Arizona and New Mexico. General Carleton was already in that part of the country, and he had been moved forward to Santa Fé, New Mexico. To raise a large force, overtake him, and, thus united, successfully invade Texas, striking perhaps a fatal blow in the rear of the Confederacy, was surely a feasible plan, and gave promise of important results. The Lieutenant-Colonel, thousands of miles away on the Potomac, knew all this, and he felt that the

35

time had arrived to make the move. He then would have greater scope, and, untrammelled and free, be able to do greater service for his country, and win greater glory for himself. The lieutenant-colonelcy did not offer the same field for the dashing and ambitious officer that the expedition to Texas would.

He returned to California full of enthusiasm, thinking that in a few short weeks he would be marching at the head of a victorious army of invasion into Texas. Immediately, on his arrival in California, he intended to raise the necessary force for the carrying out of his project. His ability as an organizer of troops would again, he thought, come in good play.

Reaching Downieville, he addressed the following letter to the Governor of California, making the necessary application. As will be perceived the real intent is veiled, for the obvious reason of not letting the information by any chance or accident be conveyed to the enemy. Once the real object known, the success of the expedition would be imperilled, if not defeated. In those days, when spies and traitors were lurking in Government offices, high and low, it behoved the prudent man to be guarded and circumspect, even in official communications. The plan of the Colonel having, as already stated, received the favorable consideration of the Government, he expected the instant co-operation of the Governor of California. Hence he was eager to be on the spot to commence the organization of the force necessary for its accomplishment.

Under date of August 25, 1862, he writes the Governor, as follows:

"DEAR SIR:

"I have just returned from the Atlantic States, having served in the Army of the Potomac as Lieutenant-Colonel of the Thirty-sixth New York Regiment, from August 5, 1861, till July 1, 1862. I would like to again take the field, and as a matter of pride would feel highly gratified to do so at the head of a regiment from my own State, California. I therefore beg to submit to your Excellency the idea of raising one or more regiments for active service in the East.

"I do not question for a moment that the men can be raised for the purpose, and it has been a source of mortification to many Californians that their State has not been represented in the grand fighting army of the Union.

"Therefore, in accordance with their views and my own desires, I write you as above, and I trust that you will not consider my correspondence an intrusion on your time. Before my arrival, this was suggested to me by Mr. Phelps, our representative in Congress, who, at the same time, informed me that a project for entering Texas from this coast was engaging the attention of the department, and he thought it would eventually receive favorable consideration. My object in addressing you is to obtain your views concerning the tender of one or more regiments to our National Government, in advance of the government call, should they make one upon you.

"Hoping that the above may meet with your Excellency's favorable consideration, and awaiting your reply,

"I remain your obedient servant,

"D. E. HUNGERFORD.

(Signed)

"To His Excellency, LELAND STANFORD,

"Governor of California."

For the East, the Lieutenant-Colonel states that he wants the troops, a literally true assertion; but in his own mind it was east in Texas that the destination was to be. He expected an immediate response to this important communication, but none came. Impatient to take the field, he writes again to the Governor, this time under date of September 18, 1862.

"DEAR SIR :

"On the twenty-fifth of August I wrote you, proposing to raise one or more regiments of volunteers for service in the East, expecting you would communicate with the general government to ascertain if that number of troops would be accepted for such service. A considerable time has elapsed and, I have received no answer to my proposition; and learning through the newspapers that a regiment is in course of organization at San Francisco, and that you are about to issue your call for another, may I hope that such is your intention, in furtherance of my proposals? I have already had many proffers from various parts of the State, and continue, by each mail, to receive encouragement and offers of co-operation, but can do or effect nothing until I have authority from Your Excellency, or the War Department. I am satisfied that two full regiments can be easily raised, provided they may be immediately sent to the seat of participation in active military operations.

"If at all within your province, I would be pleased to engage in the work at the earliest moment. Troops are more necessary just now than at any other time during the war. Awaiting your reply," etc., etc.

Again he had thought prudent to veil the real object of the raising of the troops. To that letter the Governor replied as follows :

"STATE OF CALIFORNIA,
"EXECUTIVE DEPARTMENT,
"SACRAMENTO, Sept. 26, 1862.

"COL. D. E. HUNGERFORD —

"DEAR SIR : Your favor of the eighteenth instant is at hand. I would say in answer that I have received no advices from the War Department relative to the raising

of a regiment in this State. Until such advices reach
me I cannot act in the premises.

> "Very respectfully,
>> "Your obedient servant,
>>> "LELAND STANFORD."

More delay. Time was slipping by and
he was chafing at the slowness of the Government in moving. He had expected to
receive the necessary instructions as soon as
he reached California; but the weeks were
going, and he was not yet on the march
to invade Texas. But the delay did not
damp his enthusiasm: it only increased it.
He felt (and the highest competent men in
the nation had endorsed his views) that the
expedition would have important results,
and he determined to carry it out against
all obstacles.

Here is what a California paper says of
the project for raising a regiment of troops.
It seems that even the press had not pene-
trated the real design:

"A CALIFORNIA REGIMENT.

"There is some talk of raising a regiment of volunteers in California to proceed directly to the East to take
part in the war. From what we have heard, we think,
if the matter was taken hold of in the right way, that
a full regiment could be raised in the State of men

who would equip themselves and pay their passage to New York. One company at least, and perhaps two, could be recruited in Nevada County; and many who cannot go themselves would furnish the outfit and pay the expenses of a substitute. This State has not been called on for its quota of troops, under the late calls, in consequence of the great expense and delay that would be occasioned in transporting them to the East; but in the present period of gloom and disaster to the national cause, many feel that it is the duty of California to take a more direct part than she has been called upon to take, in the great work of maintaining the national integrity. Perhaps, if a regiment was raised and equipped, some arrangement could be made to defray the expense of their transportation to the seat of war, either by the State, or by means of a public subscription. We notice by the *Downieville News* that Colonel Hungerford, who has lately returned from the East, is moving in the matter of raising one or more regiments in this State. The *News* says: 'We understand that Colonel Hungerford, but recently returned from the Army of the Potomac, has applied to the Governor for permission to raise one or more regiments of volunteers, to be conducted directly to the field in Virginia. If at all within the power of Governor Stanford, we have no doubt that the application will be successful. With the assurance that the men will be taken directly to the scene of war, there will be no difficulty in procuring enlistments. The main difficulty last fall was that the volunteers expected, what afterwards occurred, that they would be kept in inactivity on this coast. Colonel Hungerford has a reputation as a military man, has come direct from the hard-

fought field of the Peninsula, and is desirous to return
with a regiment or two of California fighting men.
Whoever goes with him will have no difficulty in getting
into business, or in getting sight of the belligerent ele-
phant. We eagerly hope his application may be successful. We don't think any military leader could be found
more competent, certainly none braver, or more effectually tried in the hottest fires of Mexico and Virginia.'"

The receipt of the letter from the Governor came as a bitter disappointment to
the Colonel. He had conceived a project of
great magnitude, and one that promised far
reaching results. It had been favorably considered by the Government, and he had returned to California, feeling that the proposed expedition was already an assured
success. But California was slow moving,
and the War Department apathetic. The
Cabinet, and in fact the whole country, had
been thrown into consternation by the ra-
pidity of Jackson's movement in Virginia ;
Washington itself they thought was threatened, and, in the almost panic that then prevailed, the gallant Colonel's proposition appears to have been lost sight of. Galling
and maddening as was the delay, and eager
and restless under his forced inaction, his
ardor and patriotism would not permit him
to lose heart in the undertaking, despite the

many discouragements and apparent lack of
support that he had to encounter. He therefore turned his attention to another field —
Nevada. He was already well-known in that
Territory. His services there in the Indian
War in 1860, and the brilliant manœuvres
he had made during the engagement with
the hostiles, whereby the camp was saved
and a second massacre prevented, were all
remembered with gratitude by the people.
Identified prominently not only in the com-
mercial development of the coast, he had
also the confidence of the State as a thorough military man, knowing every detail of
his profession. Men of his stamp were not
too common in those days of gold-seeking
and wealth-hunting. Indeed, on the statute
books of California there is hardly a law
that in any way relates to the military organization of the State that he is not entirely familiar with, or else had some part
in its being placed there. The oath taken
by the militia of that State, binding themselves to obey the mandate of the general,
as well as the State government, was written by his pen and incorporated in the law
mainly through his efforts. Therefore, if
California had failed him, he had no reason

36

to expect that Nevada would ; so his enthusiasm and hopefulness were not abated. A
requisition had been made upon the Governor of that territory for a regiment of infantry, and two more companies of cavalry,
four companies of cavalry having already
been raised. The Colonel made immediate
application for the command of the infantry.
The return mail brought his commission.
The Governor knew the reputation of the '
Colonel, and he could not forget how the
arrival of the Colonel in Virginia City a few
years before had come as a deliverance to
the population of the territory from Indian
attacks and atrocities. He rightly felt that
he could not make a better choice. The
Governor's selection was heartily approved
by the people. The principal paper in the
Territory refers in the following manner to
the Colonel's appointment :

"The new regiment of mounted infantry being raised
in this Territory is progressing finely. It will certainly,
at all events, not suffer because of the inexperience of
the officers to whom its command has been intrusted.
Daniel E. Hungerford, the Colonel, is an experienced
and brave soldier, and has been proven so on many a
hard-contested battle-field. So long ago as 1841, he held
a commission in the New York State Militia, and was
one of the first to raise and offer to the government a

company for service in Mexico. In that country, he participated in all the battles from Vera Cruz to the capital, and was wounded in one of the battles in front of the City of Mexico. He came to the Pacific coast at an early day, and came to this Territory as major of the troops sent here from California in the spring of 1860, to protect the inhabitants against the Pay Utahs. In this campaign he came up with, and defeated the savages at William's Ranch and Pyramid Lake. Soon after the first battle of Bull Run, he was at once appointed Lieutenant-Colonel, and served all through McClellan's hard-fought campaign.

"Coming to California, he sought for authority to raise a brigade, but was prohibited from doing so by the circumlocution office.

"If thorough military knowledge, long experience, and undoubted personal bravery are good criterions, Colonel Hungerford would seem to be the right man in the right place.

"He has been engaged in the following battles, where there were few that showed more bravery and gallantry: Vera Cruz, Nueva Rancho, Cerro Gordo, Amazoec, Contreras, Churubusco, Chapultepec, Garita de Belen, all in Mexico; William's Ranch and Pyramid Lake in Nevada Territory; Young's Mills, Yorktown, Bottom's Bridge, Fair Oaks, and Malvern Hill in the Peninsular campaign."

Armed with the necessary authority the Colonel immediately set to work to fill the requisition. The task was an arduous one. Nevada was sparsely settled. The distances to be traveled were great, and much care and keen discrimination were necessary in the selection of the men. In the capacity of Assistant Adjutant-General he superintended the recruiting. Regardless of the many difficulties he was not daunted, and, in a short time, succeeded in filling the quota of two companies of cavalry and six companies of infantry. At this point recruiting was suspended by general orders from the headquarters of the division. This was a hard fate for the Colonel; all his labor and expectation had gone for naught. Working night and day, making many sacrifices that he could ill afford, he was buoyed up with the hope of soon taking the field, and doing much for his country, the official records of whose wars had already borne his name more than once for gallantry and bravery. That order seemed to deprive him of the cherished hope. He had spent several thousand dollars out of his own pocket which he could not afford; but, what he valued far more, his military command, he was now without. Again a private citizen against his own will, his sword sheathed, but eager to draw it once more in the service of his country. The Mexican commissioners sought him, and solicited him to enter the service of that Republic, and assist them in driving out the foreign invaders of their soil. The Colonel had many friends in Mexico, and had considerable reputation in that country as a military man. His humane treatment of the distinguished captive, Don Juan Carno, that he had taken prisoner at Chapultepec, endeared him to the Mexicans, and won their respect as a generous foe in time of war, but a sterling friend of their Republican institutions and government in time of peace. As history tells, Napoleon the Third was about putting in execution his dream of a Latin Empire in the New World. To obtain a foothold on the soil of Mexico, despoil the Mexicans of their government and territory, and, when the United States would be torn asunder by the internal strife then raging, to pour myriads of his legions into our country, and thereby establish the supremacy of his dynasty on the Western Continent, was the stupendous project that dazzled the usurper's brain. A part had already been fulfilled. Mexico had been invaded, a quasi-empire had been established, the Republican Government had been driven from the capital, though its

troops were fighting bravely against the
despotic sway of the foreigners, and con-
testing every inch of their native land.
Maximilian was sitting on the throne, sustained — not by the will of the people — but
by French bayonets, a poor and trembling
support for any throne. But might during
those days was overcoming right. The
monarchical governments of the Old World
were looking on in indifference, some perhaps with joy, at the spoliation of a free
people. The Great Northern Light, the
Giant of Republics, was being rent by
internal strife, and could render no aid to
the threatened sister.

Upon whom else could the Mexicans call
than the patriotic and liberty-loving military
men of the North who, in drawing their
swords for their struggling neighbor, would
be but fighting on another soil the battles
of their own country. When the offer was
made to the Colonel, he saw the real state
of affairs and the portentous significance
of the events then being enacted. The dan-
ger-cloud was looming, growing day by day,
and forming another powerful menace to
our threatened National sovereignty. The
Government in those times could not well

make an armed protest against the flagrant
aggression on its Southern border. Its very
existence was already in jeopardy, it could
not afford to divert even a single regiment
to enforce its just demand. Clearly, to
private citizens on their own responsibility
would have to fall the duty of the maintenance of the Monroe doctrine then openly
violated. Colonel Hungerford with his accustomed habit of looking ahead, felt that
to help drive the invaders from Mexico
and prevent a foreign government from
obtaining a foothold upon the free soil of
America would be the means of rendering
signal service to his own county. He knew
that once in Mexico, at the head of an
armed force, there would soon be thousands
of Americans to join him, and who could
fail to foresee the beneficent results that
would flow from such a generous display
of American valor and patriotism, in the
aid of a helpless Republic? What an ever-
lasting debt of gratitude Mexico and her
people would have ever felt to us. The
expansion of trade that would result, the
closer union of the two races, their fra-
ternization in a common cause, all this,
besides the immediate and glorious conse-

quence of ridding the United States of a
menace, and Mexico of a tyrant's rule.
With these fruitful reflections, and the hope
of a speedy realization of the brilliant ideal,
Colonel Hungerford accepted the offer. The
policy of the United States Government
being neutral, the strictest secrecy had to
be maintained. The Colonel's plan was to
sail from San Francisco with a large force
of men, fully armed and equipped, and
land in Mexico, then combine with the
Mexican army. To do this required a man
of capability, sound judgment, and energy,
yet cautious and possessing a keen knowledge of men. When the Colonel arrived in
San Francisco, he forthwith began his preparations.

In conjunction with the Mexican Commissioners, Generals Placido La Vega and
Sancho Ochoa, he succeeded in recruiting
about five hundred men. Everything had
been done in the quietest possible manner;
not a suspicion was aroused. To blind the
public as to the real objects of the expedition, it was given out that they were an
organized body of "prospectors" bound for
Arizona, and for protection against the
Apaches and other hostile Indian tribes,

they had thought best to arm themselves and assume the character of a military organization. The plans had been so well laid, and carried out with such carefulness and forethought, that ten thousand stand of arms, ammunition, quartermaster and commissary supplies, and telegraph material, with men were on board the barque *Brontes,* and the day of sailing fixed, before the true nature of the movement was even suspected. The clearance and other necessary papers had been obtained. The American flag flying, they awaited only the order to make sail, and bid goodbye to the golden gate. For once keen newspaper men were completely deceived. As for the Government officials, it can be surmised that it was not difficult to throw them off the scent. To undertake, and successfully put in execution, an affair of such magnitude in a populous city like San Francisco, without exciting the least suspicion, was a work that few would have had the ability to carry through. The men were oathbound: their sworn obligation being to fight against all the enemies of Mexico, but never to take up arms against the United States. The latter proviso was not necessary, as

37

they were all staunch Unionists, but the
Colonel, not knowing what complications
might arise, thought prudent to insert it.
The whole undertaking was on the point
of success. All arrangements had been
made. In a day, a few hours, they would
have been at sea sailing to their destination.

But this great and important movement,
fraught with the prospect of vast good to
both the United States and Mexico, was
doomed to fail, through the base treachery
of one from whom it was the least expected. An American newspaper man had
betrayed the Colonel to the French Consul
at San Francisco. The Colonel had gone
to this man and imparted to him, in the
most sacred confidence, the real object of
the expedition, which he was at liberty to
reveal when the *Brontes* was well out to
sea. The Colonel had selected his paper,
as it had always professed such intense
patriotism, that he thought the secret would
be safest with him. The result was that
the French Consul made formal protest to
the Custom House authorities, who had not
been well "posted." They delayed the sailing of the barque, and, in the meantime, the
Consul and the local police concocted to-

gether an affidavit that some of the weaker
members of the party were induced by
means of French gold to sign.

On these Judas Iscariot affidavits, the
gallant Colonel and twenty-two of the
officers were apprehended, the barque was
unloaded and the arms and material stored:
thus temporarily frustrating the well-conceived design, through the stupidity of a
Custom House official, who ought to have
known better, and the vile perfidy of an
American journalist. No blame can be
attached to the French Consul. It was his
duty, if he could, to prevent the barque
leaving port: but to have his plans thus
thwarted by a member of the American
press, whose paper had always proclaimed
its great patriotism and loyalty, was . so
revolting in its hideousness, as to be hardly
believable.

The trial was one of the "causes
célèbres" in the history of the State. The
sympathy of every right thinking and
patriotic man, woman, and child in the
community was with the Colonel and his
companions, and nothing but loathing and
contempt were felt for the miscreants, who,
for a handful of the foreigner's gold, would

betray their own citizens, and stain their
manhood with a perjurer's taint. The best
counsel in the State offered their services
to the Colonel; but, not needing their assistance, he declined it, preferring to argue
and plead his own case, though not the
semblance of a case was made out against
him. His speech to the jury was a scath-
ing denunciation of the corrupt methods
that had been used against them, and fierce
in the condemnation of the emissary of a
foreign government, plotting in the city of
San Francisco against a struggling American Republic, and aided and abetted in his
nefarious work by men who claimed to be
Americans.

At times during his speech he was bit-
terly sarcastic, and the crowded court was
often convulsed with laughter at his witty
references to the bribed witnesses, and the
contradictions of their evidence. In the sacred name of justice, he demanded an immediate acquittal, without the jury leaving
their seats. When the Colonel had finished,
the foreman arose and announced that they
rendered a verdict of " Not guilty," which
was received with ringing cheers by the entire court. Indeed, during the trial, the pro-

ceedings often degenerated into a farce, and the prosecuting attorney and the bribed witnesses, it was thought, could hardly brazen it out to the end, so great was the ire and sentiment of the people against them. The Colonel's speech to the jury attracted considerable attention, and was widely read. His crime was patriotic zeal, and he knew no honest American citizen could award punishment for such an offense. His eloquent words to the jury, lofty in sentiment, and expressing high patriotism and firm resolve, and as dealing with an event of great importance in the annals of California, will be read with interest. The Colonel said :

"I appear before you in defense of myself against the wicked and malicious persecutions of perjured wretches and shameless officials, whose tender regard for truth and honesty has been polluted by the magic influence of French gold, aided and abetted by a public journal, and that, too, while professing a deep sympathy for a sister Republic now struggling for existence against the wicked and unholy usurpation of an Austrian tyrant, sustained by French bayonets. How men so base could be found in this American community, whose element is universal liberty, is indeed most wonderful, a community whose proverbial sympathies are ever with the oppressed, and whose aid and succor has, upon all occasions, been extended, and, most especially, to a patriotic people struggling for the maintenance of Republican liberty and national existence.

"But so does it seem, and how do they appear? This scum of filth has arisen upon the surface of the waters as an obnoxious poison, unfitted and incompatible to mix and combine with the purer elements of the truly great principles of American republicanism, whose sympathies are justly aroused when the cries and wails of their suffering brethren reach them, as wafted along upon the gentle breeze of heaven from the several quarters of the globe. If to be held guilty for my personal sympathies for Republican Mexico is a crime, then I am content to be guilty. 'Tis but a few years gone by, when I could have been found in the ranks of my fellow countrymen, combating in the deadly strife of war, these very people who now so excite my every sympathy that I will aid them by every honorable means in my power, even to the jeopardy of my own life, to the re-establishment of their republican form of government. If to assist the weak against the strong, the right against the wrong, then do I propose to be a criminal. Believing as I do in the truth and the righteousness of the Monroe doctrine, I must so direct my every act that they may be consistent with its teachings; and I most fervently pray and hope to live to see placed upon the National Palace of Mexico the eagled-flag of the Republic, in fraternal association with our own beloved starry-banner. The one there by right, the other as a guardian — a warning to the tyrants of the Old World that America belongs to Americans."

The Colonel then went on to review the evidence, showing clearly the falsity of the charges, and taking occasion to excoriate, by bitter invective and sarcastic references to

the bribed officials and their dastardly endeavors to subvert justice. In closing, he
said :

" Now, gentlemen, if you can find anything in the
evidence to even excite a suspicion of guilt, then I am
willing to abide by your judgment. I ask no charity or
leniency ; will receive none. Again assuring you, gentlemen of the jury, that I know no more of these alleged
transactions than you do, yourselves ; and, in conclusion,
having established my entire innocence, I ask not in
charity, but demand in the most sacred name of justice
a free acquittal from your seats, without resorting to the
jury-room."

The jury could do only one thing, acquit
him instantly and unanimously. All the
allurements of French gold, and the vile
attempts of the shameless conspirators could
not hold against the twelve honest men who
had listened to the truthful and eloquent
words of the Colonel, so convincing of his
innocence and the patriotism of his motives.

About two months after, the Colonel, still
enthusiastic and determined, left San Francisco, with a much less force, for the mouth
of the Colorado River, at the head of the
Gulf of California, to which place the arms
and military stores had been already transferred. Taking them on board another
vessel he proceeded to La Paz, Lower Cali-

fornia. Here he found that General La
Vega, with a portion of the Colonel's men,
had crossed over to the State of Sinaloa,
with a view of revolutionizing that State
in behalf of himself. The Colonel could
not engage in anything of this kind. The
engagement that he had entered into was
to serve the Federal Government of Mexico,
and assist them in repelling the invasion of
their soil, and thereby establish the supremacy of the Monroe Doctrine, which was being openly violated. He could not, in honor,
oppose the Government, or take part in any
manifestation in favor of any individual, no
matter whom. He was bound to respect and
recognize the lawfully-constituted authority.
He therefore sent two agents to General
Corona, who commanded in Sinaloa, offering
to deliver the arms and stores to him on
payment of the amounts still due to American merchants for the same. This General
Corona was unable to do, so the Colonel ordered the return to San Francisco of the
vessel and properties belonging to the merchants, thereby saving them from capture.
the French having several men-of-war in the
Gulf and upon the coast.

The Colonel remained at La Paz watching developments, not knowing what part he would be called upon to take. The War Department at Washington was informed of his arrival, and something he thought might arise that would demand his services, either for his own Government or Mexico.

During a space of one month, four separate revolutions occurred, none of which he could be induced to have anything to do with; they made every attempt, and all manner of persuasion was used, but he stood firm, holding that he came there to fight for the Federal Government, and not to take part in the partisan disputes and warfare among themselves. By this attitude and the uprightness of his acts he gained the confidence and respect of all parties.

Soon the news came of the battle of Queretaro, and the capture of Maximilian and the renegade Mexicans, and their final disposition. Napoleon the Third had awakened from his dream, and his generals and satellites were paying by their lives for their desperate attempt at the violation of the rights and subjugation of a free people.

Now, it may be asked, what was the result of the Colonel's efforts and sacrifices in the raising of these expeditions to help Mex-

38

ico, and assist by force of arms in the assertion of the inviolability of the Monroe
Doctrine? Who can doubt their potent effect in the final withdrawal of the French
troops, when referring to the correspondence
and interview of William H. Seward, our
Secretary of State, with the French Minister
of Foreign Affairs? We find Mr. Seward
using these expeditions of Colonel Hungerford and others as his principal argument,
he saying, "as must be evident to you, it is
impossible to control our people; it is plainly
apparent what they are doing."

This endorsement by the Secretary of
State of the value of Colonel Hungerford's
well-directed movements in Mexico for the
higher and national interests of the United
States and the entire continent, give to it
the consequence it is by just right entitled
to. It must have been very gratifying to
Colonel Hungerford, for it closed the last of
his military endeavors; and no one who has
read the preceding chapters, will fail to acknowledge that he has ever done all his opportunity allowed him to do, and has always
fulfilled his duty in a worthy and patriotic
manner.

During the Colonel's stay in California,

engaged in the raising of expeditions to Mexico, and before Grant had left Washington to command the Army of the Potomac, he wrote the following to a publication, regarding the Virginia campaign. Coming before Grant had made a move, it is remarkable as pointing out in advance the exact plan of the General's and its general similarity with that of McClellan's. The communication is as follows:

"The general plan of Grant's campaign against the rebel capital is not very dissimilar to that of McClellan's, in 1862, except so far as General McClellan's army was very considerably diminished, leaving him to an entire front attack, without the aid of demonstrations to divert, even momentarily, the enemy's attention. It was expected that General Wool, and subsequently, General Dix from their departments, and General McDowell from Fredericksburg, would make such demonstrations; more particularly was it expected from General Dix, who then occupied Norfolk, Portsmouth, and Suffolk, and might easily have threatened, if not have captured, Petersburg. McDowell should, at the same time, have made a strategic manœuvre, with a view of turning the rebel position. These movements would have compelled the rebels to send out a corresponding force to meet them, when the rebel capital would have been at the command of McClellan. The defeat of Banks and Shields would not have occurred, and the great terror for the safety of the national capital, and subsequent disasters of the seven days' fight we would have been spared the humiliation

of; there would have been no second Bull Run, Fredericksburg, Chancellorsville, South Mountain, Antietam,
Gettysburg to mourn for, and the war much nearer its
termination. It is not the purpose here to discuss as to
who was at fault in these defeats; but to show a similarity in the two campaigns, so far as the general plans are
concerned. At present, we have a concerted combination
of action on the part of the armies, all centering to, and
for, a fixed point and purpose. McClellan was not the
General-in-Chief, he commanding only his immediate
army. McDowell, it is true, was, at the very early part
of the campaign, under his orders, but before it was time
to make the movement, he withdrew from the Army of
the Potomac, leaving McClellan entirely upon his own
resources, without the hope of aid or assistance from
those necessary demonstrations, or the means of military
combination. General Grant, however, has full control
and command of all the armies of the Union, and can
order such movements, attacks, feints, or manœuvres, as
he may seem disposed, and is now using all the available force in combined and harmonious concert, having in
view one real and principal object : from Butler on the
South of the James, Smith on the Peninsula, Burnside
from the direction of Fredericksburg, and Meade, with
the greatest army on the inland route, all converging to
the center of attraction, Richmond, whose doom is sealed,
and has but a few days to run.

                                        "CORTES."
    "*Semper Paratus Patriæ.*"

While the Colonel was at La Paz, an accident happened whereby a prominent citizen was seriously injured by a gunshot

wound, breaking his right arm above the
elbow. There being no surgeon at La Paz,
the Colonel was importuned by many, and
expressly asked by the United States Consul,
Mr. Elmer, to attend the case. The Colonel
had no diploma; but seeing at once that it
was a case of necessity, and with his usual
characteristic of doing the best he could under all circumstances, he took upon himself
the responsibility and attended the patient
with the happy result of successfully treating him. As will be remembered from the
preceding pages, he had already had considerable experience in the study and practice
of medicine, and, though lacking the diploma, was quite as well qualified in point of
ability as if he had possessed it. His time
was so constantly occupied while he was in
California, that he was unable to fulfill all
the formalities necessary to obtain the sheep-
skin.

As the case was an exceedingly difficult
one, the Colonel's skill in the management
of it gained him considerable reputation.
The population of La Paz being poor, and
much sickness and disease prevailing, he
felt it his duty to practice the profession in
general, as the facilities for obtaining medi-

cal assistance were very meagre. He soon
had a large practice, though his tender heart
and generosity of character were not adapted to the gathering of large fees from his
patients. No one ever hesitated to consult
him because of their poverty. They knew
too well his charitableness and kindly feeling, and they felt that their inability to pay
would never ensure any less sympathy or
less able treatment at his hands. Not only
did he soon become reputed as a successful
doctor and surgeon, but among the entire
community his benevolence and charity endeared him to all.

On numerous occasions the Doctor held
consultations with the Surgeons of the
United States Navy. La Paz, being a coal-
ing station, was frequently visited by our
men-of-war. There were, at one time, five
anchored in the harbor. These gentlemen
never for a moment questioned the right of
the Colonel to the title of Doctor. Men of
proven professional knowledge themselves,
they knew that the mere possession of a
diploma did not always make a man worthy
of it ; and, as they recognized the ability
and capacity of the Colonel (as evidenced by
his success in the profession), they were al-

ways quite ready to exchange opinions and
courtesies with him. In later years, however, in order to satisfy the demands of formal etiquette, he pursued a regular course
at the Toland Medical College at San Francisco, where he was highly esteemed. There
he filled the important position of Assistant Demonstrator in Physiology, assisting in
many intricate and difficult operations.·

In 1874, he left La Paz for a tour in Europe. In leaving, he met with an unexpected
demonstration upon the mole, a long wharf
of about three hundred yards from which
passengers embark — to go on board the
steamer. This wharf was lined by two rows
of women and children dressed in their holiday attire, through which the benevolent
Doctor had to walk to gain the stairway, all
kneeling, and with clasped elevated hands
imploring God's choicest blessings upon their
friend and benefactor, the kind-hearted Doctor. The Colonel's heart has been touched
many times in his life, but never has he felt
so deeply moved as when he witnessed the
gratitude of such a multitude, spontaneously
rendered, springing from the heart of each
one of them. Those poor people had nothing to give, but they knew who had done

much for them ; the philanthropic " Doctor
Americano" was leaving them, and they
would fain testify by all in their power
their gratitude and appreciation for his
many good works. But the thanks of those
poor simple folk, so genuinely and feelingly
given, were sweeter and far more accepta-
ble to the Colonel than the largest fee he
had ever collected.

CHAPTER XI.

Arrival in Europe — Tour of the Continent — Visiting
Battlefields — In Paris — Reception to General Grant
— Return to the States — Building Railroads — En-
joying Life at Villa Ada, Rome, Italy.

L EAVING La Paz, the Colonel journeyed
to Bruxelles, Belgium, where he joined
his family. He had had an eventful and
stirring life in the States; from New York
to the Mexican War, in which battles he
had made a brilliant record, back to New
York, where his regiment was received by
such a reception of public joy and demonstration that has never been exceeded in
point of spontaneous enthusiasm and grateful welcome; then through Mexico again,
this time as a pioneer of California, taking
the overland route from Vera Cruz to San
Francisco, after undergoing innumerable
difficulties, sufferings, and dangers; in California as a prominent citizen, taking a
prominent part in the development of the
coast, and fighting at the head of a command that he himself had organized against

the Indians in Nevada; at the breaking
out of the Civil War, on the Peninsula,
ever ready to the call of his country, and
mentioned in the official reports of those
bloody conflicts for 'gallantry, bravery, and
coolness; after, the Mexican expeditions,
and then settling down in Mexico to an
arduous practice as physician and surgeon
in a foreign community. He therefore considered that he had well earned a vacation,
the first he had ever taken in his busy life.
During four years he traveled all over the
Continent, visiting historic places and points
of interest. The battle-grounds of Metz and
Strasbourg were gone over by him, and the
scenes of great campaigns in Europe, from
Waterloo in Belgium to the ancient fields
of strife of the old Roman Emperors in
Italy, had all an eager attraction to the
close-observing Colonel. Of keen and appreciative nature, those four years of observation and study were well-enjoyed pleasure
to him. Writing from Mexico, his letters
have portrayed his vivid impressions of the
beauties of nature. In the Old World, the
Italian skies, artistic and beautiful France,
picturesque Switzerland, the storied and
castled Rhine of Germany, and the art and

sculpture treasures of the Continent were a
revelation of delight and instruction to one
that had hitherto known but the majesty
and grandeur of the scenery of his own
country. Of a practical bent, he took
special note of the ways of living, and the
difference of customs, between Europeans
and Americans, and enriched his mind with
information and statistics that are of such
value to the educated traveler. Fortunate
is he who has the pleasure of listening to
the reminiscences of one who has had such
an experience, living an active and adventuresome life during the most stirring times
and events in his own land, and having a
mind stored with the result of four years
of keen observation and appreciation of the
scenery and the manners and customs of
the people of the Old World.

In 1878, the Colonel, after finishing his
tour, came to Paris, where his beautiful
home was the scene of many hospitalities
extended to his countrymen, that would
find their way to the gay city. Nothing
gave him more pleasure than the greeting
of his friends and acquaintances; but there
was no one more welcome at his board
than an old soldier, nor no topic more con-

genial than that which recalled the Mexican
War, the early days of California, or the
Civil War. Speaking fluently French and
Spanish, and having the entrée of the best
official and civil society, the Colonel gave
many brilliant entertainments to the élite
of the Parisian world, and fully sustained
the reputation of his countrymen for their
liberal and magnificent hospitality.

On the evening previous to the opening
of the Exhibition of 1878, he gave a reception to the American visitors and the
distinguished people who had gathered in
Paris to witness the opening ceremonies of
the next day. It was a happy thought to
unite all in a splendid entertainment, as a
kind of prelude to the round of official
gaieties that were soon after to begin. To
welcome so many of his countrymen on a
foreign. soil, and bring about the meeting
of so many of the noted people of America
with the celebrities of France and other
European countries, in such a cordial, in-
formal, and fraternizing manner, was the
delightful act of hospitality that he conceived and brilliantly carried out.

Another equally delightful and appreciative act of courtesy was the reception ten-

dered to General Grant. He had come to
Paris on his tour around the world. He was
a comrade-in-arms of Colonel Hungerford,
during the Mexican War. The latter proposed to his daughter, Mrs. Mackay, to thus
honor the General who had won the proud
title of the most distinguished American
soldier, and had twice held the highest office
in the gift of the people. Mrs. Mackay determined that, although on a foreign soil, her
father's renowned comrade-in-arms should be
welcomed by such a scene of dazzling brilliancy that all the glories of the Empire
could not excel. In Paris have been given
many entertainments of splendor and mag-
nificence, but never one that surpassed in
gorgeousness and beauty, the reception offered by Mrs. Mackay to the "Hero of Appomattox." Generals, statesmen, celebrities of
the world, and noted men from all countries
participated by their presence in this fête of
admiration and esteem for the great soldier-
statesman. The resources of luxurious and
artistic Paris were drawn upon to their utmost, in the adornment and decoration of
the magnificent residence of Mrs. Mackay.
The Champs Elysées that night gleamed
with the light and glitter of the most cele-

brated social event that was ever held on
that world-noted avenue.

The French journals were amazed at the
grand tribute of a private American family
to one of their countrymen, eminent in war
and the pursuits of peace. The respect and
regard of Americans for their public men,
regardless of politics, could not have been
better illustrated than by this regal banquet
to one who had been twice President of
their country and leader of its armies. To
describe an affair which has been already
fully chronicled in almost all the journals
of the globe would indeed be superfluous.
Suffice to say, however, that in all the famous tour of General Grant around the
world, when splendor of Occident and lav-
ish richness of Orient were rivaling in the
entertainments that kings and potentates
were vying with each other in his honor,
there was none that excelled, in beauty and
dazzle, the reception given him by his old
comrade-in-arms in the art center of the
Old World.

How times had changed! Thirty years
before, both subaltern officers in Mexico,
the General a lieutenant, the Colonel a captain, their swords flashing together in a se-

ries of dashing victories; that day, both
private citizens of the great Republic. One
had been twice commander of its armies,
and the twice-elected of the Nation; the
other had made a gallant record in three
wars, and had had an honorable career in
civil life, yet the latter was then giving the
former the finest reception he had ever received. The General said, during the course
of the evening, to a distinguished statesman, as they were conversing together in
one of the gilded saloons, that he had always considered the day he was made a
second-lieutenant in the United·States army
as his proudest and happiest day; but he
must thereafter reckon another with it in
equally joyous remembrance, — the reception
given in his honor that evening by his old
comrade-in-arms, Colonel Hungerford.

In the fall of '78, the Colonel returned to
the United States, making a trip through
the Western and coast States, and living his
early life over again in the seeing once
more of the scenes of former days. He visited Fort Defiance, which he built twenty
years before and which he found still standing. When he first traversed that country
it was as a pioneer, when all was virgin,

forest soil and prairie. The treasures of
gold and silver were locked in nature's embrace. But pushing, energetic Americans
had transformed the unknown land into a
region of thrift and prosperity, that, in point
of material civilization and progress, is nowhere surpassed. Men like Colonel Hungerford, brave and strong hearted, were the
forerunners that hewed the way for the
thousands and millions that were to follow.
What a keen delight to return after those
years, to talk over old times and struggles
with others like himself, who had borne the
brunt, and had come out of it all, men of
mark and standing. Accompanied by his
daughter, Countess Telfener, his son-in-law,
Count Telfener, and Mr. Mackay, all won-
dered and were delighted at the wealth and
enterprise of the great West. Everywhere
they were welcomed with the welcome that
only the big-hearted Westerners know how
to give. A California paper speaks of the
party as follows :

"Distinguished visitors, Count Telfener, Ada, Countess
Telfener, Colonel Daniel E. Hungerford, and John W.
Mackay, left here yesterday morning for Lake Tahoe
and California. Colonel Hungerford looks no older than
in the early days of the Comstock. He appears to be

a hale and rugged man of about forty or forty-five
years of age. He is a very young-looking man to be
the father-in-law of Mr. Mackay and the Count. Judg-
ing from what he has thus far passed through, he is
good for one hundred years. Colonel Hungerford met
in this city many old-time California and Nevada friends,
with whom he was greatly pleased to talk over the joys
and sorrows, the excitements and adventures of the early
days. He is now the same earnest, cordial, unassuming
man that he was in the camps of California, and in the
tents, brush shanties, and canvas houses of this town,
when the Comstock was young."

"Colonel Hungerford arrived in California in 1849.
He started from New York, and went to Vera Cruz,
then struck across the country and finally reached the
Pacific at Mazatlan. Then he and eleven others bought
a schooner; but, after knocking about in it for a time,
found it unmanageable on account of some defect in the
steering apparatus, and abandoned it, taking to the land
again. The party suffered terrible hardships before
reaching California. On one occasion they were four
days without food, and three days without water. The
Colonel says he can sympathize with Dr. Tanner. He
says he has been in many battles, and endured many
hardships in the Mexican War and in the late Rebellion;
but in all of it he never suffered as he did on the trip
from Mazatlan to San Francisco. In a battle there was
always some excitement to brace him up to endure, but
in marching and starving in a wilderness it was a dreary,
dead drag."

"The Colonel is full of military spirit, and, when there
is any fighting going on within his reach, he has always
been in it. He even took a hand in our Pinte War in

40

order to keep in practice. He received a military education, not at West Point, but at a private military academy in New York, his native State."

"He was in the War of the Rebellion, and in some of the hottest of the battles. He was a Lieutenant-Colonel of the Thirty-sixth New York Volunteers. At the Chickahominy he crossed the first troops that got over the river, holding his position with fifteen hundred men, until a destroyed bridge was rebuilt and support reached him. In the early days of California, he says he was broke fourteen times in one summer, in mining, and finally came out eight thousand dollars ahead in the fall. In 1850, he wintered at Foster's Bar in a tent so small that he could not sit erect in it, was obliged to crawl in and out on his hands and knees. Often the snow fell to such a depth as to completely cover his tent, and he would have to dig his way out in the mornings."

"From Lake Tahoe the party will go to San Francisco, when the Colonel and the Count and Countess will return overland to St. Louis, thence will go down the Mississippi to New Orleans, and from there will go directly to the city of Mexico. The Count goes to Mexico to look after railroad interests held in that country. He is also interested in mines in Mexico, but will not visit them on this trip as it is necessary for him to be in Rome in November."

In Texas the Colonel went into the railroad business. Active and energetic, he could not look on in the theater of busy life and bustle. In the early days he had

cut his way through forest and thicket, in
his pioneering and prospecting expeditions.
That same country he was now laying railroads in, and joining Mexico to the States
by one more powerful bond, hastening to
the union of the two peoples. Surely the
march of progress and civilization has been
wonderful. What has taken centuries in
the Old World to accomplish is done in
the New in the short space of fifty years.
Colonel Hungerford had fought in early
manhood in Mexico, and the brilliant triumphs of the gallant little army had gained
an empire of territory, containing precious
metals and bounteous soil. That territory,
inhabited only by the red man, he had ex-
plored as pioneer, prospector, and soldier.
Civilization and prosperity had changed all,
and in middle life he returns to build a
vast network of railway through that same
territory, become populous with cities and
villages, and smiling with fields of golden
grain, and the hand of the husbandman
reaping an abundant harvest, and securing
for himself the blessings of peace and
content.

The Colonel was president of the New
York, Texas & Mexican Railway for five

years, until 1885, when, unable any longer
to withstand the solicitations of his family,
he left Texas, and crossing the continent
took sail from New York to join them at
the beautiful Villa Ada, Rome, Italy, a
castled residence that has played its part
in Italian history.

Situated on high ground and overlooking
Rome, the panorama of the Eternal City is
before one's gaze from its windows. The
meandering course of the Tiber can be followed by the eye, until its yellow waters
meet the waves of mighty ocean at Ostia.

Historical incidents and pages in the development of the world's civilization and
Christianity are brought vividly to the
mind, in the contemplation of the very
spots in which the scenes have been enacted. The Sabine Hills, Frascati, Tivoli,
bring the thoughts back to the days of the
old Roman Empire. The lofty towers of St.
Peter's, and the glittering cross surmounting
all, rising above the clouds, is embraced in
the same vista, which includes in its scope
the Coliseum, where, in the time of pagan
Rome, Christ's followers were torn by wild
beasts, and suffered martyrdom for their
faith's and civilization's sake.

Far away in the distance, but easily perceived when Italian skies are radiant, lie the dancing blue waters of the Summer Sea.

The Colonel's study overlooks the Campagna, where in ancient times were marshaled the rival hosts for Rome's subjugation. The fields of manœuvres of the Roman Legions are there, as they existed in the ages when the world was new. The sound of the battle drums could be heard by him, were the sleeping warriors to be aroused by the tocsin, for the assembling of their forces.

Athens and Sparta are not as rich in historic lore, nor do they present such a scene of classic beauty, as is unrolled before the Colonel's gaze from his window in the Villa Ada.

In no other spot on the world's surface are there so many ruins and monuments, marking such portentous events in the earth's history.

It is in this inspiring and beautiful home that fate has decreed that the golden sands of Colonel Hungerford's life should run out. One would never suppose that "Fra gli arcadia" Roma is the same cordial, unpretentious Colonel Hungerford, of Californian days; yet such it is, for he has been made a member of the Society, and that is his scientific appellation. Also, a member of Academy of Sciences of California (corresponding), much of his time is spent in research and the acquirement of special knowledge. Traveling often on the Continent in the evening of a well-spent life, he is enjoying a well-merited repose. And, though his declining years are being passed far from his native land, and under another flag than his own beloved starry banner, yet his heart is loyal and true to America, the land of his birth.

Men like him never change. The kindly heart, the generous nature, the unassuming manner are with him to-day, as in the days of yore. With kindred, family, and romping grandchildren, in his study among his books, the American flag above his desk, reminding him of native land beyond the sea, nobody will deny the old soldier the peace and contentment that a life of devotion to country, family, and friends has justly earned for him.

It may be permitted for me to repeat, in closing this brief narrative of the life of a worthy citizen and a gallant soldier, what has been already said in the opening chapter of this book, that:

Long may the reaper spare him,
To those that love him best;
And green may be the turf above him
When they lay him to his rest.

THE END.